TYPE O, ESPRESSO, DADDYO

"Wait a minute," Brewster said. "Dracula wasn't an *elf*. He was a fictional vampire. An undead creature who survived by drinking human blood."

The dragon shrugged. "Sounds like an elf to me."

Brewster said, "You mean to tell me that elves drink *human blood?*"

"Sure, and everybody knows that," said Brian, the werechamberpot. "They hang about at night 'round their campfires, wearing black, playing guitars, spouting poetry, arguing philosophy and drinking coffee. The only thing they love more than human blood is coffee."

"Coffee-drinking beatnik vampire elves?" said Brewster.

"Aye, 'tis a foul tasting brew," said Brian. "Unfit for human consumption, if you ask me. Keeps you from sleeping. A cup or two and you're up all night. 'Tis made from a peculiar bean grown in the kingdom of Valdez. Has a pungent sort of smell when it brews. If you're walking through the forest and you smell it, then sure and there'll be elves about."

"Methinks I smell one coming now," said Rory, sniffing the air experimentally.

No sooner had the dragon spoken than a piercing scream shattered the stillness of the night...

Also by Simon Hawke

THE WIZARD OF 4TH STREET
THE WIZARD OF WHITECHAPEL
THE WIZARD OF SUNSET STRIP
THE WIZARD OF RUE MORGUE
SAMURAI WIZARD
THE WIZARD OF SANTA FE
THE RELUCTANT SORCERER

Published by
WARNER BOOKS

SIMON HAWKE

THE INADEQUATE ADEPT

WARNER BOOKS

A Time Warner Company

WARNER BOOKS EDITION

Hand lettering by David Gatti
Cover illustration by David Mattingly
Cover design by Don Puckey

Questar® is a registered trademark of Warner Books, Inc.

Warner Books, Inc.
1271 Avenue of the Americas
New York, NY 10020

W A Time Warner Company

Printed in the United States of America

First Printing: March, 1993

10 9 8 7 6 5 4 3 2 1

For Leanne Christine Harper,

with special thanks to Pat McGiveney, Darla Dunn, Doug and Tomi Lewis of The Little Bookshop of Horrors in Arvada, Co., Joe DeRose and the staff of Muddy's Cafe in Denver, Co., H. Trask Emery, David Mattingly, Brian Thomsen, Mauro DiPreta, Fred Cleaver, Chris Zinck, the Mad Scientists Club of Denver and all the understanding friends who supported me during this madness. You all know who you are, and some of you have asked not to be identified. It's okay, I understand.

➤ CHAPTER ➤
ONE

Once upon a time...

No. Let's try that again.

Long, long ago, in a universe far, far away...

Nah, that doesn't work, either.

Oh, hell, you think it's easy being the narrator? *You* try it. Only don't send your manuscripts to me, whatever you do. I've got enough problems of my own. Such as trying to figure out how to begin this book, for instance.

Let's see now, according to conventional wisdom, you're supposed to begin a story with a narrative hook. What's a narrative hook, you ask? It's a slam-bang opening sentence that's so compelling, it "hooks" your interest right away and makes it damn near impossible not to read on further. Well...I guess I've already blown that.

On the other hand, another tried-and-true technique is to get into the action right away, just plunge the reader headfirst into the story with the speed of an express train and never let up for an instant. Hmmm...too late for that, I suppose.

Well, there's always the classic approach used by all those literary authors. You know, Dickens and that whole crowd. First, you set the scene with lots of colorful, evocative, descriptive writing, then you gradually introduce the main characters as you develop the plot, but then that's a rather dated approach and modern readers aren't really all that patient with—

"*Get on with it,*" said Warrick.

What?

"I said, get *on* with it," Warrick Morgannan repeated, looking up toward the ceiling as he sat behind his massive desk, bent over his ancient vellum tomes and scrolls.

"Get on with what, Master?" asked his troll familiar, Teddy.

"I wasn't speaking to you," said Warrick.

The hairy, little troll glanced around the sorcerer's sanctorum apprehensively, noting that the two of them seemed to be alone.

"But, Master..." he whined, plaintively, "there is no one else here!"

"Of course, there is no one else here," snapped Warrick irritably. "I was speaking to the voice in the ether."

"The voice in the ether, Master?" said Teddy, picking his nose nervously.

"Yes, you know, the one that calls itself the narrator," Warrick replied.

Teddy swallowed hard and seemed to shrink into himself, which isn't easy to do when you're only two feet tall. He'd heard his master speak of this narrator before, this mysterious voice in the ether that only he could hear, and it always made him feel frightened. Now, the fact is, there's not much that frightens trolls, because although they may be rather small, they are extremely strong and aggressive. However, Teddy had no idea what to make of this invisible, omniscient presence that his master kept referring to. It made him very nervous.

"What is it saying, Master?" Teddy asked.

"It's talking about your nerves now," said Warrick with a wry grimace.

"My *nerves*?" said Teddy, becoming increasingly more nervous.

"Yes, and wasting a great deal of time, I might add," said Warrick, frowning. "If there is one thing I cannot stand, 'tis a storyteller who hems and haws and cannot seem to get the tale started properly.''

Of course, not being a storyteller himself, Warrick was not really in a position to appreciate the difficulties involved with beginning the second novel in a series, while at the same time trying to take into account the reader who may not have read the first one.

''Well, why don't you simply do one of those 'in the last episode' things?'' asked Warrick impatiently. ''Now do get on with it, will you? I have work to do.''

Ahem . . . In our last episode, we met Dr. Marvin Brewster, a brilliant, if pathologically vague, American scientist in London, in the employ of EnGulfCo International, one of those huge, multinational conglomerates that owns companies all over the world and has lots of large buildings with bad art in their lobbies. Brewster had what many men might call an enviable life. He was making a great deal of money doing what he loved, working out of his own private research laboratory with virtually unlimited funding, and he had become engaged to a highly intelligent and socially prominent British cybernetics engineer named Dr. Pamela Fairburn, who also happened to be drop-dead gorgeous.

Pamela patiently kept trying to get her absent-minded fiancé to the altar, only Brewster kept failing to show up for his weddings. It wasn't that Brewster was gun-shy about marriage, it was simply that he couldn't seem to keep his mind on little things like weddings when he was on the verge of perfecting the greatest scientific discovery the world had ever seen. Assuming, of course, the world would ever get a chance to see it. And therein lies our tale.

For those of you who were thoughtless enough to miss our first installment (*The Reluctant Sorcerer,* Warner Books), never fear, your faithful narrator will bring you up to date. The rest of you, hang in there while we wait for the late arrivals to catch up. Or simply skip ahead to the next chapter. It's okay, I don't mind.

What Brewster had constructed in his top-secret laboratory, high atop the corporate headquarters building of EnGulfCo International, was the world's first working model of a time machine. We'll skip the details of how he did it, because that was covered in our first episode (*The Reluctant Sorcerer,* Warner Books), aside from which, explaining time travel always gives your narrator a frightful headache. Suffice it to say that the thing worked, which should have assured Brewster's fame and fortune and made him as much of a household name as, say, Gene Roddenberry, or maybe even Isaac Asimov, except for one, minor, little problem. . . .

Brewster lost it. That's right, the time machine. He lost it. How do you lose something the size of a small helicopter? (Yes, that's how big it was, and if you'd read our first episode—*The Reluctant Sorcerer,* Warner Books—you'd have known that already.) Well, it had to do with a faulty counter in a timing switch that was part of the auto-return module. It's really rather complicated, but if you've ever owned a British sports car, then you'll understand how little things like that can really screw up the whole works.

As a result of this malfunction, Brewster accidentally sent his time machine off on a one-way trip. To get it back, he had to build a second time machine, go back in time with it and find the first one . . . well, you get the idea. It seemed simple and straightforward enough. So Brewster built a second time machine and that was when his trouble *really* started.

Due to some kind of freak temporal version of an atmospheric skip (either that, or the bizarre machinations of the plot), Brewster wound up in a parallel universe that suspiciously resembled the setting of a fantasy novel. And since he'd crash-landed his second time machine, Brewster was stuck there, with only one chance to make it back. Unless he could find the first time machine he'd built, there was no way for him to get back home again. Unfortunately, the first time machine was nowhere to be found.

(*The reason it was nowhere to be found*: three brigands had found it in the Redwood Forest and sold it to a nearby sorcerer, who managed to stumble onto a spell that tapped into its energy field.) However, the time machine was not designed to be operated by magical remote control, and as a result, it hadn't functioned quite the way it was supposed to.

There was a temporal phase loop, or maybe a short circuit, and the sorcerer disappeared, while the time machine remained exactly where it was. When the sorcerer did not return, his frightened apprentice took this mysterious and terrible device to Warrick Morgannan, the most powerful wizard in all the twenty-seven kingdoms, and the bane of your faithful narrator's existence.

"What?" said Warrick, glancing up from his vellum tomes and scrolls.

Nothing. Go back to work.

Warrick scowled and went back to his paperwork again while Teddy the Troll continued to sweep the floor, nervously glancing up toward the ceiling.

Now where were we? Right, we were discussing Brewster's strange predicament. The first person Brewster ran into in this primitive and magical new world was Mick O'Fallon, whom he first took to be a midget, but who actually happened to be a leprechaun. Mick witnessed Brewster's dramatic arrival in his world and naturally assumed that Brewster was a mighty sorcerer. He also mistakenly assumed that "Brewster" was a title, not a name, as in "one who brews." In other words, an alchemist. And since Brewster habitually told everyone he met to call him "Doc," Mick called him "Brewster Doc," and the name, as well as the mistaken assumption it engendered, stuck.

An amateur alchemist himself, Mick was seeking the secret of the Philosopher's Stone, which in this particular universe had nothing to do with turning base metals into gold, but into a much rarer metal known as nickallirium, the chief medium of exchange in the twenty-seven kingdoms. The secret of making nickallirium was controlled by the Sorcerers and Adepts Guild, which meant they also controlled the economy in all the twenty-seven kingdoms. They guarded this power jealously, and allowed no one to practice magic unless they were a dues-paying member of the Guild. Brewster was ignorant of all these details, however, and in the universe in which he found himself, ignorance was anything but bliss.

When word began to spread that a new wizard had

arrived, the residents of the nearby town of Brigand's Roost began to drop by to make the new sorcerer's acquaintance. As the town's name might lead one to believe, the residents of Brigand's Roost were mostly outlaws who plied their trade along the trails and thorny hedgerows of the Redwood Forest. They were known as the Black Brigands, for the black masks they wore in imitation of their leader, the infamous Black Shannon, a deceptively angelic-looking woman with the disposition of a she-wolf and the morals of an alley cat. Now while such character traits might be regarded as shortcomings in most social situations, they happen to be extremely useful in conducting business, and Shannon quickly saw certain advantages to having a wizard in the neighborhood.

Meanwhile, Warrick was busy trying to solve the mystery of Brewster's missing time machine.

"Yes, what is it *now*?" snapped Warrick.

Teddy gave a guilty start and dropped his broom.

"I am very busy, Teddy," Warrick said. "Whatever it is, it can wait."

"But, Master—"

"I *said*, it can wait!"

Teddy stuck his lower lip out petulantly, picked up his broom and resumed sweeping, mumbling under his breath.

Now, due to unforeseen circumstances, your narrator has to be extremely careful when it comes to writing about . . . you-know-who, because as we have already discovered back in our first episode, the Grand Director of the Guild is a very powerful adept, indeed. So powerful, in fact, that he can detect the presence of the narrator. This could make things rather sticky.

The thing is, as any good writer can tell you, characters who are properly developed tend to take on lives of their own and . . . you-know-who is certainly no exception. His characterization demanded highly developed thaumaturgical abilities and magical sensitivities of a very high order. The trouble is, when you start playing around with things like magic, there's no telling what might happen, and in this case, what apparently happened was that your faithful narrator did his job a shade too well.

As a result of overhearing some narrative exposition in the previous episode, War...uh, Teddy's master has already discovered that the mysterious apparatus now in his possession is something called a "time machine," though he has yet to figure out exactly what that means. He has deduced that it is a device for transporting people somewhere, but he has no idea where or how. To solve this mystery, he has offered a reward for the capture of the brigands who had found the strange machine, in the hope that they can lead him to its creator.

Brewster was unaware of all these ominous machinations, and when last we left our unsuspecting hero, he had made an agreement with a dragon by the name of Rory, who promised to help Brewster find his missing time machine. In return, Brewster would tell the dragon stories of the world he came from. Unfortunately, Brewster neglected to take into account the fact that dragons live forever, and they love hearing stories almost as much as they love to frolic in the autumn mist, so this could develop into a rather open-ended deal.

Having set up housekeeping in a crumbling, old keep, Brewster must now reluctantly live up to his reputation as a sorcerer, which is a bit of a trick, since he can't do any magic. However, as Arthur C. Clarke once said, any knowledge that is sufficiently advanced would seem like magic to those who didn't understand it, and while Brewster knew nothing about magic, he did know a thing or two about science.

In exchange for help in seeking the whereabouts of his missing "magic chariot," Brewster has set about the task of bringing progress—and, hopefully, some profit—to the muddy, little town of Brigand's Roost. He is aided in this task by Mick, the leprechaun; Bloody Bob, the huge, nearsighted brigand; a local farmer named McMurphy, who has visions of becoming a tycoon; and Brian, the enchanted werepot prince, who many years ago had been turned into a golden chamberpot by an irate sorcerer whose daughter Brian had seduced. During each full moon, Prince Brian reverts to his human form, which has remained agelessly youthful, while the child he had fathered has grown up to become none other than the Grand Director of the Sorcerers and Adepts Guild, Warrick Morgannan.

"*Now* what?" snapped Warrick, looking up from his ancient vellum tomes and scrolls once more.

"But, Master, I said nothing!" Teddy the Troll protested.

"I distinctly heard my name mentioned," Warrick said severely.

Teddy swallowed hard and glanced around anxiously. " 'Twasn't me, Master. It must have been the narrator." However, he looked very guilty and his denial was not entirely convincing.

Warrick narrowed his eyes suspiciously. "Are you certain 'twas not you?"

"Nay, Master, I said nothing! *Nothing!*"

"I do not care for pranks, Teddy."

"But I could never play a prank on you, Master," Teddy insisted vehemently. "I would not know how! Trolls have no sense of humor."

"Aye, 'tis true," said Warrick, scowling. "It must be that the narrator has begun the tale."

"It has a *tail*?" said Teddy with alarm.

Warrick rolled his eyes. "Oh, never mind. Fetch me that stack of scrolls over there."

Teddy put down his broom and went over to the stack of ancient scrolls Warrick had indicated. "All of them, Master?"

"Aye, all of them. Somewhere, there has to be an incantation that will allow me to summon up this narrator and compel him to do my bidding. I shall not rest until I find it."

Fortunately, Warrick would never find such a spell, because your faithful narrator has no intention of writing it into the plot. So there.

Warrick slammed his fist down on the table, then angrily swept all the scrolls onto the floor, making Teddy jump back in fear.

"There shall be a reckoning," he said, through gritted teeth. "You mark me well."

"But, Master, you *said* to fetch the scrolls!"

"Blast it, Teddy, I wasn't speaking to *you*!"

"Oh," said Teddy. "Forgive me, Master, I thought—"

"*Don't think*!"

"Yes, Master. I mean, no, Master, I shan't."

Warrick shut his eyes in patient suffering. "Of all the familiars I could have chosen, I had to pick a stupid troll. I could have had a nice black cat, or an intelligent owl, perhaps, but *nooooo....*"

Teddy looked stricken. He sniffled, then waddled back to his grubby little corner in the sorcerer's sanctorum, where he sat all hunched up, hugging his hairy little knees to his chest and pouting.

"I *hate* the narrator," he mumbled to himself. "I hate him, I hate him, *I hate him!*"

A large glass beaker filled with noxious fluid suddenly fell off the shelf above where Teddy sat and shattered on his head, covering him with foul-smelling ooze.

"*Teddy!*" Warrick shouted.

With a whimper, the little troll bolted out the door.

➤ CHAPTER ➤
TWO

The stone keep looked decidedly odd with the solar collectors mounted in place. Angling up from the roof of the lower section of the keep, the collectors ran up to the tower, just below the fourth floor. Mick had been puzzled by the project from the very start, and thought that the collectors looked "bloody peculiar," but Bloody Bob, the immense old brigand who was Brewster's self-appointed "loyal retainer," thought that they looked pretty. But then again, he had been the foreman in charge of their construction, and had developed quite a proprietary attitude about them.

Ever since Brewster had appointed him construction foreman on the projects at the keep, Bloody Bob had undertaken his new duties with an earnest zeal. He insisted that everyone address him as "Foreman," and any brigand who forgot and called him Bob was fetched a mighty clout upon the head that usually rendered him unconscious. And when Foreman Bob stood back for the first time to take a good look at the fruit of all his labors, his massive chest had swelled with pride.

The construction of the solar collectors had entailed building wooden frames on which were mounted loops of copper pipes, made by bending copper sheets around rods of pig iron and then forming them and soldering them together.

They were then painted black with pitch and connected to the water tank on the fourth floor with a loop running through Brewster's brand-new Franklin stove, which Mick insisted on calling an "O'Fallon stove," since he had made it in his smithy to Brewster's specifications and had already taken orders for half a dozen more from the residents of Brigand's Roost. The water tank was kept filled by the cistern on the roof, and the collectors stored the solar heat that would enable Brewster, for the first time since his arrival in this primitive, medieval world, to take hot showers.

This, in itself, was a source of puzzlement to many of the brigands. As a rule, they didn't like to bathe at all, and considered it an unhealthy practice. Since the infrequent baths they took at the insistence of Black Shannon, who was averse to body odor, were normally taken in the ice-cold waters of the rushing stream, it wasn't difficult to see where they had come up with this notion. As for the shower Brewster had designed, they had no idea what to make of that, at all. Nor could they comprehend Brewster Doc's other new alchemical mystery . . . a strange concoction he called "soap."

They had all crowded around to watch as Brewster directed Bloody Bob and Robie McMurphy in rendering the fat from butchered spams, which were squat and ugly, hoglike creatures with rodent faces and hairless, pink-speckled bodies. Their fat content was high, McMurphy had explained, and the meat tasted so vile that even starving hunters passed them up. However, since animal fat had been required for Brewster's "alchemical recipie," the brigands had slain half a dozen spams they found rooting in the forest.

Standing over a boiling cauldron that Mick had brought out from his smithy, McMurphy and Bloody Bob worked under Brewster's direction, skimming the top until the "sorcerous brew" was clear. Then Brewster had them pour it through some hand-woven cloth which they had filled with ashes, to add lye to the mixture, into a mold where it was left to solidify. Mick had wrinkled his nose as he gazed at the soap solidifying in the molds.

"And you say the purpose of this magically rendered fat is to cleanse the body?" he'd asked dubiously.

"Well . ... yes," Brewster had replied.

"And how does it do that?" asked Mick. He wrinkled his nose again. "You're not going to eat it, surely?"

Brewster laughed. "No, no, of course not, Mick. You stand under the shower and scrub yourself with it."

"Aye? And then what happens?" asked McMurphy.

"Well, then you rinse off," said Brewster. "And the dirt washes away, leaving you fresh and clean."

McMurphy shook his head in amazement. "Think of it!" he said. "A magical dirt remover!"

"And it only works when the water is hot?" asked Mick.

"No, it works whether the water is hot or cold," said Brewster. "Only it's a lot nicer when it's hot."

" 'Tis something I will have to see," said Mick.

"You can try it for yourself," said Brewster. "In fact, I encourage all of you to try it. There's plenty of soap to go around."

Of course, once he had said that, they all wanted to see him try it, first. And no amount of recalcitrance on Brewster's part would dissuade them from witnessing his first hot shower. Brewster felt a bit self-conscious about the prospect of taking a shower in front of a crowd, but since it was in the interests of science and general cleanliness, he decided he could put up with a small amount of embarrassment. The only condition he'd insisted upon was that none of the women could watch.

Once the solar collectors had been installed and the water in the tank adequately heated, a small crowd gathered in front of his spacious shower stall, which Bloody Bob had constructed out of stone, mortar, and copper, with Mick handling the plumbing, which he was rapidly becoming quite expert at. Even the peregrine bush was present, having learned to climb the stairs to Brewster's quarters in the tower, where Bloody Bob had placed a large wooden planter filled with earth, so the bush could burrow its roots in while Brewster slept.

The little red-gold thorn bush had taken to following

Brewster around everywhere, so Mick had given it to Brewster, for the curious little ambulatory shrub had attached itself to him like an affection-starved puppy. It had always been afraid of Mick, who had caught it while it was wandering around the forest near his smithy, and the fact that Mick always yelled at it and constantly kept threatening to throw it in a pot for his next batch of peregrine wine had made it very nervous. Its branches shook violently whenever Mick came near, and when he yelled at it, its leaves drooped disconsolately. However, Brewster had always spoken nicely to it, remembering that Pamela had always spoken to her houseplants, and the peregrine bush had responded to his kindness. Its leaves had taken on a brighter sheen and its branches were sending forth new growth shoots.

"Sure, and you can keep the bloody thing," said Mick, "for 'twas forever getting underfoot and being a damned nuisance. Mind you, though, 'tis but a wee shrub now, and you'll have yourself a thorny problem when it grows to its full height. When you tire of it, let me know, and I'll brew it up for wine."

"Oh, I couldn't possibly do that, Mick," protested Brewster. "It . . . trusts me."

"Well, don't be saying that I didn't warn you, then," Mick had replied.

"Oh, I'm sure that Thorny and I will get along just fine," said Brewster.

Mick had raised his eyebrows. *"Thorny?"*

"Well . . . that's the name I've given it," admitted Brewster sheepishly.

Mick shook his head and sighed. "First you go speaking to the shrubbery, and now you've taken to naming it, as well. Faith, Doc, and you're a different sort o' man entirely."

So with even his pet bush in attendance to watch the inauguration of the soap, Brewster stripped down awkwardly as the others watched curiously. He turned away, blushing, as he took off his boxer shorts with the little red lips on them. The shorts had been a gift from Pamela, who had thought that they were "cute," but none of the brigands snickered when they saw them. They knew that adepts often went in for all sorts of cabalistic symbols on their clothing, each of which had a sorcerous purpose, and when they saw the shorts, they merely looked at one another significantly. Though Brewster wouldn't be aware of it, the women of Brigand's Roost would soon be busy sewing boxer shorts with little red lips on them, the better to improve their menfolk's potency.

Brewster stepped into the shower. He turned on the tap, and as the warm water flowed through the perforated copper showerhead Mick had constructed, he began to soap himself. The brigands gasped and drew back when they saw the soap begin to lather up.

" 'Tis the foam of madness!" Pikestaff Pat cried out.

"No, no," protested Brewster, looking back over his shoulder at them. "It's *supposed* to do this. The lather . . . the foam is what gets you clean, you see."

With a rustling sound, the little peregrine bush reacted to the sound of water dripping. It shuffled forward quickly on its roots and jumped into the shower with Brewster, so it could get under the spray.

"Thorny! No!" shouted Brewster, crying out as the bush's thorny branches scratched him. He hopped about in the shower stall as the confused bush scuttled about beneath the spray with him, its sharp little thorns pricking his skin.

Unable to help themselves, the brigands burst out laughing uncontrollably as the dejected little bush hopped out of the shower stall and went to huddle, quaking, in a corner, water dripping from its drooping leaves. Facing them, naked, wet, and foamy, Brewster saw Black Shannon standing in their forefront, her hands on her hips and a mocking little smile on her face.

She had come in while his back was turned, intent on not missing the demonstration, and now her gaze traveled appreciatively up and down his body. As the laughter died down, Brewster blushed furiously and covered himself up with his hands.

Shannon merely smiled and held out a cloth towel for him to dry himself off with.

Brewster stepped out of the shower, hunched over, took

the towel from her, and hastily wrapped it around his middle. "Th-thank you," he stammered. "Well . . . anyway . . ." he added, clearing his throat awkwardly, "that's how it works."

"We shall all try this magic soap," Shannon said, with a glance around at the others, who looked rather uncertain about this new development.

Pikestaff Pat shook his head. "If you ask me, 'tis not seemly for a man to be all lathered up, like some bloody horse run half to death."

"I *didn't* ask you," Shannon snapped. Her blade scraped free of its scabbard and she put its point to Pikestaff Pat's throat. "I said that we shall *all* try it. *Any questions*?"

"Uh . . . no," replied Pikestaff Pat, with a nervous swallow, his gaze focused on the sword point at his throat.

"From now on, each and every brigand will possess a piece of this magic soap," said Shannon. "And each of you will use it, *understood*?"

There was a chorus of grumbled, "Ayes." With a satisfied nod at Brewster, Shannon sheathed her sword, turned on her heel, and strode out of the room.

"Well," mumbled Pikestaff Pat, as the remainder of them filed out, "at least we found a use for the bloody spams."

Sean MacGregor had spent the better part of the evening sharpening his blades by the campfire. It took a while because he was meticulous about their being sharpened properly and because he had better than a dozen of them, of various shapes and sizes, worn on his belt and in crossed bandoliers over his chest. He also had his sword, which was a true work of art indeed, as was only fitting for MacGregor the Bladesman, who had yet to meet his match.

Attached to the breast of his brown, rough-out leather tunic was the coveted badge of the Footpads and Assassins Guild, in the shape of a double-edged dagger. MacGregor's badge was different from all the others, in that it also had a star inscribed upon its blade, which identified him without question as the number-one assassin in the Guild, entitled to command top rates. He had been the number-one assassin ever since he had assassinated the previous number-one assassin, which was generally how rank was determined in the Guild. Since inept assassins did not usually last very long as a result, this practice ensured a consistent, high level of professionalism.

Seated across from him, on the other side of the campfire, were his three apprentice henchmen, the brawny brothers Hugh, Dugh, and Lugh. They were as alike as peas in a pod, and hardly anyone but Mac could tell them apart. They were strapping, young bruisers with straw-colored mops of hair and amiable, round, peasant faces that generally wore expressions of bovine placidity, except for when they had to fight or think. When they were forced to think, their faces contorted into such pained expressions that one might have thought they were suffering from terminal constipation. But when faced with a fight, their ploughboy faces lit up with an innocent, childlike joy.

Mac had first met them in a Pittsburgh watering hole known as The Stealers Tavern, famed hangout of assassins, cutpurses, and alleymen. The three brothers had just finished taking on all comers and the tavern was a shambles, with limp bodies slung about all over the place. Recognizing potential when he saw it, Mac had offered them positions as his apprentices and they had eagerly jumped at the opportunity of learning a good trade, and from no less an accomplished instructor than the famous Mac the Knife.

They had been on the road for several weeks now, on the trail of three men sought by Warrick the White, who was paying not only Mac's top rate, but offering an attractive bonus, as well. This was the first actual assignment in the field the three brothers had ever participated in, and they were eager to learn as much as they could. The only problem was, there was only so much their dense craniums could handle at any given time, and instructing them in the finer points of stalking and assassination was a taxing process. It was fortunate that MacGregor was a patient man.

He grimaced as he glanced across the campfire at his three apprentices, who were busily stuffing themselves with roasted spam. They had killed two of the creatures earlier that afternoon, and despite Mac telling them that spams didn't make good eating, the brothers had cooked them up anyway and now they sat there, chewing and belching happily, brown fat juices dribbling down their chins onto their tunics.

"You actually *like* spam?" MacGregor asked with disbelief.

"Aye, 'tis powerful good, Mac!" Dugh replied. " 'Ere, tear yourself off a chunk!"

He held out a dripping, suety mass of roasted, pink-speckled flesh. Mac winced and recoiled from it. The smell alone was enough to stunt your growth, he thought.

"No, thank you, I am not very hungry," he replied with a sour grimace of distaste.

"Suit yourself, then," Dugh replied, elbowing his brothers gleefully. "Just means more for us, eh, lads?"

Mac reached for the wineskin and squirted a stream into his mouth. He sighed, leaned back against a tree trunk, and lit up his pipe. "Right, then," he said, when he had it going. "Time to review our progress, lads."

They all sat up attentively, like acromegalic schoolboys.

"What have we learned thus far?"

"About what, Mac?" asked Lugh with a puzzled frown.

MacGregor rolled his eyes and drew a long, patient breath. "About our quarry, lads, the three men we are seeking for our esteemed patron, Warrick the White."

"Well . . . there's three of them," offered Dugh.

MacGregor shut his eyes in patient suffering. "Yes, very good, Dugh, there are three of them. But if you will recall, we knew that to begin with, did we not? What else?"

The brothers screwed their faces up in expressions of fierce concentration. "One of 'em likes wee wooden horses!" Hugh finally said triumphantly.

MacGregor reached into his pouch and removed a small, hand-carved, wooden chesspiece. "Right," he said, holding it up. "And what, exactly, does this wee wooden horse signify?"

"Uh . . . a knight?" asked Lugh.

"Very good, Lugh! It signifies a knight. And what is the name of the game in which this knight is a game piece?"

"Cheese!" said Dugh.

"Close," said MacGregor with a wry grimace. "Actually, 'tis called chess. Try to remember that. Now, let's all say it together, shall we?"

"Chess," said the brothers in unison.

"Very good," said Mac. "And what is the significance of this information?"

Silence.

"It tells us that at least two of the men we seek are players," said MacGregor, "and it also tells us that they are probably somewhat clever, as chess is a game for clever men. Further, the fact that they had brought this game with them on their journey indicates that they are avid players, and chances are that they had probably played this game whenever they had stopped to rest. So. . . ." He gave them a prompting glance, hoping for the best.

Silence.

"Hugh?" said MacGregor. "Come on, now, lad, you can do it. . . ."

Hugh concentrated with such intensity that he let loose a tremendous fart.

"Oh, blind me, what a bloody stench!" cried Dugh, scuttling away from his brother. Lugh grabbed his own throat dramatically and made gurgling, choking noises.

"You shut up now!" shouted Hugh.

"Argh!" said Lugh. " 'Tis like a bloated corpse, all burst apart and squirmy with bleedin' little worms and maggots . . ."

"You shut up!" cried Hugh, fetching his brother a clout on the head. "I'll bloody well kill you, I will!"

"Argh! Kill me, too!" cried Dugh, performing a mock swoon. "A quick death would be merciful!"

Hugh leaped upon his other brother and in seconds, the three of them were scrabbling around in the dirt, pummeling each other and laughing hysterically.

MacGregor looked up toward the heavens and addressed a quiet plea to the gods. "For pity's sake," he said, "don't just look down. *Help* me."

Whereupon the sky was suddenly split with lightning, followed by the crash of thunder, and it began to rain, a deluge that quickly put out the campfire and had the hot coals steaming.

MacGregor glanced up at the sky again and murmured, "That wasn't quite what I had in mind." He frowned and pulled his cloak over him for shelter. Meanwhile, the narrator, feeling playfully omniscient, smiled smugly and went on to the next scene.

Bonnie King Billy sat leaning back against the headboard of his royal bed, wearing his royal nightgown and his royal nightcap and feeling royally depressed. He frequently felt depressed when it was raining, but on this night, he felt especially depressed, and not just because of the rotten weather.

Next to him, the beautiful Queen Sandy reclined gracefully with her head on her down pillow, her long and slim legs bent at an attractive angle underneath the covers, the slinky outline of her body underneath the sheets making a fine, aesthetic counterpoint to the way her long, golden hair was spread out across the pillow, like an angel's halo. (None of this has anything to do with the following scene, of course, your narrator simply likes to entertain himself every now and then.)

"Petitions," mumbled King Billy disconsolately.

"Mmmmm?" murmured Queen Sandy.

"Nothing but petitions," said King Billy, sticking out his lower lip in a royal pout. "Petitions, petitions, and more petitions. Each one worded more nastily than the one before it, too."

Queen Sandy sighed. "Are you *still* on about that?" she murmured. "Go to sleep, William. 'Tis late."

"How can I sleep with all these petitions hanging over my head?" asked King Billy grumpily. "I always thought my subjects loved me. You always told me that they did."

"They did, and they do," replied Queen Sandy, burrowing down into her pillow. "Now go to sleep."

"Well, if they love me, then why do they assail me with this avalanche of petitions?"

Queen Sandy sighed wearily. " 'Tis because of the new edicts," she replied.

King Billy frowned. "What new edicts? I have issued no new edicts."

"You did," she insisted. "The royal sheriff issued them in your name. And he continues to issue new ones all the time, as quickly as he can think up new laws for the people to break."

"Really?" said King Billy. "Well, what's he doing that for?"

Queen Sandy sighed again and sat up in bed, turning toward her husband. "He's doing it because Warrick told him to," she said. "And you gave Warrick your blanket approval, don't you remember?"

"I did?" King Billy asked. "Why did I do that?"

"To restock the royal dungeons," explained Queen Sandy, "so that Warrick could use the prisoners for his magical experiments, instead of simply having his minions snatching people off the streets."

"Ah, quite so, quite so," King Billy replied, nodding. "I remember now. I was receiving petitions complaining of my subjects being snatched off the street and I told Warrick he could use the prisoners, instead." He frowned. "I thought that solved the problem."

"It would have," replied Queen Sandy, "except that Warrick had already depleted the royal dungeons, and in order for there to be more prisoners, there had to be more arrests, and in order for there to be more arrests, there had to be more laws for the people to break, and in order for there to be more laws, there had to be new edicts. And Warrick suggested that you give the royal sheriff your approval to issue some new edicts, announcing some new laws. Do you remember now?"

"Aye, of course," King Billy said. "So that should have taken care of matters. But then why all these new petitions?"

Queen Sandy gave him one of her special looks.

"I just hate it when you give me one of your special looks," complained King Billy. "It always makes me feel as if I've done something particularly foolish."

" 'Tis because you always *do* something particularly foolish to provoke such looks," Queen Sandy replied.

"Well . . . what have I done *this* time?"

"You have solved a problem with another problem," said Queen Sandy. "Warrick's minions were snatching people off the streets, and so the people sent in petitions of complaint. You chose to allow Warrick to use the prisoners in the royal dungeons, so that he wouldn't need to snatch people off the streets, only he had already used up all the prisoners without asking your permission, so instead of giving him a royal reprimand, you agreed to his suggestion that the royal sheriff issue some new edicts, which would bring about increased arrests, so that now, instead of Warrick's minions snatching people off the streets, *your* minions are snatching people off the streets and giving them to Warrick. Nothing's changed, my dear, except that instead of the people blaming Warrick, now they are blaming you. And *that* is why you are receiving more petitions."

"Oh," said King Billy. "I see." He put his fingers up to his lips in a gesture reminiscent of David Niven (at least, it would have been reminiscent of David Niven if anyone in this universe had known who David Niven was). "Well, I suppose I shall have to do something about that."

"That would be nice, dear," said the queen, lying back underneath the covers once again.

King Billy brightened. "I know! I shall issue a new edict outlawing petitions!"

"Oh, go to sleep!" Queen Sandy said.

At approximately the same time, in another part of town, a rather seedy part of town, specifically, the corner of Cutthroat Avenue and Garotte Place, it was nearing closing time in The Stealers Tavern and the tavern keeper announced last call.

"Last call!" announced the tavern keeper redundantly.

"I'll have another," said the small, dark, feisty-looking, hawk-faced man sitting at the end of the bar. He tapped his mug for emphasis.

The tavern keeper grimaced and brought the man another

mineral water and lime. "You sure you don't want a *real* drink, now?" he asked the hawk-faced man for the fourth time."

"For the fourth time, I don't drink," the hawk-faced man replied.

"You know something? They say you can never trust a man who doesn't drink," the tavern keeper grumbled.

"You know something? They're right," the hawk-faced man replied. "Now shut up and leave me alone."

Harlan the Peddlar drank his mineral water and scowled at the retreating back of the tavern keeper. He was not in a particularly cheerful mood. Business was slow. In fact, business was downright awful. At the rate things were going, he thought, he'd soon be reduced to eating the spam stew handed out at the local soup kitchens. It was all part of Bonnie King Billy's FTP Program, which stood for Feed The Poor, although most of the poor people in the kingdom called it Something-Else The Poor.

"I never should have picked this business," Harlan the Peddlar mumbled to himself through gritted teeth. "I should've been a bard, instead. Bloody bards have all the luck. Wandering about, strumming on their blasted zithers, telling fantastical lore. . . . S'trewth, 'tain't workin'. That's the way to do it. Making money telling fantasy. Aye, 'tain't workin'. That's the way to do it. Money for nothing and your maids for free."

Knopfler the Bard walked up behind the peddlar and tapped him on the shoulder. "Watch it," he said.

"Sod off!" said the peddlar. He finished off his drink, took a deep breath, and exhaled heavily. "What I need is something new," he said to himself. "Something people will want, and that no one else has to offer. Something unique, so I'll be able to control the price. Only where is one to find such a commodity? What could it be?"

He paid for his drinks and left the tavern, going back out to his peddlar's cart. He paid the ruffian he'd hired to watch it while he was inside, scowling as he counted out the coins, yet knowing full well that if he hadn't bought such protection, not only would all his wares have disappeared, but probably his cart and horse, as well.

"Whatever it may be," he mumbled to himself as he climbed up into his cart, "I shan't find it in Pittsburgh. Too many craftsmen here, too many peddlars stopping by to call on them. I'll need to find some craftsman somewhere who hasn't been discovered yet. Aye, that's what I'll need to do. Scour the countryside and find some unknown, starving craftsman somewhere who's got something completely different. What could it be, though, what could it be?"

The determined peddlar whipped up his horse, and the cart slowly lumbered off, heading toward the road leading out of the city. He'd bought provisions enough for a long journey. Somewhere out there, in the wilds, he knew he'd find what he was seeking. He had no idea what it was yet, but when he found it, he'd know.

➤ CHAPTER ➤ THREE

"Doc, wake up!"

"Mmmmm?" Brewster opened his eyes and started when he saw Shannon standing by his bed, looking down at him. She stood in her habitual, aggressive posture, legs spread apart, hands on her hips, close to the pommels of her sword and dagger. All things considered, it was quite a sight to wake up to first thing in the morning.

"Doc, we need to talk," said Shannon, sitting down on the edge of his bed.

Belatedly, Brewster realized that it had been a warm night and he had kicked most of the covers off himself. He realized this when Shannon cast a lingering, appreciative gaze down along his body, stopping at . . . well, you know where she stopped. She smiled as he made a quick grab for the covers and pulled them up over himself.

"You seem pleased to see me," said Shannon with a smile.

"That . . . uh . . . often happens with men . . . in the morning," Brewster explained, blushing furiously.

"Indeed?" said Shannon, raising her eyebrows. "I hadn't known. I'd never lingered long enough to find out."

"Yes, well. . . ." Brewster cleared his throat awkwardly. "What was it you wanted to discuss?"

"We can speak while you get dressed," said Shannon.

"Uh, no...that's okay," said Brewster hastily. "That can wait. Go ahead, I'm listening."

" 'Tis about my men," said Shannon.

"What about them?"

"You have the greater part of them laboring here upon your sorcerous works," she said. "Now, 'tis not that I'm complaining, mind you, I quite understand that there is much to do, what with Mick and Robie requiring help in making the many-bladed knives, and tending to the brewing and the manufacture of the magic soap, and then there are the stoves to make, and the wire to be pulled and the copper pipes to be formed...well, 'tis all most wondrous, you see, but Bob has almost all the men assisting in these various works, which leaves me but a few to dispose about the forest trails to ply our brigand trade. We are taking in less booty now than ever before, and I fear that at this rate, we shall soon be in rather dire straits."

Brewster nodded. "I see," he said. "You're worried about your income."

"Income?" Shannon asked with a puzzled frown.

"Uh, yes, the booty, as you put it," Brewster explained. "The profits that come in. In-come, you see?"

"Ah," said Shannon, comprehending. "In-come." She nodded. "A useful expression. I shall have to remember it." She crossed her long and lovely legs and Brewster shifted uncomfortably beneath his covers. He wished she'd wear more clothing. "So...you see my difficulty," she continued. "You said there would be profit to be made from this manufacturing process of yours. My concern is that you have most of my men working here day in and day out, yet thus far, we have seen none of this profit, this in-come, as you call it."

"I understand," said Brewster. "However, you must understand that this sort of thing takes time."

"How much time?" Shannon asked.

"Well...first, we have to establish the process and work out all the problems," Brewster explained. "Then we have to build up our inventory...our stock, as it were. And then, we have to institute our marketing program. Now, I've been giving that a lot of thought, because it's not really my area of expertise, you see, and I'm not quite certain how to go about it yet, but once we have—''

"All this means nothing to me," Shannon interrupted impatiently. "And it sounds as if 'twill take a great deal more time. I fail to see the wisdom in this. As brigands, we reap our profits much more quickly."

"Yes, I suppose that's true," said Brewster. "However, it's a much more uncertain business. I mean, you can't depend on it for steady work, if you can see my point. Aside from that, the risks are greater. And it's dishonest."

"What has that to do with anything?" asked Shannon.

"Well . . . wouldn't you rather have a steady income, with a far greater potential for profit and much less risk?" he asked.

"Aye, I would," said Shannon, "only when does all this come about? How long shall I have to wait?"

Brewster sighed. "Shannon, we're barely getting started," he replied. "Please, try to be a little patient. These things take time. However, I promise you, if you can only be patient a little while longer, it will be well worth it. You'll see."

Shannon pursed her lips thoughtfully. "Very well," she said. "I shall wait a while longer and try to be more patient, as you ask. But we had best see some profit soon."

She turned and strode out of Brewster's room, leaving him sitting up in bed, clutching the covers to himself and feeling very anxious. She was the most unpredictable young woman he had ever met, and the most difficult to figure out. Not that he'd ever been much good at understanding women in the first place.

He looked around the room as he sat in the crudely made wooden bed, clutching the coarsely woven blanket. What he saw were bare stone walls, with several sconces mounted on them for torches. There was a tall, standing brazier, a wooden trunk for storing his clothing, several crude wooden benches, a wooden table with a bowl and pitcher for washing up, and a couple of goblets for drinking. A crudely woven carpet covered part of the stone floor. There was no glass in the narrow windows, and he was suffering from mosquito bites. At least, he thought they were mosquitoes. In a world like this, he thought, they were liable to be almost anything. All in all, it was the most Spartan, primitive existence he had ever known.

He had already lost track of how long he'd been here. He estimated it to be about a month, perhaps a little more. Pamela must be frantic, he thought. He'd disappeared before, but only for a day or two at most, never for this long. He imagined that she'd probably called all the hospitals in London, and then gone to the police and filed a missing persons report. He was a valued asset to EnGulfCo, so they would probably have detectives looking for him, as well. Only they'd never find him. The days would stretch on into weeks, the weeks into months . . . how long would she wait? What must she be thinking?

In the quiet hours of the night, Brewster had always concentrated all his thoughts upon the task at hand, the next project, and the next one after that, the best way to design a solar heater, the most feasible way to install the plumbing, the problem of electricity and whether or not it would be possible to design some sort of crude light bulb, anything to keep him from thinking the thought that was going through his mind right now. . . .

Suppose he never made it back? He could, quite conceivably, be stuck here in this primitive, medieval world for the remainder of his life. He tried to force his mind back to a more pragmatic frame. There was a great deal of interest in this world, a great deal to learn. It could easily become the research project of a lifetime. But of what use would it be if he could never bring any of this information home with him?

On one hand, he could probably have a good life here. With what he knew, he could become an important man in this world, another da Vinci, and he could become wealthy and respected. And there was much that he could do for these people. Yet, on the other hand, he did not belong here.

He already had a life, a good life . . . a life he'd left behind. Chances were, he'd left that life behind forever.

A momentary feeling of panic overwhelmed him. And then he heard a rustling sound as Thorny, the little peregrine bush, uprooted itself from its planter and scuttled across the floor toward him. It stopped beside his bed and tentatively, very gently, stretched out its branches to touch him very lightly, so as not to scratch him. Almost like a puppy, sensing its owner's depression and offering a little love in an attempt to ease it.

Brewster stopped himself as he was about to stretch out his hand and stroke the thorn bush, as he would a dog. In spite of himself, he had to smile.

"Thanks, Thorny," he said. "You're a good friend. I feel better now."

Thorny's little, red-gold leaves seemed to perk up and it rustled its branches in response.

"Man's best friend is his bush," Brewster said with a chuckle. "I wish Pamela could see you. Well . . . who knows? With any luck, Thorny, maybe someday soon, she will."

In the meantime, like it or not, I'm here, he thought, and I might as well make the best of it. That meant not only doing what he could to improve his own situation, but to pull his own weight, as well. In some cases, he'd already done that. Bloody Bob had been so nearsighted when they'd first met that the brawny, aging brigand had been practically blind. Now, with the "magic visor" that Brewster had designed for him, with crudely ground glass lenses sandwiched between the two riveted bronze pieces that made up the visor, Bloody Bob could see. Even if these home-ground lenses weren't quite up to the modern optometrical standards Brewster was accustomed to, for Bloody Bob, it was like a miracle, and there was nothing the old brigand wouldn't do for the mighty sorcerer who had cured his blindness.

In Mick's case, the paybacks were still coming. Brewster owed a great deal to the muscular, little leprechaun. If not for Mick using his tremendous physical strength to rip open the buckled door, he never would have managed to get out of the crash-damaged time machine, and when the liquid oxygen tanks exploded, he would have gone up with it. On top of that, Mick had taken him in, and fed him, and given him the use of the stone keep. And it was Mick who had facilitated his reasonably smooth entry into this world, by introducing him to the brigands and the local farmers and vouching for his character, as well as his "magical abilities."

Yes, he certainly owed Mick a lot, but in some ways, he had already paid him back at least some of what he owed him. The still he had designed for Mick would dramatically increase his production of peregrine wine, brewed from mash derived from the roots of the ambulatory peregrine bushes, and the Franklin stove he'd shown Mick how to make for his own use in the keep would be another source of profit for the industrious leprechaun, who had already taken orders for more. The "many-bladed knife" production, which had seemed to generate the most excitement, was underway and soon their first batch of Swiss-Army-style knives would be complete. Mick clearly understood the benefit in all these things, just as he understood the profit to be made. Likewise, the brigands who were helping on these projects were equally enthusiastic. The problem was Black Shannon. She kept growing more and more restless and impatient.

He sighed and shook his head. "I just don't know what I'm going to do about that girl," he said to himself, out loud.

"Belike you are the only man who'd think of asking such a question," the gem-studded, golden chamberpot replied from its place on the chair across the room.

Brewster started and glanced at the pot sharply. "Damn, Brian, you startled me," he said.

"Sorry," the pot replied. " 'Twasn't my intention, I assure you."

"I know," said Brewster, getting up to put on his clothes. "I just can't seem to get used to the idea that you're actually a person, under an enchantment. I keep forgetting and thinking I'm alone in the room. Thoughtless of me. I'm really the one who should apologize."

"Think nothing of it, Doc," said the pot. "I'm quite accustomed to it."

"Well, just the same, I'm sorry for forgetting," Brewster said.

"Doc, my friend, believe me, you have nothing to apologize for," said the pot. " 'Twas a long time I spent locked up within that wizard's trunk and I am grateful for a civilized man to speak with for a change. Especially one who never thinks of using me for the purpose for which chamberpots were all intended. 'Tis a wonderful thing, this toilet you've invented. For that alone, you have my eternal gratitude."

"Yes, well . . . thank you, Brian," Brewster said awkwardly.

"However, returning to the point at hand," the pot continued, " 'tis a mystery to me why Shannon is of such concern to you. You are a man, she is a wench, and a rather fetching one, at that. She also finds you comely. I say throw her down and mount the pony and she'll cease to trouble you."

Brewster shook his head. "It would take a better man than I to throw *that* 'wench' down," he said. "Quite aside from the fact that 'throwing a woman down and mounting the pony,' as you put it, is a rather disrespectful way of treating the opposite sex, and not at all my sort of thing. On top of which, it's a rather simplistic solution and one that I doubt very much would work."

"It's never failed me before," the pot said.

"Yes, and look where it's gotten you," said Brewster.

"Aye, well . . . sad to say, 'tis a point that I can ill dispute," the pot replied.

Brewster stared at the enchanted werepot prince and marveled. "I still can't get over it," he said. "What's happened to you defies all known science. How a human being's molecular structure can be altered in such a radical fashion, not to mention the fact that you can speak, when you have no visible means of doing so . . . it's absolutely mind-boggling."

" 'Tis magic, Doc," the pot replied. "And 'tis in the laws

of magic, and not your science, that you will find the solution that you seek. And I do earnestly hope you find it.''

"One way or another, Brian, I'll find a way to turn you back, permanently," Brewster said. "I just don't know how, yet. It'll be the greatest challenge of my career. But if a man found a way to do this to you, then there has to be a way for me to find out how to reverse the spell."

"Then 'tis magic you shall need to learn, Doc," the pot said. "And from being kept by a succession of adepts— who, admittedly, failed to restore me—I've nevertheless learned a good deal about sorcery. I shall help you to the full extent of my abilities."

"Yes, well, it's past time I started doing something about that," said Brewster, as he pulled on his leather breeches and reached for his shirt. "I know I promised that I'd try to help you, but I've simply been so busy with the projects at the keep that I haven't had much time to devote to your problem. You've been very patient, Brian, and you deserve better."

He could almost hear the shrug in the pot's voice as it replied, " 'Tis a long time I've been the way I am, Doc. I can suffer it a while longer, if I must."

"I only wish Shannon had your attitude," said Brewster. "She's starting to become a problem. I think I know what the trouble is, too." He paused in lacing up his shirt. "Until I came along, Shannon was in charge and her leadership was undisputed. Of course, I would never presume to dispute her leadership, but at the same time, I can see where she'd perceive her position as being of secondary importance ever since I arrived."

"Which is as it should be with a woman and a man," said the pot.

"No, Brian, you're wrong," said Brewster. "Especially when it comes to a woman like Shannon. If she truly perceived me as her rival, how long do you think I'd last? I'd never survive a test of strength against her. And let's face it, without the brigands, we wouldn't be making any kind of progress here at all. I need to find some way to get her more involved. And at the same time, I promised her greater profit than she could achieve by stealing. I'm going to have to make good on that promise, and I'm going to have to do it soon, or else she'll take matters into her own hands and that'll be the end of it.''

He slipped into his tweed sport coat and stood there, looking down at himself. He spread his arms out in a shrug. "Don't I look a sight?" he said. He was wearing rough, brown leather breeches and a loose-fitting shirt that laced up at the chest. On his feet, he wore soft leather boots. The houndstooth Harris tweed jacket with the leather elbow patches and brown leather buttons didn't quite go with the outfit, but his gray flannel trousers had worn out and his white Oxford shirt was soiled and frayed. "This kind of life is rather hard on clothes," he observed wryly.

"I think the wool doublet looks rather dashing," the pot replied. "Except for where you had to patch it where the sleeves had worn out at the elbows."

"They're not worn out," said Brewster. "The patches are really just for decoration. It's just the style."

"You mean that where you come from, the fashion is to make the clothing look worn out?" asked the pot.

"Well . . . I suppose it is," said Brewster. "The first thing the kids do when they buy a new pair of pants is rip the knees out."

"Why?" asked the pot.

"I really don't know," said Brewster with a frown. "Anyway, let's go see how things are coming along. Maybe I'll come up with some ideas about where Shannon could fit in. Unless I can get her involved in something that can put her abilities to good use and make her as enthusiastic as the others, she's going to keep feeling left out and she'll wind up growing resentful. And that's one lady whose resentment I would *not* want to incur."

He tucked the chamberpot under his arm and went downstairs. The little peregrine bush followed like a shadow, scrabbling after him on its twisted roots.

It was still quite early, but there was already a great deal of activity on the grounds of the keep. As Brewster crossed the great hall on the first floor of his tower, he was greeted by the brigands already gathered there, who rose to their feet respectfully as he came in.

"Good morning, Doc," said Fuzzy Tom, pausing in his ingestion of copious quantities of scrambled eggs to stand and incline his great, hairy head and face toward Brewster as he passed. The gesture was almost, but not quite, a bow. His greeting was echoed by Lonesome John and Winsome Wil, who likewise stood and inclined their heads respectfully.

"Morning, Tom, John, Wil," said Brewster, hastening past them to the kitchen, so they could sit back down and finish their breakfast.

He'd done nothing to encourage this formality and, in fact, he'd done his best to discourage it, but there seemed to be little he could do about it. It was, doubtless, Bloody Bob who was responsible.

The aging brigand had once been a famous warrior, serving under kings and dukes and princes, and it was in such service that he learned courtly behavior and the proper way to act around a liege lord. After Brewster had restored his sight by making a crude prescription visor for him, the brawny old ex-warrior had formally sworn allegiance to him and appointed himself Brewster's "loyal retainer." Reverting to his old habits, Bloody Bob had taken to addressing Brewster as "milord" and even dropping to one knee in his presence, a practice he gave up with some reluctance only when Brewster insisted he desist. However, he continued to display at least a token formality toward his "liege," something the other brigands had begun to emulate.

It was hardly the sort of thing that Shannon could fail to notice and Brewster was concerned that she might take it the wrong way. She was, after all, the leader of the brigands and she had won her position the hard way. Brewster didn't want her to think that he was trying to usurp her place. If Shannon started to regard him as a serious threat to her position, she was liable to take matters into her own hands and Brewster was under no illusions as to what would happen if that came to pass. The results, for him, were liable to be fatal.

He came into the kitchen, where Pikestaff Pat's wife,

Calamity Jane, was busy supervising the preparation of the meals for the day. The kitchen, they had discovered, was the safest place for her. As her name implied, she was the most accident-prone woman Brewster had ever seen. Allowing her to wander about the construction site on the grounds of the keep was a sure fire way to guarantee disaster.

If there was a ladder within ten miles, Jane would find a way to trip over it and knock down whoever had climbed up it. If there was a bucket placed on some scaffolding, somehow it would contrive to fall at the exact moment that she passed, and in such a way that it would spill its contents all over her and wind up on her head, causing her to stumble and knock into something else, which would start a chain reaction of injuries among the workers that would bring everything to a halt. In the kitchen, however, her jinx did not seem to affect her for some reason and she was completely in her element, cooking up meals that would rival those served in the finest restaurants in London.

Saucy Cheryl was over at the cutting table, along with Juicy Jill and a couple of other fancy girls from Dirty Mary's Emporium and Hostelry, dressing out the spams for the soap-making operation. She saw Brewster come in, grinned, and waved a bloody cleaver at him. Jane stopped cutting up the vegetables to bring him his morning cup of tea. She handed him the steaming mug, watching his face with an anxious expression as he took a tentative first sip.

"Very good, Jane," Brewster said with a smile. "Thank you."

"Have I got it yet, Doc?" she asked hopefully.

"Well . . . no, not quite," Brewster replied, and when he saw the disappointed expression on her face, he quickly added, "but you're getting closer all the time."

She smiled, satisfied that she was making progress, and went back to slicing up the veggies. Jane had set herself what seemed to be an impossible task, namely, trying to duplicate English breakfast tea without access to any tea leaves. It had started when Brewster once remarked, rather wistfully, that he missed having good English tea for breakfast and Jane had decided then and there that she'd find a way to duplicate the beverage.

She took it as a challenge to her culinary and homeopathic skills, and she kept experimenting with all sorts of strange herbal infusions. She had managed to come up with a rather pleasant and tasty brew that was somewhat reminiscent of black Ceylon tea, but there was something about the taste that still wasn't quite right. As a result of her efforts, she had developed a number of recipies for blends of herbal teas, which she kept in ceramic jars on the kitchen shelves, and having once seen her crushing up some peculiar-looking beetles with a mortar and pestle, Brewster had decided that he was not going to inquire about any of her ingredients.

The brigands were now taking daily tea breaks in the afternoon, when Jane would brew up a number of different blends and serve them in steaming pots in the main hall of the keep. They had helped her name them, too, and some of the more popular blends were Dragon's Breath Brew, Fairy Mist, and a tea that Jane herself became quite partial to and drank throughout the day, which her husband, Pikestaff Pat, had christened Jane's Addiction. It seemed to make her very giddy and Brewster wasn't sure what she put in it, but the one time he had tried it, he found himself starting to hallucinate and had avoided it ever since. Still, with all these teas being produced, Brewster thought there was a good chance they might find a way to market them, which would be yet another potential source of profit for the brigands.

They now had a number of projects underway that would produce marketable commodities. There were the "many-bladed knives," the first batch of which were almost ready for assembly. There was the soap-making operation, and Mick's "O'Fallon Stoves," and then there was the still, which was producing a good yield of peregrine wine—more properly, a sort of moonshine whiskey brewed from the boiled roots of peregrine bushes. Mick said it was a lot more potent now, something Brewster was willing to take his word for, as the old, cold-brewed stuff had been enough to render him nearly comatose.

The big question now was how would they market these commodities? The little village of Brigand's Roost was much too small to provide a proper market for their production, and most of the residents were already involved in their new cottage industry. The nearest city, according to Bloody Bob, was miles away, and Brewster did not think Shannon would react too well to the idea of her brigands being used as teamsters to haul the goods to market. Quite aside from which, every one of them had a price on his head, which could make deliveries rather precarious.

Developing a market posed yet another problem. There wasn't much that they could do in the way of advertising except, perhaps, for putting up some placards. Their business would have to depend primarily on word-of-mouth advertising. And that would take time.

So there it was again, thought Brewster. Time. The eternal enemy. No matter how he looked at it, it would take time to develop a market, and time for the profits to materialize, time he didn't really have. As far as Shannon was concerned, this "magical manufacturing process" of his was a bit too much like work. Nor would it take too long before the rest of the brigands began to realize that manufacturing, for all the wonders it produced, was remarkably similar to labor. And at that point, he might well wind up encountering the first concerted labor action in the twenty-seven kingdoms.

The other problem was, of course, that all this left him with no opportunity to search for his missing time machine. It could be anywhere. He hadn't really seen anything of this new world yet. He simply couldn't get away. Somehow, somewhere, there had to be a solution to these problems.

He went outside, past the boiling kettles where Robie McMurphy and Pikestaff Pat were rendering the spam fat into soap, and around the outside of the keep to the riverbank. Behind him, Thorny rustled along in his wake, like a faithful puppy dog with leaves.

Brewster walked along the riverbank, thinking to himself, trying to come up with some solutions to the problems that he faced. At a bend in the stream, the water rushed through a small ravine, where the rock outcroppings poked out of the clay banks and made a sort of miniature canyon. There was a pool down there, where the brigands often bathed, and Brewster climbed down to it and sat upon one of the large flat rocks above the water. He reached down and picked up a handful of pebbles from the clay slope and proceeded to toss them into the water as he contemplated this strange state of affairs.

Absently, he reached down again to pick up a few more stones to toss and his hand came up clutching a blocky lump of clay. He stared at it curiously and broke it up in his palm. It came apart in little square chunks.

"Doc! Doc, where are you?"

He looked up toward the sound. "Over here, Mick!" he called out.

A few moments later, the powerfully built leprechaun came bustling up, pushing his way through the underbrush. He stood up at the top of the small ravine, slightly out of breath.

"Doc?"

"Down here, Mick."

"What are you doin' down there?"

"Thinking," Brewster replied, as Mick clambered down to him. He gazed thoughtfully at the mineral material in his palm.

"I came to show you the first finished blades," said Mick, plopping down on the rock outcropping beside him. He seemed very excited as he reached into his belt pouch and withdrew several gleaming knife blades, as yet unassembled. He handed them to Brewster.

"Well?" he said anxiously. "What do you think?"

They were larger than the blades in Brewster's Swiss Army knife. Larger blades were slightly easier to make and Mick had thought that they would be more useful and appealing than the smaller blades. The main cutting blade was six inches long and the smaller one measured four inches. There was also a three-inch awl blade and a six-inch saw blade, as well. They were keeping it simple, using just those four blades, to begin with. They were the end result of weeks of unceasing toil on Mick's part, and he was justifiably proud of them.

To produce the steel, Brewster had designed a large, double-action bellows powered by a belt running off the water-wheel shaft. Mick, Robie, and Bloody Bob had painstakingly constructed it to Brewster's specifications, making it out of leather and a large wood frame. It took up almost the entire room where the grinding stones were, so the milling room of the keep had now also become Mick's second smithy.

The bellows functioned like a piston, pushing air through the furnace in both directions through a ceramic pipe that came up around the crucible and vented through the ceiling. To turn it off, it was necessary to disconnect the crude, yet effective, rosined belt made from plaited vines. Pig iron was heated in the crucible to the melting point, and the impurities were then removed by adding lime to the molten iron, which resulted in a huge flash of smoke and flame going up the smokestack. When the smoke dissipated, air was blown over the mixture to add carbon dioxide and when there were only small flames left burning atop the molten iron, it was poured out into the molds, where it solidified into steel.

Without nickel, molybdenum, and chromium, they could not make stainless steel, of course, but what they did get was a fairly good grade of steel that would not rust if it was kept oiled and properly cared for. Mick had originally balked at the idea of using coal, because he said it made "dirty iron," metal with impurities. He had always used charcoal in his foundry, but Brewster showed him how to make coke by preburning coal, burying it, and burning it for a couple of days in a reduced oxygen atmosphere. The impurities were thereby burned off, resulting in coke, which burned hotter and simplified the making of steel.

Once the steel was solidified in the molds, the next step was to take the blades out for polishing and sharpening, which was done before the tempering process, so that the crystals wouldn't break when the blades were sharpened, thereby enabling them to hold an edge better. The blades were then heated until they were red-hot and plunged into oil. Finally, they were wiped down and polished on a wheel run by a leather belt. The wheel itself was made of iron, with leather glued to it for buffing. Brewster held the end result in his hands. All that remained now was for the pieces to be riveted together with the handles and the spacers.

"Beautiful, Mick," said Brewster, admiring his handiwork. "An excellent job. Outstanding. Very nice, indeed." He gave the blades back to Mick.

Mick beamed with pride. "The best blades I've ever forged," he said with a huge grin. "Truly, Doc, your magical knowledge has improved my craft beyond all my expectations! Think of the swords and daggers I shall be able to make now! S'trewth, there will be no armorer anywhere in the twenty-seven kingdoms to compare with Mick O'Fallon!"

"I'm glad, Mick," Brewster said. "It was the very least I could do for all the kindness you've shown me."

"Aye, and 'tis the better part of the bargain I've received," said Mick. "Sure and 'twas a great day for Mick O'Fallon when you arrived in your magic chariot."

"And I have yet to find the one that's missing," Brewster said.

"Never fear, Doc, 'twill turn up. You'll see. You've got Rory flying over the forest, keepin' his dragon eye out for it, and he's told the fairies to be on the lookout for it, too. We'll find it, never you mind."

"I hope so, Mick," said Brewster. "I certainly hope so."

"Aye, well, in the meantime, things are coming along splendidly," the leprechaun replied. "Now all we need to do is decide what material we'll be using for the handles. Gold, perhaps? Or maybe silver? Faith, and that's all been done before, though. For such a wondrous many-bladed knife, the handles must be something truly special and unique. Unicorn horn, perhaps? Of course, that wouldn't be in plentiful supply. . . ."

Brewster stared thoughtfully at the broken-up mineral lumps he'd dropped. He reached down and picked them up again.

Mick stared at him with a puzzled expression. "What's

that you've got there, Doc?'' His eyes grew wide when he saw what Brewster had picked up. ''Faith, Doc, and 'tis just clay!''

''Not clay, Mick,'' Brewster replied. ''Bauxite.''

Mick frowned. ''Box-ite?''

Brewster smiled. ''Yes, Mick, bauxite.'' He glanced around at the sloping ravine. ''And it seems as though we've got a plentiful supply.''

''I don't understand, Doc,'' Mick said, still puzzled.

''You will,'' said Brewster. He clapped the leprechaun on his muscular shoulder. ''Mick . . . how'd you like to learn how to make aluminum?''

➤ CHAPTER ➤
FOUR

As Teddy the troll dragged the hapless, screaming prisoner across the floor, Warrick stood watching with his arms folded, frowning in concentration. It was difficult to concentrate with all that screaming going on, but he was getting used to it. What he wasn't used to was the frustration that he felt.

Each time a subject was strapped into the device, and Warrick spoke the spell that activated it, there was a crackling of energy and a peculiar stench, followed by an annoying clap of thunder that had a tendency to break all the glassware in the sanctorum, and then the subject disappeared. Thus far, nothing Warrick had done had succeeded in bringing any of the subjects back, consequently, there was no way of knowing where they had disappeared to.

Warrick stood back from the device each time he activated it, and when the process was complete, he approached it once again and cautiously glanced inside, where he could see that some of the symbols displayed upon the control panel of the time machine had changed mysteriously, but he had no idea what any of it meant.

"Control panel?" said Warrick, frowning. "What is a control panel?"

Teddy paused in his task of strapping in the struggling prisoner and glanced at his master uneasily.

"Were you talking to me, Master?" he said.

"No," snapped Warrick irritably. "Get on with your work."

"Yes, Master," said Teddy, with an apprehensive glance up toward the ceiling.

"*Noooo*!" screamed the prisoner as Teddy strapped him in. "No, *please*! Don't! Don't kill me, Master Warrick, please, I beg you! I'll do anything, anything, I *swear* it!"

"Oh, do be quiet!" Warrick said, with an abrupt, sorcerous gesture toward the prisoner. The prisoner jerked as if struck, then fell unconscious. Teddy finished the task of strapping him in and hastily backed away from the machine. It frightened him, not only because everyone he strapped into it kept disappearing, never to be seen again, but because Warrick himself hesitated to come too close to it. And anything that made Warrick nervous made Teddy doubly so.

"It does *not* make me nervous," Warrick protested.

"What, Master?" Teddy asked.

"I am merely exercising proper caution," Warrick said.

"What, Master?"

"I was not speaking to *you*, Teddy," Warrick replied.

"Ah. Sorry, Master."

"My wand," said Warrick.

Teddy simply stood there, staring at the time machine with nervous anticipation.

Warrick cleared his throat. "I said, my *wand*."

Teddy remained motionless.

"*My wand, you misbegotten wart hog!*"

Teddy jumped, startled. "Oh! Forgive me, Master, I thought you were speaking to the one you call the narrator again."

He hurried over to the table to fetch his master's wand while Warrick sighed heavily and shook his head. "You are making my life very difficult, you know," he said.

"I am sorry, Master, I do not mean to," Teddy said, handing him his wand.

"No, not *you*, Teddy, I was speaking to the narrator."

Teddy bit down on a hairy knuckle. This whole thing with his master speaking to the invisible narrator all the time was making him very uneasy and confused. He was starting to develop a nervous tic. Not to mention the effect that it was having on the narrator.

"Well, 'twould make matters a great deal easier if you were simply to tell me what I wish to know," said Warrick.

"And what would that be, Master?" Teddy asked.

Warrick rolled his eyes. "Not *you*, Teddy, the narrator!"

"Oh. Sorry, Master."

"And stop doing that!"

"Stop doing what, Master?" Teddy asked.

"No, Teddy, not *you*, the narrator! I was speaking to the *narrator*! Each time I address a comment to him, he makes *you* reply, thereby avoiding the necessity of answering me."

"He *makes* me reply? You mean, I am being *controlled*?" asked Teddy, glancing nervously from side to side and wringing his hairy hands with concern.

"You see? He's done it again! Now cease, blast you, and face me like a man! Teddy, leave us alone."

The little troll hesitated uncertainly.

"No, you don't," said Warrick. "Teddy, go to your room. *Now*."

"But, Master. . . ."

"I said, go to your room! At once, do you hear? And none of this hesitating nonsense. I will send for you when I need you. Now come along. And before the little troll could think to reply, the wizard took him by the arm and walked him to the door, opening it and urging him on through, then closing it behind him."

That was sneaky.

"You left me with no other choice," said Warrick with a crafty smile. "And none of this cutting to another scene business, either. I'm wise to that game."

All right. You win. For the moment. So . . . what is it you want?

"You know very well what I want. I wish to know the secret of the time machine," said Warrick.

Now you know perfectly well I can't tell you that. You already know a great deal more than you're supposed to. If you start finding things out in advance of the plot, you're really going to screw up the story.

"That is your problem, not mine," Warrick replied.

There was a loud knocking at the door.

"Forget it," Warrick said. "I'm not falling for it."

The knocking was repeated, louder this time.

"Sorry, 'twon't work," said Warrick. "You can put a squad of men at arms with battering rams out there for all I care. I am not budging from this spot until I receive an answer, so you might as well give it up."

Warrick yawned. He suddenly felt extremely tired. He'd been a long time without sleep and—

"Stop that," Warrick snapped. "I am *not* tired and I will sleep when I am damned good and ready."

In spite of himself, he felt his eyelids growing very heavy. He could barely keep them open. He—

"Oh, no, you don't! Warrick wasn't in the least bit sleepy. He suddenly felt a fresh, invigorating burst of energy and the narrator realized that 'twas pointless to resist. Despite himself, he felt the immeasurable strength of will the wizard brought to bear upon him and he felt irresistibly compelled to do the sorcerer's bidding."

No, he didn't.

"Protesting vainly, the narrator nevertheless felt his will weakening in the face of Warrick's power. Whether he wanted to or not, he was going to tell the sorcerer the secret of the time machine, who made it, and where it came from, and where—"

Without warning, the narrator typed in a space break and cut to another scene.

Sean MacGregor and his three henchmen dismounted in front of the roadside hostelry and tavern, and not a moment too soon, either. They were dusty from riding all day and the small hostelry looked like a good place to spend the night. The wooden sign hanging over the door identified the hostelry as The Dew Drop Inn, which testified to the fact that clichés not only withstand the test of time, but cross its boundaries, as well.

There were several horses tied up outside at the rail and, by the look of them, they did not belong to peasants. Their tack was not only lightweight and functional, to facilitate fast traveling, but well-made and expensive, as well. Sean MacGregor did not fail to note this as they tied up their own horses and went inside. The three brothers went in first, making a beeline straight for the bar. MacGregor stopped just inside the doorway and looked around.

It was a simple, country roadside inn, with planked wood flooring stained by years of spills, a rough oak bar ringed with the circular stains of wet mugs of ale being placed upon it, and a roaring fire in the hearth, over which hung a large black kettle in which stew simmered. The tables and the benches were all made of heavy, rough-hewn redwood; the better to withstand the occasional disagreement among the patrons.

The man behind the bar was large, ruddy-faced and heavily bearded, with shaggy brown hair that was liberally streaked with gray. He looked quite capable of taking care of any trouble, despite his years, and his face bore the disinterested, noncommittal expression of a man who'd seen most everything at one time or another. However, he wasn't the one who caught MacGregor's attention. Mac was far more interested in the group of men sitting together at a table in the corner, near the hearth.

While Hugh, Dugh, and Lugh were interested in nothing more than quaffing copious quantities of ale, MacGregor took a long look at the men huddled together at the corner table. And they, in turn, took a long look at him, as well. There were six of them, and they were a rough and surly looking lot. Several of them had scars upon their faces and all of them had shifty eyes. They were all bristling with weapons, too. MacGregor saw one of them spot the Guild badge on his tunic and nudge the others.

A pretty, young, dark-haired serving wench was busy filling several plates of stew on a wooden tray, which she then proceeded to carry over to the group in the corner. She did not fail to notice MacGregor as she crossed the room, for Mac was a rugged and good-looking man whom pretty, young serving wenches invariably found attractive, as this one apparently did. She gave him a coy look and an inviting smile, which he returned. He took a table on the opposite side of the room, where he could have a clear view of the others, and left the three brothers to their chug-a-lugging contest. A moment later, the serving wench came over to him.

"Welcome, good sir," she said, with a dazzling smile, which is a required attribute in any pretty, young serving wench. It goes with the long, flowing hair, the dimples, the clear blue eyes, and the saucy wiggle. "And what would be your fancy on this fine evening?"

The way she said it suggested that she might not necessarily be referring to anything on the menu, which was probably just as well, as menus hadn't been invented yet. This was hardly a five-star dining establishment and the deal was that if you didn't like whatever was simmering in the pot, then you were pretty much left with whatever was fermenting in the keg. Either way, Sean MacGregor wasn't particularly choosey, at least not when it came to food, although he did draw the line at eating spam.

"My fancy on this evening would be a bowl of your fine stew, a tankard of good ale, and that twinkle in your eye, my love, together with your smile, which is nearly sustenance enough all by itself."

Now a line like that would normally produce a rather pained expression in the average modern waitress, and possibly even a tart rejoinder, but that's only because the fine art of courtly flirtation has, unfortunately, become outmoded. Chances were, however, that even a modern waitress would have reacted favorably to such a line coming from a man like Sean MacGregor, because he was a fine, dashing figure of a man, indeed, rather like a cross between Errol Flynn and Sean Connery, with a bit of Harrison Ford thrown in, and his delivery would have had Shakespearean actors calling their vocal coaches in despair. The knives in the crossed bandoliers didn't hurt, either.

"Why, thank you, kind sir," the serving wench replied, blushing prettily. "I do believe we have at least a bowl or two of stew left in the pot, and of the ale and the rest," she added with a wink, "you may drink your fill."

"Have a care, my love, I am a very thirsty man," MacGregor replied with a grin.

"Then I shall make every effort to see your thirst is quenched," the serving wench said, gazing directly into his eyes.

Ah, well, you just don't hear dialogue like that nowadays, unless you hang out with the Society for Creative Anachronism. Personally, I think it's the clothes. Lines like that simply don't play when you're wearing jeans and polyester. However, put on a rough-out leather doublet, some tight breeches, a pair of high, swashbuckling boots, and buckle on a blade or two, and the next thing you know, you'll be declaiming like Scaramouche. Unless, of course, you're rather dim, like Mac's three apprentice henchmen, who couldn't turn a phrase if it had power steering. They were already on their third pitcher, and trying to see which of them could belch the loudest.

"What is your name, my love?" MacGregor asked.

" 'Tis Lisa, good sir. And yours?"

"Sean MacGregor," he replied. "Tell me, Lisa, those men over at the corner table, have you ever seen any of them about before?"

"Why, no, they are all strangers to me," she replied. And then she grimaced. "And a rather coarse lot they are, too."

"They haven't been giving you any trouble, have they?" asked MacGregor with a frown.

"Not really, but I have seen their sort before," said Lisa. "Mostly, they have been asking questions about some men they're seeking."

"What men?"

"Three men, they said, who were traveling together. One tall, with a long face and dark hair, one of medium height and balding, with a fringe of light-brown hair, and one with dark-red hair and a beard, who doesn't speak."

"Indeed?" MacGregor said. "And have you seen such men?"

Lisa drew closer. "Truth to tell, I do remember three such men who stopped here once," she said, "but I have told those buzzards nothing, for their rudeness and coarse ways."

"And it serves them right, too," said MacGregor. "Tell me, Lisa, when those three men were here, did they by any chance while away the time by playing chess?"

"Funny you should ask that," Lisa replied. "I do recall it, for they seemed upset that one of their game pieces had been lost. They asked me if I had a thimble they might borrow, so they could use it in its place."

"Would you know, by any chance, if it was *this* piece they were lacking?" asked MacGregor, removing the carved wooden knight from his pouch.

"Why, yes, I do believe 'twas a knight," said Lisa. "I heard two of them arguing about it, each blaming the other for its loss. Were they friends of yours, then?"

"Not exactly," said MacGregor, "but I am most anxious to make their acquaintance. Thank you, Lisa. You have been most helpful. And very charming, to boot."

"And you are a shameless flatterer, Sean MacGregor," she replied with a smile.

"I only speak the truth," he replied.

"Why is it that I think you only speak it rarely?" she responded with an arch look.

"Because 'tis true," said MacGregor. "You see? I am completely honest with you."

She laughed. "Go on with you."

She went over to the bar to draw a tankard of ale, giving a wide berth to the three brothers, who were beginning to have some trouble making a connection between the rims of their tankards and their lips. She brought the ale over to MacGregor, then went to get his stew. As she crossed the room, one of the men sitting at the corner table got up from his bench and sauntered over to MacGregor's table, his hand resting lightly on the pommel of his sword.

"I see you wear the badge of the Assassin's Guild," the burly stranger said. He was a big man, powerfully built, with long brown hair hanging to his massive shoulders. His steely gaze flicked from MacGregor's face to the badge on his tunic, and back again. "And I also see it has a star upon it. Unless it be a counterfeit to impress pretty serving maids, that would make you Mac the Knife."

"My friends often call me Mac," MacGregor replied, "but I fear I do not know you, sir."

"The name is Black Jack," the stranger said. " 'Tis a name that is well-known in certain quarters."

"Indeed? And whose quarters would those be?" MacGregor asked innocently.

"You seek to mock me, sir?"

"I seek only enlightenment," MacGregor said.

"Well, then, perhaps you would be so kind as to enlighten *me* as to your business in these parts?"

"I fail to see where my business is any of yours," MacGregor replied.

"Well, then perhaps *this* will improve your vision," Black Jack replied, drawing his sword with lightning speed and holding its point to MacGregor's throat.

Mac remained seated, calmly gazing at the man before him. He did not even glance down toward the sword point held at his throat. The three brothers remained slumped over the bar, oblivious to what was going on behind them. The tavern keeper merely watched, his face expressionless, but Lisa gasped and dropped the bowl of stew that she was bringing to MacGregor. Her hand went to her mouth in alarm.

"I believe I see your point," MacGregor said calmly, taking a sip of ale. " 'Tis a bit too close for comfort, I might add."

"If I do not receive an answer very soon, the discomfort is liable to increase," said Black Jack, pressing home his point ever so slightly.

"Well, in that case, I suppose that I had best oblige you," MacGregor replied. "My business is with a client who has employed my services to seek out certain individuals."

"By any chance, would these be *three* individuals?"

asked Black Jack while his companions watched intently from across the room.

"Perhaps," replied MacGregor, taking another sip of ale.

"And would one of them happen to be tall, with dark hair and a long face?"

"Perhaps," replied MacGregor, once again.

"And would another happen to be of medium height and balding, with a fringe of brown hair?"

"Perhaps," replied MacGregor, for the third time.

"And would the third happen to have dark-red hair, with a beard, and have been never heard to speak?"

MacGregor calmly sipped his ale. "Perhaps," he said, yet again.

"In that event, perhaps we seek the same three individuals," said Black Jack, his sword point never wavering from MacGregor's throat.

"Perhaps," MacGregor said.

"And since there is a handsome bounty on those individuals, which my friends and I hope to collect, perhaps it would be in my best interests if I were to eliminate any potential competitors. And if such a competitor happened to be the number-one-ranked member of the Assassin's Guild, then perhaps it would only add to my reputation if I were to dispatch him."

"Perhaps it would, if you were to succeed in such an effort," said MacGregor, ignoring the sword held at his throat as he once again raised the tankard to his lips.

"Well, considering that I have you at something of a disadvantage, then perhaps I shall," replied Black Jack with a smile.

"Perhaps not," MacGregor said. He took another sip, then suddenly spat a spray of ale into Black Jack's face. As Black Jack recoiled instinctively, MacGregor slammed his tankard down, pinning Black Jack's blade beneath it to the table.

With a curse, Black Jack jerked back his blade, which gave MacGregor time to send his bench crashing to the floor as he sprang to his feet and drew his own sword.

"You shall pay dearly for that!" snarled Black Jack.

MacGregor grinned at him. "Come and collect," he said.

As their blades clashed, Lisa cried out and Black Jack's companions quickly rose to join the fray. However, all this commotion finally awoke the three brothers to the fact that something was going on behind them.

Hugh turned around as MacGregor engaged Black Jack and saw the five men getting up and reaching for their weapons. "*Fight!*" he yelled out gleefully, and hurled his empty tankard with such force that the man whose head it struck was killed instantly. The sturdy tankard only suffered minor damage.

Dugh took three running steps and leapt up on a table top, from which he launched himself in what would have been a graceful swan dive, except that Dugh was built less like a swan than like a grizzly bear, and bears aren't really all that graceful. In any case, there was nothing graceful about the way he landed, right on top of two of Black Jack's companions, and they all went tumbling to the floor.

Lugh was the slowest to react, which gave the man nearest him time to lunge at him with his blade. Lugh tried to dodge, but he was still a little slow and the blade penetrated his shoulder, missing his heart, which had been the swordsman's intended target. Lugh grunted, grabbed the exposed part of the blade and kicked his attacker in the groin. The man's eyes got all bulgy and he made a sound like a pig being fed into a meat grinder as he doubled up and clutched himself.

"That *hurt*," said Lugh, pulling the sword out of his shoulder and proceeding to belabor his attacker about the head with its ornate, basket hilt.

That left one man to face Hugh, and he decided on the spur of the moment that he didn't really feel like facing such a large opponent at close quarters. He reached for his dagger, drew it, and flipped it around so that he could hold it by the point and throw it. Unfortunately for him, this rather showy gesture gave Hugh time enough to snatch up a bench and hold it up as a shield just as he threw his knife. The blade stuck in the bench, which Hugh then proceeded to use as a battering ram, running at his opponent with it.

Caught in the act of trying to draw his sword, the fifth man screamed as Hugh slammed into him, benchfirst, and carried him back against the wall.

Meanwhile, without his friends to support him, Black Jack suddenly found he had his hands full. Not that he wasn't a good swordsman, for he was, but Sean MacGregor had yet to meet his match and Black Jack just wasn't it. He retreated rapidly before MacGregor's dancing blade, parrying like mad, and if he'd had time to think, he would have thought that instead of wasting time earlier with all that snappy repartee, he should have simply run MacGregor through.

"What, no more snappy repartee?" MacGregor taunted him as he advanced. With a deft twist of the wrist, he hooked Black Jack's blade and sent it flying across the room. This time, with his sword point at Black Jack's throat, he backed him up against the bar. "Now... about this reputation of yours," MacGregor said.

As MacGregor spoke, Dugh was busily smashing his two antagonists' heads together. They were making very satisfying, thunking sounds, but Dugh had a rather limited attention span and he was growing bored of this game. He decided to see if his brothers needed any help, and so he flung his two stunned antagonists away from him, one in either direction. Unfortunately, the one he flung off to his right happened to strike MacGregor, knocking him right off his feet. Black Jack was quick to take advantage of this fortuitous reprieve by kicking MacGregor as he went down and then bolting for the door, snatching up his sword *en route*.

"You've not heard the last of Black Jack!" he cried, and then he ran out the door, mounted up, and galloped off down the road.

"Somehow, I knew he was going to say that," said MacGregor, wincing with pain as he pushed himself up to a sitting position.

"How did you know that, Mac?" Dugh asked, giving him a hand up.

"Because that's what they always say," MacGregor replied with a sour grimace. "Oh, and by the way, in the future, when you decide to toss someone around, do check to see which way you're tossing him, will you?"

"I'm sorry, Mac," said Dugh, looking down at the floor.

"Want we should chase him for you, Mac?" asked Lugh.

"I shouldn't bother," MacGregor replied. "He has a fast horse and he's had a good head start." He frowned. "What's making that noise?"

He turned around and saw Hugh still bashing away with the bench. He had his man pinned up against the wall and he would pull the bench back, allowing the man to fall forward just a little bit, and then slam him back against the wall with it once more, which was producing a sound not unlike that made by a washing machine with sneakers in it. (I know, the analogy is out of period, but that's exactly what it sounded like.)

MacGregor walked over to Hugh and tapped him on the shoulder. "Hugh . . . I think he's dead."

Hugh pulled the bench back and the bloody corpse collapsed to the floor.

"Oh," said Hugh, sounding a trifle disappointed.

"One of the things you'll need to know, Hugh, if you're ever going to be a good assassin, is that you only need to kill somebody once," said MacGregor. "Once is usually sufficient. Now then, I don't suppose any of these chaps are still alive?"

"I think this one's still breathin', Mac," said Dugh, bending over one of the prostrate figures.

MacGregor turned him over with his foot. He grimaced at the sight of the man's face, which had been dramatically rearranged. "Well, I fear this one won't be talking any time soon," he said. "Pity. We might have learned a thing or two."

"I'm sorry, Mac," said Dugh. "Did I hit the fella too hard?"

"Oh, well, it couldn't be helped, I suppose," MacGregor replied. "You see, lads, in the future, if we are ever set upon by unknown assailants, we must try to keep at least one of them alive, and preferably in some shape to answer questions. That way, we can find out who they are, whom they are working for, and how much they know."

"Gee, Mac, this assassin stuff is really complicated," Lugh said.

"Aye, well, never fear, you'll get the hang of it eventually," MacGregor said. "You did well, lads, you did very well, indeed. And, fortunately, we are not left completely in the dark about this situation. We do know that the man I fought, presumably their leader, is named Black Jack, and from what he told me, it seems that they were working freelance, in the hopes of collecting the bounty on the men we seek."

"You mean, they were working for Warrick, too?" said Hugh.

"Not exactly," replied MacGregor. "You see, while Warrick the White keeps me on retainer, he has also offered a bounty for these men he's seeking, which increases the odds of those men being found, since enterprising men such as our friends here will attempt to find them on their own in order to collect the bounty."

"But I thought *we* were supposed to find them," Dugh said.

"Indeed, we are," said MacGregor, "but we are not the only ones looking, you see. The bounty increases Warrick's chances of having someone find those men, but it does make our job a bit more complicated, in that we shall be competing with everyone else who's looking for them."

Lugh shook his head. "It doesn't seem right to me," he grumbled.

" 'Tis not meant to be right to you," MacGregor replied. " 'Tis meant to be right to the client."

"Difficult work, this," Hugh observed.

"Aye, well, if it wasn't, then everybody would be doing it, wouldn't they?" MacGregor said.

"Who's going to pay for all this, then?" the tavern keeper asked, surveying the damage to his establishment, which was relatively minor, all things considered. The Stealers Tavern was still undergoing repairs, from the three brothers' last visit.

MacGregor bent down and quickly searched the man lying at his feet. He found the man's purse and examined its contents. "These fellows will, I think," he said. "I'm sure that, between them, they have more than enough to compensate you for your loss."

The tavern keeper grunted and proceeded to relieve the other bodies of their purses.

Lisa came up to MacGregor, her eyes shining. "I thought for certain he was going to kill you," she said. "You were wonderful!"

"I still am," MacGregor replied with a wink. "This Black Jack fellow, I don't suppose you've ever heard of him before? He seemed to think he had some sort of reputation."

"Aye, that he does," said Lisa. "I never knew his name, nor laid eyes on him before, but sure and I've heard of him."

"Indeed? What have you heard?"

"He is a thief, a brigand, and a cutthroat," Lisa replied. "And not above any dubious enterprise that promises to bring him profit. 'Tis said he killed a man once in Pittsburgh, in The Stealers Tavern, merely for breaking wind beside him."

"Mmmm. Well, considering the offal served for food there, I can't say as I blame him," said MacGregor. "So he frequents The Stealers, does he? That must be where he heard about the bounty on those men we seek. And now that his friends have succeeded in delaying us, he's got himself a good head start."

"Not really," replied Lisa with a smile. "He galloped off down the wrong road. The three men you're seeking took the east fork."

"Did they, indeed?" MacGregor grinned. "Well, in that case, there's no great rush, is there? We'll spend the night and take the east fork first thing in the morning. Innkeeper, we'll be needing rooms for the night!"

"Mine is at the end of the hall," said Lisa softly.

► CHAPTER ►
FIVE

Mick O'Fallon had no idea what Brewster Doc was up to this time, and he had no idea what this "aluminum" was that they were going to make, but it was shaping up to be yet another mysterious and complicated project. Until he had met Doc, he had never heard the word "project" before. He had heard the word "projectile," which referred to something that was launched through the air as a weapon, such as an arrow fired from a bow or a large stone hurled by a catapult. Doc, however, used this word "project" in an entirely different sense, referring to various alchemical and sorcerous works. Perhaps, thought Mick, it had something to do with the energies projected through the ether in order to bring these works about. In any case, the energy required for Doc's sorcery had to be prodigious, because each time he launched one of his projects, it usually meant a lot of work for everyone, especially for Mick O'Fallon.

Even the brigands who worked with him had to admit that these sorcerous projects of Doc's entailed a lot more sweat than they were used to shedding. Nevertheless, they took part without complaint, partly because there were few people who could boast of participating in sorcerous works, and partly because they were curious to see what wondrous miracle Doc would produce this time.

While Mick worked with a team of assistants at his smithy to produce the metal vessels Brewster required, another team of brigands had been organized to collect the grayish substance Brewster had called bauxite. Much of it they found on the surface of the banks in the ravine, but they also had to dig in order to find more. Brewster had taught them how to recognize it and while one group pursued that task, another worked to grind the bauxite up with mortars and pestles. This ground-up bauxite was then mixed with potash, ground limestone, and water, which produced something Brewster called "sodium hydroxide." For simplicity, Brewster had said that it could simply be called a "caustic soda," but everyone enjoyed saying "sodium hydroxide," because it sounded magical and powerful.

The ground bauxite was then mixed with a solution of this sodium hydroxide in the first of the vessels Mick had made, which Brewster called a "pressure tank."

"In this heated vessel, which is a crude sort of pressure cooker," Brewster had explained, as everyone gathered around, "the ore will be dissolved under steam heat and pressure. The sodium hydroxide will react with the hydrated aluminum oxide of the bauxite to form a solution of sodium aluminate. The insoluble impurities, which will look like red mud because of the iron oxide content, will settle to the bottom. The remaining solution will then pass into the second vessel, the one with the pressure release valve, which is called the blow-off tank, because it lets the steam out, you see. The cloth filters we're using will have to be changed each time, because they're going to get all clogged up, but that shouldn't really present a problem.

"We're actually going to be using a somewhat simplified process," he continued, "but then we're not really making a high, commercial grade of aluminum, so I don't think we'll need a whole series of reducing tanks and heat exchangers and precipitators. We'll sort of be playing this by ear, and we may have to modify the process somewhat, but it should work. Once we have the alumina distilled, we'll scrape it off the sides of the tank and put it into the reduction pot, that's the one we've lined with carbon, you see, and then we'll melt the cryolite in it. That's the white substance I found in Mick's laboratory. Eventually, we'll probably need more of it, but Mick assures me he can get more from the dwarves who work the mines. We'll run electricity through it using the generator and the voltage regulator I've salvaged from my time machine . . . my, uh, magic chariot, that is. We'll use carbon rods for the anodes and put about 750 volts of direct current through it. That should do the trick. The aluminum will melt and sink down to the bottom, and the impurities will float up to the top. After that, all that's left will be to draw the aluminum off the bottom and pour it directly into the molds. At that point it should be pure enough to work, and that's all there is to it.''

They had all simply stared at him, without comprehending a word of what he'd said. It all sounded terribly impressive, but no one had a clue as to what any of it meant.

"Well," said Brewster with a shrug, "if it sounds confusing, don't worry about it. Not everyone can be expected to understand this kind of sorcery, you know. It's a special kind of sorcery called 'science.' You'll see. Once we get all the bugs worked out of the process, it should work just fine."

"Seems like a terrible lot of trouble to go to just to make handles for the knives," said Mick dubiously. "T'would be a lot easier simply to use horn."

"Well, you said you wanted something special, didn't you?" Brewster replied. "Besides, aluminum will be a lot more practical, and it'll probably make the knives more valuable, too. It certainly won't be something people will see every day. And we'll be able to use it for other things, besides. You'll see. It may be a lot of trouble, but I think it will be worth it."

Brewster didn't tell Mick the main reason they were doing it was that he simply got caught up in the idea and wanted to see it done. And Mick didn't tell Brewster that his biggest misgiving was that the process would use up all his alchemite, which Brewster had called by the strange name of "cryolite." Apparently, thought Mick, they had a lot of different names for things in Brewster's Land of Ing.

One of the first things Brewster had done, after he moved into the keep, was ask Mick if he could take an inventory of the alchemical laboratory. Mick had agreed without hesitation, because although, in a sense, it was his laboratory, in another sense, it really wasn't. Most everything that it contained had belonged to that unknown, bygone sorcerer who had once lived at the keep at some point in the past, farther back than anyone in Brigand's Roost could remember. And what few things Mick had added to it had not really amounted to a hill of beans. Despite all the things he had mixed together, burned, melted, and reduced, he had come no closer to the secret of the Philosopher's Stone than when he'd started. Doc's knowledge, on the other hand, had been more than amply demonstrated and it was clearly far more extensive than that of any adept Mick had ever heard of. Perhaps even more extensive than that of the Grand Director of the Guild himself. So Mick was anxious for the opportunity to learn everything he could.

However, although he'd said nothing to Brewster, he had some anxiety about letting him use up all the alchemite. He could, indeed, get more from the dwarves who worked the mines up in the mountains, but it would cost him dearly. In order to obtain the supply he already had, it had been necessary for him to make half a dozen of his finest blades, designed to dwarf proportion, and at that, he'd negotiated long and hard to talk them down from the dozen blades they'd first demanded. Still, he would have paid even that price, had it been necessary, for the dwarves normally sold all their alchemite to the Master Alchemists of the Treasury Department of the Sorcerers and Adepts Guild.

When Mick had found out, quite by accident, that the dwarves regularly supplied this substance to the Master Alchemists of the Treasury Department, he had correctly deduced that alchemite was one of the necessary ingredients in the magical process that was the secret of the Philosopher's Stone, so he had bought some under the table, as it were. Yet, no matter how he'd tried, he still hadn't been able to discover the secret of the spell. He had used up about one-third of the supply he'd bought, and now it appeared that Doc was going to use up all the rest in this aluminum-making project. And Mick didn't even know what this aluminum was.

Nevertheless, he hadn't been able to refuse him. In the short time they had known each other, Mick, never the most sociable of individuals, had developed a greater liking for Doc than for anyone he'd ever known. And his respect for Doc's knowledge increased daily.

Thanks to Doc, he was now making better blades than he'd ever hoped to make, and in time, Mick was convinced that he'd achieve a reputation as the finest armorer in the twenty-seven kingdoms. And thanks to the still Doc had invented, Mick was now making more peregrine wine than he'd ever been able to make before, and it was a superior distillation, easily twice as potent as the wine produced by his old method. Soon, they would be bringing it to market outside Brigand's Roost and Mick had little doubt that he'd be able to sell all the wine that he could make. Doc had expressed the opinion that it shouldn't really be called wine, but that it should properly be called a "whiskey," whatever that was. "It's strong enough to knock you out," Doc had said. "It's a regular Mickey Finn." And then and there, Mick had decided that when they brought the peregrine wine to market, he would call it "Mickey Finn."

Privately, Doc had confessed to him that he wasn't really an adept, but for all his denials, Mick couldn't understand why Doc persisted in claiming he knew nothing of true sorcery. If these "scientific works" he had embarked upon weren't sorcery, what were they?

"Mick," he said, "you and Brian are the only ones to whom I've told the truth, that I'm not really a sorcerer. I know you find that difficult to accept, because you've seen me do some things that seem like sorcery to you, but the fact is that *anyone* could do those things if they knew how."

"Aye, well, I suppose that anyone could do magic if they knew how," Mick replied. "Knowing how's the trick."

"I don't seem to be getting my point across," said

Brewster. "All right, let's try it this way. Of the things I've told you about the world I come from, what seems to impress you the most is the airplane. Granted, it sounds very impressive, and I suppose it is to someone who's never considered the possibility of a flying machine. However, the fact is that there's really nothing magical about it. These airplanes are powered by devices called jet engines. The jet engines propel the airplane along a runway, which is a very hard, straight road. Now, as the speed of the airplane increases, the force of the air rushing over its wings eventually causes it to lift, which allows the plane to fly. Now to you, this undoubtedly sounds like magic, but in fact, it isn't. It's merely science, the knowledge and application of certain natural laws."

He unrolled a scroll, picked up a quill, dipped it in the inkwell, and began to draw. First he sketched an airplane, then a diagram of the engine.

"This is merely a rough sketch, you understand," he said. "The actual engine is a bit more complicated than what I'm drawing here. And it's much larger, of course. Now this part here is called the turbofan. As its blades turn, they suck air into the engine. The air then enters devices called compressors, which raise the pressure of the air inside them, which then flows into the combustion chambers. Fuel is sprayed into the combustion chambers, where it is mixed with the air and ignited. The hot gases resulting from the combustion pass through devices called turbines, which drive the compressors and the turbofan, then out the rear nozzle of the engine, which forces the airplane forward. It rolls along the runway on large wheels, and as the force increases, the speed of the airplane increases. As it moves forward faster and faster, the air rushes over the wings. Now, if we look at one of these wings from the side, it looks like this."

He made another drawing, a cross section of a wing, as Mick watched intently.

"Now you will notice that on the bottom, the wing is flat, while on the top, it is curved. As the engine drives the airplane forward, air flows around the wings. This is called the airfoil principle. Some air flows around the bottom of the wing, some flows around the top. But because the top of the wing is curved, the air that flows over the top of the wing moves faster than the air flowing beneath it, which makes the pressure of the air greater beneath the wing than above it. This pressure forces the wing upward, and lifts the plane, allowing it to fly. There's nothing magical about it. It requires no spells or incantations, merely a knowledge of the science of physics.''

Mick seemed unconvinced. "This science seems as powerful as any sorcery I ever heard of," he said.

"Well, perhaps," said Brewster. "However, I happen to be a very well respected scientist, yet I can't even *begin* to understand how Brian was turned into a chamberpot. It goes against all the known laws of science. Where I come from, people would say it was impossible."

"I only wish it were," said the chamberpot wryly.

"If you would teach me more of this science," Mick said, "I shall teach you all the magic that I know, which may not be very much, I admit, but with my slight skill and Brian's knowledge, gained from several lifetimes of living with adepts, we could instruct you in the methods of the Craft to the best of our ability."

"I would like that very much, Mick," Brewster said. "Not only because I'd like to find a way to free Brian of his enchantment, but because as much as science seems to fascinate you, magic fascinates me."

"If you ask me, this science still sounds very much like sorcery," said Mick. "Perhaps science is merely sorcery of a different sort."

"I guess it all depends on how you look at it," said Brewster with a shrug. "Maybe sorcery is merely science of a different sort. And as a scientist, it's my job to study it."

"Do you think you could help us make one of these airplanes?" Mick said.

Brewster chuckled. "Well, now, that would be a rather tall order. I don't know about jet engines, but I suppose it might be possible to devise some sort of primitive steam engine, perhaps. If we could come up with a way to make an internal combustion engine, it might even be possible to make a sort of ultralight. But first we need to make aluminum.''

When the aluminum-making apparatus was properly set up, it took up a great deal of space. They had to clear away most of the apparatus in the laboratory and store it in one of the upper rooms of the tower. Brewster had been too carried away with his enthusiasm for the project to notice Mick's disappointment at losing his laboratory, and Mick hadn't said anything about it. But Shannon, who had dropped in from the Roost to observe what Doc was up to with her brigands now, saw how Mick was feeling and drew him aside while they were preparing to initiate the process.

"It seems that you have lost your laboratory," she said, drawing him aside.

"Aye, well, I never had much luck with my alchemical experiments, anyway," said Mick, in an attempt to downplay his disappointment.

"Just the same, you have given up more for Doc than any of us," she continued. "You have given him the use of your keep, you have labored for him ceaselessly, and now you have given up your laboratory. And to what end? What profit have you seen from all of this?"

Mick glanced at her sharply. "Speak plainly, Shannon," he replied. "Is it that you believe we are all wasting our time and effort? You think Doc is taking unfair advantage of us?"

"I am beginning to wonder," Shannon said. "True, he has worked some mighty sorcery, but what gain have we received from any of it?"

"You may answer that question for yourself," said Mick. "You enjoy my brew as much as any of the brigands, and Doc's still has vastly improved not only its quality, but it has enabled me to increase my yield. How often have I heard you complaining that your brigands do not bathe enough? Well, Doc's magic soap not only keeps them clean, but they enjoy it so much that they bathe more often now. Some of them even do it every day. We shall soon be bringing the many-bladed knives to market, and in learning how to make them, I have learned to craft blades that will be superior to any I have ever seen. When I apply this newfound knowledge to the swords I make, you and your brigands will be better armed than any force in the twenty-seven kingdoms. Doc's presence here has been a boon to all of us, yet 'tis not something that you choose to see. Truth to tell, 'tis the jingling of stolen purses that you miss, and 'tis jealous you are over the respect and loyalty that Doc commands. 'Twas you, yourself, who agreed to let the brigands assist Doc in his works," Mick pointed out.

"Aye, that I did," she replied in a sullen tone, "but only because he promised me far greater profits. Thus far, I have seen much work, but precious little profit. I have too few men to watch the trails now, and there is no telling how many opportunities for plunder have been missed as a result."

"You are a greedy woman, Shannon," Mick said, "and what is worse, you have no patience. And I, myself, have none to listen to such talk. There is much work left to be done. If you wish to see these profits you are so impatient for, then I suggest you let me alone to do it."

And with that, he turned and walked away. Shannon's hands clenched into fists and her lips compressed into a tight grimace. Had anyone else dared to speak to her that way, she would have given them a taste of steel, but Mick wasn't just anyone. He was more than armorer to the brigands, he was her friend, as well, and what he'd said struck home that much harder as a result. She turned on her heel and stalked off to where her black stallion waited obediently. She swung up into the saddle, put her heels to Big Nasty's flanks, and galloped off furiously down the trail leading through the forest.

At this point, the narrator will exercise his prerogative to control the flow of space and time by going back to London to check up on the other woman in Brewster's life, the lovely Pamela Fairburn. Poor Pamela hasn't had a very easy time of it. With a body that would leave even construction workers speechless, a face that could have easily graced the cover of any fashion magazine, a personality that could make even the most misanthropic individuals feel comfortable in her presence, and a level of intelligence that made her one of the top cybernetics engineers in Europe, you'd think that Pamela would have it made. She had everything . . . everything, that is, except the man she loved.

None of her friends, her colleagues, or her family could understand what the hell was wrong with Brewster. Nor could they understand what Pamela saw in him. To their way of thinking, any man in his right mind, faced with the prospect of marriage to a woman like Pamela Fairburn, would set land-speed records in racing to the altar. However, Marvin Brewster hadn't made it there at all. He had missed not one, not two, but *three* scheduled weddings, and now he'd disappeared again. Her family was absolutely furious and her father had stopped speaking to her. But in spite of everything, Pamela still remained loyal and faithful to Brewster.

She understood not just because she loved him, but because she knew the type of man he was. A most uncommon type, a genius, and Pamela understood that for genius, one often had to make allowances. Most geniuses possessed erratic personalities, and in the circles Pamela Fairburn moved in, she had met her share of geniuses. However, while there were those whose personalities made it difficult to make allowances, Brewster wasn't of that sort at all.

He was more like a small boy who'd promised his mother he would be home before dark, but became so caught up in his play that he lost all track of time. He had a sweet, endearing quality that made it possible to forgive him almost anything, and in his case, there really wasn't all that much to forgive. He was not abusive, he didn't drink to excess, and he did not use any drugs. He was not threatened by her assertiveness nor intimidated by her intelligence. He did not smoke cigarettes and only smoked a pipe occasionally. He did not have loutish friends who kept him out carousing until dawn. He didn't play around and he couldn't care less about sports. His one flaw was a tendency to become so caught up in his work that he simply forgot everything else.

The last time Pamela had seen him, he had apparently solved whatever scientific puzzle he had been obsessed with and gone running out the door of their apartment, heading for his lab. Pamela had not known what he was working on, but that was not unusual. Brewster would often discuss some of his work with her, because she was one of the few people who were capable of understanding it, but he could be secretive when it came to certain, special projects. Again, like a small boy who would hide a present he was making for his mother until he had it finished and could spring it full-blown as a surprise.

She had fully expected him to be occupied in the lab until the wee, small hours of the morning, but when daylight came and he still hadn't returned, she was not really surprised. She had the weekend off, and she had waited up for him most of the night, so she decided to get some sleep, expecting him to wake her as soon as he came home, all brimming with enthusiasm for whatever breakthrough he had made. Yet, when she awoke late Saturday afternoon to find that he still hadn't returned, she began to wonder if he hadn't taken off again, in search of some essential part for some kind of electronic circuit or something, which was how he'd wound up missing for two days the last time they'd scheduled the wedding. She called his laboratory, but there was no answer. That, too, did not really surprise her. She'd known him to become so caught up in his work that he would ignore the ringing phone, sometimes even unplug it. With a sigh, she hung up the phone and waited patiently. So much for their plans of taking a weekend drive in the country.

Sunday came, and still no Brewster. Pamela's irritation turned into apprehension. She kept telling herself that this wasn't anything unusual. He's done this sort of thing before, she thought. He'd probably lost all track of time. Again. He could become so driven that he would often forget to eat or sleep. He needed taking care of more than any man she'd ever met, but she did not wish to seem overbearing. Still, she couldn't shake the feeling that something had gone wrong. By Monday morning, she was convinced of it. She got into her car and drove to the EnGulfCo building.

The director of security checked the logs and learned that Brewster had gone up to the lab on Friday night and he had never left. "No one can enter or leave the security areas without logging in and out," he said. "It's standard procedure. However, Dr. Brewster's been known to stay in his lab for days. He's got all the comforts up there. He's probably just busy working on one of his special projects. I'm sure there's no reason to be concerned."

"Something's wrong, I tell you," Pamela said. "I can feel it! What if there's been some sort of accident? I need to get up there."

"I'm afraid I don't have the authority to allow that, Dr. Fairburn."

"Then call Dr. Davies and tell him that I wish to speak with him."

The director of security called the executive secretary of the EnGulfCo vice-president in charge of research and development, who put him through to the vice-president of R and D himself. Dr. Davies asked that Pamela be brought up to his office, where she went through more or less the same conversation again. She was rapidly losing her patience.

"I'm his *fiancée*, not some industrial spy! For God's sake, Walter, you *know* me! I work for the government and I've got top-level clearance! What does it take to get permission to go up in a lousy lift?"

"Rather a great deal, I'm afraid," said Davies. "The lift won't even take us up there. It's equipped with a sophisticated scanner. He designed it himself, so he's the only one who could gain access to the penthouse floor. Even I couldn't get up there. And the door to the lab is double-thick steel, like a vault, and scanner-equipped, as well. He's the only one who can get in or out."

"That's absurd," said Pamela. "What happens if there's a fire, or some sort of accident?"

"Yes, well, we brought up the same objections, but he

was quite adamant." Davies shrugged. "You know how
stubborn he can be. And given his value to the corporation,
well, he gets pretty much anything he wants."

"Can't we simply go up to the floor below the penthouse
and take the stairs?" asked Pamela.

"Well, that's a security area, too," said Davies. "We
could get up there, but in order to get through that way,
we'd have to pass through another steel door equipped with
a palm scanner."

Pamela shook her head with exasperation. "Like a little
boy with his bloody secret clubhouse. Well, we shall simply
have to break in."

"Do you have any idea what that would involve? Besides, I don't really have the authority to make such a
decision," Davies said.

"Well, who *does* have the authority? Never mind. Let me
use your phone."

"Be my guest."

She placed a call to the CEO of EnGulfCo International.
She explained the situation to him briefly, then handed the
phone to Davies, who said, "Yes, sir" a lot, then hung up
and looked at her with a sheepish expression.

"You know, I've worked here for ten years. I'm a
vice-president and I have to make an appointment just to
call him. I had no idea you two knew each other."

"We don't, really," Pamela said contritely. "He plays
golf with my father. Look, I'm sorry, Walter, but I just *know*
that something's happened. I can't tell you how I know, I
just do."

"Well, I hope you're wrong," said Davies, "but I've
been directed to give you my full cooperation. However, it's
going to be a major project breaking through those doors."

"We may not need to do that," she said. "Let me have a
look at that scanner system."

About an hour later, Pamela had figured out the scanner
system and bypassed it. Davies and the engineer who'd
brought the tools she'd asked for stared at her with
astonishment.

"Damn, I knew you were good, Pamela," said Davies,

"but I think you've missed your calling. I know some foreign governments who would pay a fortune for your skills."

"Well, it helps that I know how Marvin's mind works," she replied. "He's camouflaged the circuitry to appear much more complicated than it really is. And there's no way to get through it without setting off alarms at least a dozen different ways. Which you were kind enough to turn off. Don't worry about your security, Walter, I'd never have gotten this far without your help."

She opened the door and they went up the stairway to the penthouse. There was no response when they buzzed the door to the lab, and it took more time to defeat the scanner that controlled it, because it was wired differently. Pamela cursed and swore and finally got it open. They went through into the lab and, needless to say, there was no sign of Brewster.

"I can't understand it," Davies said, looking around the lab, completely baffled. He had checked the bathroom and the supply closets, and he was at a total loss to account for Brewster's absence. "He *has* to be here! How could he possibly have gotten out?"

It was a locked-room mystery. There was only one way in or out of the lab, and that door had been locked until they had opened it. There was no other way anyone could have entered or left. The lab was located on the penthouse floor, so going out a window would have been out of the question. Aside from which, the windows didn't open. The ductwork was not big enough for a grown man to fit through, and there was no sign that the grills covering the ductwork had been tampered with. There was simply no other way in or out.

"Look at all this broken glass," Pamela said. "It hasn't been thrown or dropped, it's simply shattered. If there had been some sort of an explosion, it should have caused a great deal more damage. And the windows aren't even broken."

"Thick shatterproof glass," said Davies. He sniffed the

air. "No lingering odors, but then I suppose the air recirculation system would have taken care of that."

Pamela bit her lower lip. "He's pulled disappearing acts before, but never anything like *this*."

She made a quick inventory of the lab and determined that, with the exception of the broken glassware, nothing appeared to be out of place. Brewster may have been abysmally distracted and absent-minded in his personal life, but his laboratory was a model of neatness and organization, and it didn't take her long to figure out that everything appeared to be more or less where it was supposed to be. It certainly did not look as if the laboratory had been ransacked by anyone. That left her with the puzzle of the broken glassware. It had simply shattered, which suggested some sort of sonic disturbance. But there was no clue as to what might have caused such a phenomenon.

"What's this forklift doing here?" she asked, puzzled.

Davies frowned. "I have no idea. I didn't even know he had a forklift up here. I certainly don't recall any requisitions for it. I suppose he must have brought it in himself. It's small enough, it would have been a simple matter for him to drive it into the lift."

"But I don't see anything heavy enough to require a forklift," she said, looking around.

"I wonder what the devil he's been up to this time?" Davies said.

Pamela's next step was to look for Brewster's notes. She and Davies checked through his desk and bookshelves and computer files and finally found them in a filing cabinet, under "N."

"Why 'N'?" said Davies, puzzled.

"For 'Notes,' of course. Only Marvin would have filed them that way."

There were quite a few folders filed under "N" for "Notes," so they started with the last one, which yielded several slim, cardboard-bound, black composition books filled with Brewster's meticulous, cramped and nearly illegible scrawl. They made a pot of coffee and some sandwiches, then sat down at Brewster's desk and got to work. Hours later, when they found what they were looking for, neither of them could believe it. It was not until they read the notes of the preliminary experiments that they became convinced. Their next step was to convince the EnGulfCo CEO.

"He's built a *what*?" he said over the speakerphone in Brewster's lab.

"A time machine," said Davies, wincing.

"That's absurd," said the CEO. "It's more than absurd, it's impossible. What is this, Davies, some sort of joke? Are you drunk?"

"No, sir. I rather wish I was."

"It's all right here in his notes," said Pamela. "You can come and see for yourself. He's been obsessed with something for the past few months, some sort of secret project that was occupying all his time and attention, even to the point of missing three scheduled weddings."

"Yes, yes, I'd heard all about that from your father," said the CEO. "But . . . a *time machine*, Pamela? I mean, really. . . ."

"I never knew *what* it was," she replied. "He wouldn't tell me. But last Friday, he made some sort of breakthrough that had him tremendously excited. He ran out right in the middle of *Frankenstein*."

"In the middle of *what*?"

"*Frankenstein*," said Pamela. "It was on television. It was his favorite film."

"*Frankenstein*?" said the CEO. "What the devil's *that* got to do with anything?"

"It was a very special film to Marvin," Pamela replied. "He'd first seen it when he was a child and it was what set him on the path to becoming a scientist. The point is, he had it on cassette, but he still wouldn't miss a showing of it on the telly, and he never would have run out in the middle if it wasn't something terribly important. I think he finally made his breakthrough and he rushed right off to test it."

"Now, wait just a moment," said the CEO, "let me get this straight. Are you *seriously* suggesting that he'd constructed a time machine up there in his lab, right out of H.G. Wells, and took off somewhere in it?"

"It appears so, sir," Davies replied.

"That's utterly ridiculous!"

"Is it?" said Pamela. "Very well, then. *You* explain how he was logged entering the building, and going up to his lab, then never seen to come back out again, despite there being guards on duty and video monitors in all the corridors and the lift. The door to the lab was still locked from the inside, and most of the glassware in the lab had been shattered by what must have been a sonic boom. He had also been working with a quantity of Buckyballs, which EnGulfCo had obtained for him somehow, at what had to be quite considerable expense."

"*Buckyballs?*" said the CEO. "What the devil are Buckyballs?"

"Buckminsterfullerine," said Davies. "It's a carbon compound named after Buckminster Fuller, because it's shaped rather like the geodesic dome that he designed. It also resembles a soccer ball, so it's called 'Buckyball,' for short. It's very stable and quite slippery, so it's frictionless, and it's normally produced by sono-chemistry. However, all we are able to produce is F_eC6_0, but Marvin was using F_eC3_0, which is so rare it only forms in supernovas. His requisitions normally go through my department, but I knew nothing of this. I can't imagine where in God's name he could have found it."

"Oh," said the CEO. "It seems I remember something about that now."

"It *seems* you remember?" Pamela said. "How in bloody hell could you *forget*?"

"Well, I don't really understand all this scientific mumbo jumbo," said the CEO. "All I recall is that Brewster picked up something about a meteor strike on some tiny, Pacific island no one had ever heard of, and there was apparently some compound in that meteor he needed for his work. He came to me about it, all very mysterious and hush-hush. Well, you know, I decided if he needed it that badly, he was probably on the track of something that was liable to be profitable, and since he's never let us down before, we negotiated for the purchase of it. There was also something involving offshore drilling rights, as I recall, sort of a hedge on our investment, as it were. Anyway, I don't quite see your point. What is the significance of all this?''

"The significance of it is that he used the Buckyballs to construct a time machine,'' said Pamela, "and it certainly appears as if it's worked. He's gone off somewhere, Lord only knows where.''

"Or, more to the point, *when*,'' said Davies. "Not only is there no way of telling where he might have gone, but there's no way to replicate the process. Not unless we can manage to get our hands on another fragment of a star that's gone supernova.''

"You're saying there's no more of that stuff lying around the lab?'' asked the CEO.

"Hardly,'' Pamela replied dryly. "It's not the sort of stuff one generally finds 'lying around,' as you put it.''

"So what you're telling me is that this . . . hell, I can hardly believe I'm even saying it . . . this time machine Brewster constructed is the only one of its kind, and cannot be reproduced?''

"That's *exactly* what I'm saying,'' Pamela replied. "We have no way of knowing where he went, and we'd have no way of going after him, even if we knew.''

"Good God,'' said the CEO. He was silent for a moment. "Look, Pamela, don't tell anyone about this. Not a soul, you understand? Davies, I'm holding you responsible. I'm going to need a little time in order to take all of this in. If what you're telling me, incredible as it may sound, is really true, then it's the scientific discovery of the century. Perhaps even of all time. The implications are absolutely mind-boggling. I shudder to think what the media would make of all this if they knew.''

"It's not the bloody media I'm concerned about,'' said Pamela, "it's Marvin! God only knows what may have happened to him!''

"Steady on, now,'' said the CEO. "We still don't know for a fact what's really happened, but if it's what you think, then getting frantic won't do any good at all. First things first. Are you all right? I mean, are you able to handle this, emotionally?''

Pamela took a deep breath and let it out slowly. ''I'm handling it about as well as anyone in my position could be expected to handle it, I suppose. I'm absolutely flabbergasted, and I'm frightened, but I'm not in a state of shock, if that's what you mean. I'm in control.''

''Good for you,'' said the CEO. ''I'm placing the two of you in charge of Brewster's laboratory for the duration, and I'll direct security to make sure you're the only ones to have access to it. If you need anything, anything at all, don't hesitate to let me know personally. In the meantime, I'm going to have to give some thought to what we're going to do about this . . . if, indeed, there *is* anything that we can do, except wait to see what happens. But I don't want a whisper of this leaking out. I think Brewster would want it that way, too.''

''Yes, I'm sure he would,'' said Pamela. ''But I'm worried sick about him. What if something went wrong? What if he's. . . .'' Her voice trailed off and she felt a lump in her throat.

''Let's not talk about that now,'' the CEO said. ''For the moment, it appears that all we can do is wait and see.''

''Yes, but for how long?'' asked Pamela.

''As long as it takes,'' the CEO replied. ''In the meantime, go through all his notes and try to find out as much as you possibly can. Whatever happens, Pamela, don't worry. We'll see this through together. EnGulfCo will be behind you every step of the way, I promise you.''

Pamela hung up the phone, feeling some small measure of relief. At least she wouldn't be alone through this thing. The entire resources of EnGulfCo International would be behind her, and those resources were considerable. If there was anything that could be done, they'd find a way to do it. It didn't completely ease her worries, but at least it was something.

''Oh, Marvin,'' she said. ''What have you done this time?''

''He's made Einstein look like a bloody bush-leaguer,

that's what he's done," said Davies. "I can still hardly believe it. It's incredible. I wonder where he's gone."

"I don't care," said Pamela, "so long as he gets back safely. And when he does, I swear, I'll kill him!"

Meanwhile, the EnGulfCo CEO made another call as soon as he got off the phone with Pamela. When he reached the party he was calling, he gave strict instructions that Dr. Pamela Fairburn and Dr. Walter Davies were to be shadowed around-the-clock, that all contacts they made with anyone were to be reported to him immediately, that their homes were to be discreetly searched and their phone lines tapped.

He then made another call to the home of a certain official in the Ministry of Defense, who owed a great deal of his comfortable lifestyle to EnGulfCo. He told him to find out everything there was to know about Buckyballs, and to keep it quiet.

"If this stuff is only found in meteors," the CEO said, "I want to know about every meteor that's hit the planet since Day One. And if there's any more of it left anywhere in the world, *find it*. Money is no object. EnGulfCo is going to corner the market on Buckyballs."

➤ CHAPTER ➤
SIX

It took a while to get the process straightened out, and make sure that everything went properly, but after everything was set up, Brewster set about whipping up his first batch of aluminum. It was a primitive way of doing it, but nonetheless effective, and there were enough laborious steps in the process to suitably impress everyone involved with the sorcerous significance of it all.

Brewster knew he'd need to work out some of the bugs and figure out a way to do it more efficiently. For example, he'd have to work out some way to grind up the bauxite and the limestone that would be quicker than doing it manually, and he'd need to have finer cloth made up to use for filters, to catch more of the impurities. The release valve on the blow-off tank needed to be redesigned and he'd have to have Mick make another one, and probably a couple of spares, as well. But one of the biggest problems had been solved, and very neatly, purely by accident.

Brewster had been concerned about how to run the portable generator he'd salvaged from the time machine. Refining his own fuel could pose a problem, and he'd considered adapting it so that it could be run by water power, by a series of belts and reduction gears connected to the water-wheel shaft. Eventually, a setup like that could possibly provide electrical power for the keep, but working it out would be a time-consuming process. Fortunately, he was saved that trouble for the present by the fortuitous discovery that an alternate fuel was, indeed, available to power his portable generator.

While they were setting up all the equipment to make the first batch of aluminum, it had been necessary to clear out some of the kegs of peregrine wine that Mick had stored, in order to make more room. This was the new and improved, more potent brew that had been produced with the aid of the new still, and just how potent it really was they had discovered when Fuzzy Tom and Fifer Bob decided to take a short break to sample the contents of one of the kegs they had been moving.

So as not to be interrupted while they partook of their refreshment, they carried the keg outside, where Pikestaff Pat and Lonesome John were tending the fire beneath the rendering pot for the soap. They invited Pat and John to join them for a short libation, and they tapped the keg. As they did so, some of the brew inside spilled onto the ground, beside the fire. A stray spark happened to shoot out of the fire and ignite it, and the resulting explosion blew all four of them right out of their boots.

Brewster heard the explosion, followed by the sound of screaming, and rushed outside with Mick and Bloody Bob and several of the others in time to see Fuzzy Tom sitting on the ground, batting wildly at his flaming beard, while Fifer Bob ran around in circles, screaming, his clothing in flames. Pikestaff Pat lay unconscious on the ground, some distance away, smoke rising from his prostrate form, and Lonesome John was crawling about, stunned and blackened, looking as if he'd been struck by lightning. They managed to wrestle Fifer Bob down to the ground and get the flames put out, and with the exception of some minor burns and scrapes among them and the loss of a considerable amount of facial hair on Fuzzy Tom's part, there were fortunately no serious injuries. However, the combustible nature of the new, improved peregrine wine had been quite amply demonstrated and Brewster found that by diluting it somewhat, it made a perfectly acceptable fuel to power his generator.

"Hmmm," Brewster mused as he started up his generator with the new fuel for the first time. "Interesting. Runs like a top. I wonder. . . ."

"What are you wondering about, Doc?" Mick asked.

"Mmmm? Oh, I was just thinking," Brewster replied absently. "Amazing stuff, this. I can't believe you people actually drink it."

"Warms you up right and proper, it does," said Mick with a grin.

"I'll bet," said Brewster. "I shudder to think what it does to your liver. I was just thinking that this could have an application to a crude sort of internal combustion engine. We could probably sand-cast the cylinders, and there would be a lot of hand-finishing work involved, of course, but—"

"An inter-what?" asked Mick.

"Mmmm? Oh, never mind. I'll explain later. It's just another project I might have in mind."

"Ah," said Mick, "I see." Of course, he didn't see anything at all, but he didn't want to admit it.

"Well," said Brewster, "it looks like we're all set for our first production run. Let's see what happens, shall we?"

Everyone who wasn't directly involved gathered around to watch while the production team fired up the cookers. From the first step, where the ground-up bauxite was mixed with the caustic soda, to the last, where the melted aluminum was separated in the reduction pot, took several hours, and by the time the process was complete, anticipation had reached a high pitch. No one was sure what this aluminum stuff was, and they were all eager to see the final results of this latest sorcerous project. When Brewster finally upended the cooled pot and the slag from the impurities fell out, followed by about a pound of solidified aluminum, they were all too stunned to speak.

Mick drew a sharp intake of breath and glanced at McMurphy. McMurphy glanced at Long Bill. Long Bill, his jaw hanging slack, glanced at Froggy Bruce. Froggy Bruce didn't glance at anybody. He couldn't take his wide-eyed gaze off the aluminum, which he recognized instantly, as they all did, as nickallirium, the rarest and most precious metal in the land, which only the Master Alchemists of SAG knew how to make. They could scarcely believe what they were seeing. Mick could barely even breathe. Doc had just shown them the secret of the Philosopher's Stone. And, as incredible as it seemed from the way he was acting, he didn't seem to realize the true significance of what he had just done.

Brewster mistook their absolutely stunned reaction for a display of indifference. "Well," he said, "I realize that it may not look like much now, but when you see what we can do with it, you'll realize what—"

His words were interrupted by a tremendous crash as Bloody Bob's eyes rolled up behind his visor and, overwhelmed by the implications of it all, he fainted dead away.

"Bob!" said Brewster, bending over him. "Good Lord. Bob, are you all right? What happened?"

"Uh . . . must be the heat," said Mick, with a sidelong glance at the others.

"Aye, that's what done it," said McMurphy, catching his glance. " 'Twas the heat."

"Aye, the heat," echoed the others.

"Bit warm in here."

"Stuffy."

"Aye, stuffy."

"Aluminum, you call it?" Mick said, clearing his throat.

"Yes," said Brewster, slapping Bob lightly on the cheeks in an effort to revive the big old brigand. "It's a soft metal, very easy to work, and it doesn't rust. It should make some really nice handles for the knives. Polished up, it'll look very attractive, too. I should think it would really make them sell."

"Oh, aye. . . . I should think so," said Mick, clearing his throat again. He glanced at the others significantly and gave a slight shake of his head. They merely nodded, wide-eyed.

"Here, somebody give me a hand," said Brewster. "We'll take him out to get some fresh air."

As Long Bill and McMurphy helped him carry Bloody

Bob outside, Mick turned to the others and said, "Not a word about this, you hear?"

"*Nickallirium*," breathed Silent Fred, so shocked that he actually spoke a complete sentence. "We've just made *nickallirium*!"

"And Doc doesn't even seem to know!" said Froggy Bruce. "Can it be possible he doesn't truly realize what he's done?"

"Boys," said Mick, grinning as he folded his arms across his chest, "your brigand days are done. No more lurking in the hedgerows, lads. We're all going to be rich."

What sort of a name for a town was Brigand's Roost? Harlan the Peddlar had never even heard of it before. He had never journeyed this far from Pittsburgh before and a part of him was already regretting his decision to embark upon this search for some unique commodity that he could sell. He had traveled far from Bonnie King Billy's domain to the Kingdom of Frank, the smallest, poorest, and most insignificant of the twenty-seven kingdoms, in the hope that somewhere, in this pestilential province, he would find some clever craftsman whose labors had as yet gone undiscovered. It had been a long, tiresome, unpleasant journey and he was tired and dusty from the trip when he pulled his wagon up before the inn with the crudely lettered wooden sign hanging outside that said simply, "One-Eyed Jack's."

It certainly wasn't much of a town, for all its flamboyant name. The shield-shaped wooden sign erected on a pole outside the town had said:

> *You Are Now Entering The Town Of*
> *BRIGAND'S ROOST*
> *Population Small, But Varied and Vastly Entertaining.*
> *Have A Nice Day*

The town was nothing but a small cluster of ramshackle, thatch-roofed cottages, a few weathered barns, and an assortment of tumbledown chicken coops, with a narrow, rutted road winding through it. Chickens were wandering freely on the street, if it could even be called a street, and a few ugly, fat, pink-speckled, wild spams were rutting with their rodent snouts among the refuse. A skinny dog ran by, clutching a dead snake in its jaws.

As Harlan's wagon entered the town, drawn by his tired, plodding cart horse, it was encircled by a gaggle of grimy, barefoot, and bedraggled children, who shouted at him and pelted him with dirt clods. This was, of course, the Awful Urchin Gang, whose awfulness was measured by the fact that no one would admit to being their parents, and so they ran wild and unfettered, except occasionally, when one or two of them strayed way out of line and were caught and fettered by the adults of the town.

"Get the hell away from me, you weaselly, egg-sucking, little bastards!" Harlan bellowed at them, which only brought on a rain of dirt clods comparable in its fury and intensity to what the *Luftwaffe* did to London during the Blitz.

Shielding himself with his arms, Harlan reached behind him into the wagon and pulled out something he always carried with him on his travels, against the possibility of being set upon by thugs and highwaymen. It was a small, cork-stoppered, glass vial, of which he had a number in a felt-lined, wooden case, specially brewed up for him by a Pittsburgh alchemist named Morey. (His magename was actually Morrigan, but he didn't look anything like a Morrigan; he looked more like a Morey.) Hand-lettered on the label of the vial, in Morey's neat little script, were the words, "Elixir of Stench."

Cursing under the rain of dirt clods, Harlan threw the vial at the feet of the Awful Urchin Gang and the glass shattered, releasing what Morey the Alchemist called, "A stench most foul." And foul it was, indeed. It smelled worse than a dozen demons breaking wind. It smelled worse than a unicorn in heat. It smelled worse, even, than roasted spam. It would have stopped a gang of well-armed brigands in their tracks and sent them running for the hills, holding their noses.

It didn't even faze the Awful Urchin Gang.

In desperation, Harlan whipped up his tired horse, which

hardly needed the whip after it caught a whiff of the Elixir of Stench, and the beast bolted through the town, outracing the Awful Urchin Gang and almost upsetting the wagon as it galloped round a bend in the road near the center of the town. Harlan swore and pulled back on the reins, bringing it to a halt just outside One-Eyed Jack's Tavern.

"Obnoxious, little, scum-sucking troglodytes," he mumbled as he descended from the wagon.

"I see you met the Awful Urchin Gang," said a dry, slightly raspy voice from above him.

Harlan glanced up and saw Dirty Mary leaning out an open window on the second floor of the inn. "Any of those miserable guttersnipes yours?" he inquired.

"If any of them were, I wouldn't admit it," Dirty Mary replied.

"I bloody well don't blame you," said the peddlar.

"None of them are, though," Dirty Mary said. "The last child I had grew up and ran off to the war."

"What war?"

"I dunno. There's always some war going on somewhere. Anyway, it was a long time ago. I scarcely remember what he looked like. He wasn't worth much, so I can't say as I miss him."

The peddlar grinned. "What's your name, fair damsel?"

Dirty Mary sniffed. "Fair damsel, is it? Faith, and I'm old enough to be your mother. They call me Dirty Mary if it please you, and even if it doesn't please you. 'Tis all the same to me. And you can save your flattery for my fancy girls, but 'tis me you'll have to deal with, so 'twon't be getting you a cheaper price. And there's no haggling, mind."

Harlan threw back his head and laughed. "Far be it from me to go haggling with the likes of you, Mary. But for now, 'tis a meal and a drink or two I'm after, and perhaps a bit of conversation."

"Come in, then, and I'll come down and keep you company. Sure, and there's no charge for that. 'Tis precious little company I get these days."

"What's to protect my goods from yonder horrid little

swine I hear approaching?'' Harlan asked, hearing the Awful Urchin Gang bellowing as they caught up with him.

"You leave that to me," said Dirty Mary, and as the Awful Urchin Gang came racing around the bend in the road, she gave a gravel-voiced yell loud enough to crack slate. "*Eeeeeyow, you urchins!''*

They all came screeching to a halt, gazing up at her fearfully.

"You be leaving this good man and his fine wagon alone, or it'll be your ears I'll be boxing for you, each and every one of you, you hear? Now *off* with you, and find some other mischief!''

Heads down, they shuffled off, dejectedly, and the peddlar looked at Dirty Mary with new respect. "I'm much obliged to you," he said.

"No need for it," said Dirty Mary. "Come on in, then. I'll be seeing you downstairs.''

Harlan entered the inn and walked up to the bar. With the exception of a few old people lounging around in the corners, the place was empty, save for the innkeeper behind the bar, One-Eyed Jack himself, who, as it might well be surmised, wore a black leather patch over one eye. One empty eye socket, to be precise.

He'd lost his eye years earlier, in a tavern brawl, and he had purchased a lovely glass one, with a blue iris. It didn't really go with his other eye, which was brown, but he liked the effect. Unfortunately, he got drunk and passed out one night and someone had stolen it right out of his eye socket. He suspected it was one of the brigands, which was a good bet, and had vowed revenge, if he could ever figure out which one it was. (In fact, it had been Saucy Cheryl, one of Dirty Mary's fancy girls. She'd always had a weakness for blue eyes.)

One-Eyed Jack gave Harlan the Peddlar a jaundiced look as he came up to the bar. (It wasn't that One-Eyed Jack was unfriendly; he just happened to suffer from jaundice and that was the only kind of look he could give.)

"What can I get you, stranger?'' One-Eyed Jack asked.

"A tankard of mineral water and lime, and a bowl of your finest stew," said Harlan.

"A tankard of *what*?" said One-Eyed Jack.

"Mineral water and lime," replied the peddlar, with an edge to his voice. He was in no mood to be harassed over his choice of libation.

"Never heard of it," said One-Eyed Jack.

"You never *heard* of it?" said Harlan.

"That's what I said, 'tain't it? What is it?"

"What *is* it?"

"I just said that, didn't I?" said One-Eyed Jack.

The peddlar rolled his eyes. "Well . . . what *have* you got, then?"

"Peregrine wine," said One-Eyed Jack.

"And?"

"And Mulligan stew."

"No, I mean what else have you got to drink?" said Harlan.

"I've got peregrine wine," said One-Eyed Jack, again.

"That's it?"

"Did you hear me say I had anything else?"

"Well, no, but. . . ."

"Then that's what I've got."

"What's Mulligan stew?"

" 'Tis a stew Mulligan makes out back," said One-Eyed Jack.

"What's in it?"

"Dunno. Ask Mulligan."

"Well . . . where is he?"

"*Hey, Mulligan!*" bellowed One-Eyed Jack.

"*What?*" shouted Mulligan from back in the kitchen.

"*What's in the stew?*" yelled One-Eyed Jack.

There was a long pause.

"*I forget,*" yelled Mulligan.

"Wonderful," said Harlan wryly.

"So what'll it be?" asked One-Eyed Jack.

"Some choice," said the peddlar. "A wine I've never heard of and a mystery stew. World-class establishment you've got here. Do I dare ask what peregrine wine is?"

" 'Tis brewed from the root of the peregrine bush," said One-Eyed Jack. "Good for what ails ya."

"So 'tis like a herbal thing?" said Harlan. "What the hell, I'll try it. And since I'm feeling adventurous, and also starving, I'll try a bowl of the mystery stew. Bring it to that table over there."

He went over to the table he had chosen and a few moments later, Dirty Mary came down to join him. She had spruced herself up a bit, as she didn't often get much company these days. She had put on a nice dress and she didn't look even remotely dirty. No one was sure exactly how she got her name, unless perhaps it had something to do with her chosen occupation, and no one knew how old she was. She wouldn't tell anyone her age, not even One-Eyed Jack, whose memory wasn't what it used to be and who would have forgotten within five minutes of being told, anyway. In any case, she was not in the first flower of her youth. Her petals had certainly seen better days. She spotted Harlan and came over to join him at his table.

"Nice place you've got here," said the peddlar. "Given your wonderful selection, I can't imagine why you're not doing better business."

Dirty Mary shrugged. "Well, Mulligan's stew never tastes the same twice," she said. "Sometimes it's better than others, sometimes even the wild spams won't eat it. But the wine makes up for it."

One-Eyed Jack came over and set down two tankards full of peregrine wine in front of Harlan and Mary. The peddlar sniffed it experimentally.

"Smells like medicine," he said wryly. "Where is everybody? Except for those awful urchins and those old people over there, the whole town appears deserted. Not that there's much of it to begin with."

"Everyone's at Doc's place," said Mary, taking a sip of wine. "Even my fancy girls. He's got them working. My fancy girls, working. Hard to imagine, but there you have it."

"Who's Doc?" asked Harlan, lifting the tankard, but not yet taking a drink.

" 'Tis a mighty sorcerer, Brewster Doc is," said Mary, taking another gulp of brew. "Lives out at the old mill. 'Tis a keep, actually, but there's a mill there, and Doc's been working some powerful wonders out there."

"You don't say?" said Harlan. He took a drink. His eyes bulged out and he gasped for breath as he made a sound like a leaky bellows.

"I imagine you'll be wanting to see for yourself," said Dirty Mary as the peddlar clutched spasmodically at the table. "I'll be heading out that way myself before too long. Shouldn't want to miss the feast. There's feasting every night at Doc's, after the work is done. We used to have some feasting here, every now and then, but lately every-body feasts at Doc's. Jack doesn't mind. Says 'tis less cleaning up for him to do. Still, they tell me business will pick up once word of Doc's wonders starts to spread."

The peddlar was making gasping, wheezing noises as he tried to breathe. Mary simply sat there, sipping her wine, as if it were no more potent than a broth.

"He's made magical dirt remover," she said. "Works like a charm. Used it myself. Foams up nice and pleasant. Makes you look like a horse that's lathered up from being run too hard, but it dissolves the dirt like magic if you scrub a bit." Dirty Mary frowned. "What's that noise outside?"

The sound of a high-pitched, keening wail reached them and started to grow louder. Mary got up and went to the door in time to see the Awful Urchin Gang come fleeing around the bend in the road, with the three brawling broth-ers, Hugh, Dugh, and Lugh, in hot pursuit on foot, pausing every few steps to pick up some fresh dirt clods and hurl them at the urchins. The urchins ran past the open door of the tavern and turned a short distance down the road to make a stand. Hugh, Dugh, and Lugh were brought to a halt by a fresh fusillade of dirt clods from the urchins. They ducked down behind the peddlar's wagon, picked up some more dirt clods, and returned the fire. They were all having a splendid time.

MacGregor came riding around the bend at a walk, leading the brothers' three horses. He watched the battle for a moment or so, shook his head and rolled his eyes, then dismounted and tied up the horses.

"A pleasant evening to you," he said to Dirty Mary.

"And to you," Mary replied. She jerked her head toward the three brothers. "That lot yours?"

"Aye, sad to say," MacGregor replied as he watched them dart out from behind the wagon, launch a broadside of dirt clods at the urchins, then duck behind the wagon once again, giggling like schoolboys. "You want I should make them stop?"

"Ah, let them have their fun," said Mary. "It appears the urchins may have met their match."

MacGregor frowned. "I wouldn't want the children getting hurt," he said.

"There's more where they came from," Mary replied. She took in his dark, handsome appearance, the crossed bandoliers stuck full of knives, and the Guild badge on his tunic. "You're an assassin?"

"Aye, lady, that I am," said Mac. "But you need fear nothing from me. I am a professional."

"So am I," said Mary. "Come on in and let's talk shop."

MacGregor climbed the three wooden steps up to the tavern entrance and Mary stepped aside to let him in. As was his habit, he quickly cased the place as he came in. "Things appear to be quiet," he said. His gaze fell on the peddlar, choking at his table. "What's wrong with him?"

"Amateur drinker," Mary said simply.

"Really?" said Mac. "I'll try some of whatever he's having."

"Jack! Another tankard!" Mary shouted. "I'm called Dirty Mary."

"Sean MacGregor. They call me Mac the Knife. And those three overgrown boys out there are ... well, never mind." He came over to the peddlar's table. "Is the little fellow going to be all right?" he said.

Mary shrugged and took another sip of wine. " 'Tain't killed anyone yet," she said, gazing at her tankard thoughtfully. "Still, there's always a first time."

They sat down together at the table, where Harlan the Peddlar was still trying to find his voice. Or catch his breath. Whichever came first. One-Eyed Jack brought Mac a tankard of peregrine wine. Mac raised the tankard and took an experimental sip. His eyes grew wide and the color drained out of his face.

"*S'trewth!*" he said, the breath hissing between his teeth as he inhaled sharply. He shook his head to clear it. "This stuff'll pickle your innards! What in thunder *is* it?"

"Peregrine wine," said Mary, taking another healthy gulp. MacGregor watched with disbelief as it went down her throat without any apparent effect.

"I never even heard of it," said Mac, "which scarcely seems possible. How is it made?"

"Distilled from the root of the peregrine bush," said Mary. " 'Tis Mick O'Fallon's own special, secret recipie, made more potent by a magical device known as a still."

"Indeed?" said Mac. "And who might this Mick O'Fallon be?"

"He's a leprechaun," said Mary. "An armorer, by trade, and a bit of an amateur alchemist. If you want yourself a proper sword, or a fine new knife, then you should go see Mick. You won't find a better craftsman."

"Craftsman?" wheezed Harlan, still trying to recover from his first taste of peregrine wine. "Did you say... craftsman?"

"Aye, and a right fine craftsman he is, too," Mary replied. "You won't find a better blade than Mick O'Fallon's in all the twenty-seven kingdoms."

"Is that so?" said MacGregor. "Well, in that case, I shall have to make a point to seeing his work for myself. Where might one find this Mick O'Fallon?"

"He'll be at Doc's place," Mary said. "They're all at Doc's place all the time, these days. Much to do. Many wonders to perform."

"Wonders? What sort of wonders?" Mac asked.

At that moment, Hugh, Dugh, and Lugh came bursting into the tavern, grinning from ear to ear and pounding each other on the back. "Hey, Mac!" yelled Dugh. "We won! We beat their breeches off 'em!"

"Sent 'em howling in retreat, we did!" said Hugh.

"They went for reinforcements!" Lugh said.

"Have some of this wine, lads," said MacGregor with a smile. "Innkeeper! Three tankards for my boys!"

Jack set three tankards up on the bar and the three brothers made a beeline for them. As one, they lifted the large tankards to their lips and drained them in one gulp.

As one, their three heads snapped up and their eyes bulged out of their sockets.

And, as one, they stiffened and started to keel over backwards.

"*Timber!*" shouted Mac.

With a resounding crash, the three brothers collapsed full length to the floor, unconscious.

"Innkeeper, we'll be needing rooms for the night," said Mac.

Shannon galloped down the road leading from the keep to Brigand's Roost, her leather quirt slapping at Big Nasty's flanks. But no matter how hard she rode, she couldn't seem to outdistance her anger and frustration.

No man had ever got the better of her, and now Doc had somehow managed to accomplish that very thing, and without any visible effort, to boot. He had virtually all the brigands working at his keep every day, and the few she had left to watch the trails kept complaining that the others at the keep were having all the fun. They hadn't had a decent robbery in weeks.

She would have fought Doc for the leadership of the brigands, but he had never challenged her. Indeed, he kept insisting that *she* was the leader of the brigands, and that he had no interest in that position himself. He never questioned her leadership or her authority. And yet, still, the brigands seemed to give him more obedience and show him more respect than they did her.

She had tried seducing him and that had proved a dismal failure. That had been a first, as well. Never had a man resisted her successfully. Doc had claimed to be betrothed, to some sorceress from his own land named Pamela, but other men had forgotten wives and sweethearts when confronted with her charms. Shannon thought she must be slipping. Truly, she thought, it had to be magic. What other explanation could there be? And how could she fight magic?

As she rode toward Brigand's Roost, she grew angrier and angrier, her frustration mounting until she felt ready to burst. She needed to talk to Dirty Mary. The older woman was always full of good advice. Yes, she'd talk to Mary. Either that, or kill somebody. She reined in her horse outside the tavern and strode inside, her boot heels loud on the wood-planked floor.

"Well, *hel-lo*," said a deep, resonant voice. "Look at what the wind blew in."

MacGregor's style and timing were impeccable, most times. However, this was not one of those times. Shannon stopped dead in her tracks and slowly glanced at him over her shoulder.

Mac gave her his best grin. Shannon did not return it.

Had Jack or Dirty Mary been there, they might have warned him, but Mary had gone up to prepare the rooms for Mac and his companions, and Jack was occupied with putting those very companions to bed, as they were quite insensible and needed help. There was no one in the place except some of the old people, and when they saw the look on Shannon's face, they calmly started to pull their benches back against the wall.

"Were you addressing your comment to *me*?" asked Shannon, with a dangerous edge to her voice.

"To none other, my lovely," Mac replied. "Faith, and you're a fine, strapping figure of a woman. What are you called, my beauty?"

"I am not your beauty, stranger," she replied, her voice a whip crack, "nor am I your lovely. Such talk might turn the heads of brainless serving wenches where you come from, but I have no use for it. Nor for the likes of you."

Mac smiled. "My, my," he said, "what sharp claws we have."

"Sharp enough," snapped Shannon, her eyes flashing as her blade sang free of its scabbard. "Care to try your luck?"

MacGregor laughed. "So, sharp claws and a spirit to go with them! Nay, put away your blade, girl, or do you not perceive the Guild badge on my tunic? I fear you're somewhat overmatched this time. Why not join me for a drink, instead?"

"Your Guild badge does not frighten me, assassin," she replied. "Nor do all those pretty knives you wear so ostentatiously. 'Tis one thing to wear a weapon and 'tis another to know its proper use. Any common footpad can plant a knife in someone's back. It takes more courage to meet your opponent face-to-face."

"And so I have met my share," MacGregor said. " 'Tis no mere, common footpad you behold, my pretty. My advice to you is to put down your blade. Save it for threatening the farm boys hereabouts."

Shannon's eyes were narrow slits. "And my advice to you, assassin, is to draw your sword and prove your worth. Or else I'll run you through right where you sit."

MacGregor sighed and shook his head as he got to his feet. With an air of resignation, he drew his sword and made a wide, sweeping gesture with it and his other arm, as he gave her a curt bow. "Well, then, if you insist upon a lesson in humility, I am at your service."

He gave her a mocking salute with his blade and, with a condescending little smile, he came on guard.

Shannon's blade flashed at him so quickly that it was only his instinct, honed to a razor's edge from years of practicing his craft, that saved him. He brought his blade up in a parry purely by reflex, never dreaming she'd attack so quickly. With equal speed, Shannon flicked her sword around his parry and nicked one of the bandoliers on his tunic. And she kept on coming. Startled, MacGregor found himself retreating before her furious onslaught. And, with equal astonishment, he suddenly realized that she purely meant to kill him.

He recovered from his initial surprise quickly, however, and realized that this was no mere girl who paraded with a blade that he was facing, but a skilled and lethal antagonist. He became immediately serious and shifted into his professional mode. Whoever this young woman was, he realized, she knew what she was about. Someone had taught her, and they had taught her well. Well, thought MacGregor, he was about to teach her better.

He parried and launched his counterattack. His point flicked past Shannon's defense, and she barely caught it on her quillons. Suddenly, she was on the retreat.

"You fight well, my pretty," he said with a grin as he pursued his attack. "But, alas, not well enough. 'Twill be a shame to kill you."

"Talk won't get it done," Shannon replied with a parry and riposte, followed by a feint and a beat against his blade to knock it aside. Her point darted home and would have penetrated his shoulder but for being deflected by one of the knives in his bandolier. As it was, it scraped against his tunic, cutting it and drawing a little blood.

"Damn," said MacGregor. "That was my best tunic, blast you."

"Then 'tis only fitting you be buried in it," Shannon replied as she pressed home her attack.

The clanging of their blades rang out like a steel-drum tattoo as they moved back and forth across the floor, knocking into benches and tables, recovering, and ducking aside from deadly thrusts. Shannon hooked a bench with her foot and sent it crashing against MacGregor's shins. He nearly tripped, recovered, and parried her thrust just in the nick of time. He reached out with his free hand, grabbed a tankard of wine off a table, and dashed its contents into her face. As Shannon recoiled, bringing her arm up to her face, he hooked her blade and sent it flying across the room.

"Now then, my pretty," he said, "since you've been declawed, I think 'tis time I—"

However, he never finished, because Shannon spun around, snatched up a bench, and swung it at him. It struck him in the shoulder and he tumbled to the ground, momentarily stunned, giving her the time to leap up on a table and vault it, running across the room to retrieve her sword. As she picked it up, Mac came on guard with a determined expression on his face. With his free hand, he drew one of his long knives so that he could fight Florentine style, dagger in one hand, sword in the other.

"You're good, my love," he said. "A shameful waste of talent in this backwater. But I grow weary of this dance and 'tis time for it to end."

"You fight well, yourself, assassin," she replied. "You are skilled, and without scruples. 'Tis a pity you grow weary, for I am but beginning to enjoy myself." And she drew her own dagger.

Dirty Mary and One-Eyed Jack had come down, alerted by the noise.

"Shannon," said One-Eyed Jack wryly. "I might have known. I'd better stop it."

"Why?" asked Dirty Mary.

"Well, if she kills him, who'll pay the bill?" asked One-Eyed Jack.

"He seems to be holding his own," Mary observed. "Besides, you're getting old, Jack. I wouldn't be getting between them, if I were you."

"They'll wreck the place," said Jack.

Mary shrugged. "So? It's been wrecked before. At least once a week, and sometimes twice on Saturday."

"Be one hell of a mess," said Jack. "I'm tired of cleaning up after these sorts of things."

"Oh, stop your complaining," Mary said. " 'Tis a fine and proper fight. Settle back and enjoy it."

The old folks at the back of the room made room for them on the benches and eagerly beckoned Jack and Mary to join them.

Shannon and MacGregor advanced and met in the center of the room. Shannon aimed a feint at MacGregor's chest, then slashed in with a quick cut at his head. He brought up his blade in time to parry it and darted in with his dagger. She blocked the thrust with her own short blade and launched a devastating kick at his groin. It was only by twisting aside at the last second that Mac avoided it. He took it on his hip and then pushed hard against her as their blades were locked, sending her stumbling backward. Shannon recovered quickly and as he lunged, she parried, then pivoted sharply around and caught him in the temple with a spinning high kick.

The old folks at the back appreciatively applauded the unorthodox technique.

MacGregor went down and Shannon lunged in for the kill, but he brought his blade up at the last moment and deflected her thrust, so that her point went into the floor, then lashed out hard with his foot and knocked her off her feet.

Shannon retained her grip on her sword, however, and they both came up ready for more, bent over slightly, circling, looking for an opening. Both of them were grinning.

"You're the best I've ever seen," MacGregor said with admiration. "Where the devil did you learn to fight like that?"

"Fending off admiring louts such as yourself," Shannon replied. "But you're not so bad yourself, assassin."

"Not so bad?" MacGregor said with a smirk. "Faith, love, I'm the best there is."

"Then prove it," Shannon said, lunging at him.

Their blades clashed, their daggers darted in, looking for openings, but each countered the other. As Shannon blocked his dagger thrust, MacGregor quickly brought his elbow up and smashed her in the jaw. Blood spurted from her lip as she recoiled from the blow.

"Well struck," she said, recovering more quickly than he had anticipated and aiming a cut at his face. Her blade struck home and opened up a gash along his cheek.

"*Blast you!*" said MacGregor. "That'll leave a scar!"

"On you, 'twill look quite dashing," she replied as she parried his attack.

He feinted, followed up with another quick feint, and beat her blade aside. She recovered, but not quite quickly enough. Her right arm was left exposed and MacGregor's blade slid past her own and up along her forearm, ripping through her flesh.

"That *hurt*, you bastard!" she snarled, batting his blade

aside with her dagger and launching a kick at his essentials. It struck home and Mac grunted as he doubled over, but still managed to bring his blade up in time to block her thrust.

She moved in quickly, her blade locked against his, and as he stabbed out with his dagger, she caught it with her own and kept right on coming, pushing him down onto the floor. They both fell, Shannon on top of him, and she used her knee to pin his knife hand as she held his sword down with her blade. With a bloody grin, she held her knife blade across his throat.

"*Damn*, but you're good!" she said, and leaned down and kissed him full on the mouth. It was a hard, passionate kiss, and when she broke it, she looked down at him, his mouth smeared with her blood, his eyes wide with surprise, and she smiled as she pressed her blade against his throat. "Yield, assassin," she demanded.

"Fuck you," he said.

"In due time," she replied, "but first you yield to me, and grant you've met your better." She pressed the blade against his throat.

"Damn you to hell," MacGregor said. "I yield."

The audience at the back broke into spontaneous applause.

"She didn't kill him," One-Eyed Jack said with surprise.

"I think she likes him," Dirty Mary replied.

"What happens now?" asked One-Eyed Jack.

Mary gave him a sidelong glance. "You *are* getting old," she said.

Shannon let Mac up. She stood and sheathed her blades. Mac sat up slowly, rubbing his throat, still aching from the kick to his privates. He squirmed uncomfortably.

"Damn," he said. "You just about unmanned me."

Shannon smiled. "I hope not," she replied.

MacGregor grinned. "S'trewth, and 'tis the first time in my life I've ever met my match," he said.

"More than your match," said Shannon with a chuckle.

"Very well, then," admitted Mac sourly. "*More* than my match. Satisfied?"

"Not yet," Shannon replied with a twinkle in her eye. "But we'll work on it."

"You handle a sword like a demon from Hell. Who the devil *are* you?" asked MacGregor.

"I am called Black Shannon."

MacGregor stared at her. "*You*! Faith, and I've heard of you! There's a king's ransom on your head!"

"Were you thinking of trying to collect on it?" she inquired, resting her hand on the pommel of her sword.

Mac held up his hand. "Nay, lass, not I. 'Tis enough damage I've taken for one day." He rubbed his shoulder and, as he brought his hand up, it contacted his Guild badge.

He stared down at it thoughtfully, then unpinned it from his tunic. "You'll be honoring me if you would wear this," he said. "You've beaten the best, and that makes you the best now. And if there be any who doubt it, they'll have to deal with Sean MacGregor."

"MacGregor the Bladesman?" Shannon said. "You're the one they call Mac the Knife?"

"Aye, lass, that's me."

Shannon threw back her head and laughed.

"What's so funny?" Mac asked.

"S'trewth, and 'twas your own father who taught me!" she replied.

MacGregor's eyes grew wide. "Well, I'll be. . . . Faith, and I could have sworn I'd encountered that style before! How did you come to know my father?"

"You do not remember? He caught me trying to lift his purse and when I tried to stab him, he disarmed me and said that if I wished to be an alleyman, I'd best learn how to do it properly."

MacGregor's jaw dropped. "*You*! You mean to tell me that *you* were that scrawny, dirty, little ragamuffin he brought home with him?"

"Aye," she said, "and you were too good to speak with me. And but a few days later, you left home to embark upon your own career. I swore that one day I'd meet up with you again and take you down a peg or two."

"And so you have," MacGregor said. He came up to her and pinned his Guild badge on her tunic. "You've done my father proud. And my much belated apologies for being too full of myself as a young lad and not paying attention to you. Rest assured, it shall not happen again."

She smiled. "I'll wager that it won't," she said, and kissed him.

The old folks watching them smiled and went, "Awww. . . ."

"Jack!" said Shannon. "Drinks all around!"

"Who's paying?" Jack asked.

"Loser pays," said Shannon.

"Are you so sure I've lost?" asked Mac.

"Perhaps not," she replied with a smile. "But we shall see."

➤ CHAPTER ➤ SEVEN

"I wonder what he's doing with all those people?" Queen Sandy frowned as she mused aloud and brushed her long, flaxen hair.

Bonnie King Billy merely grunted as he sat on the edge of the royal bed in their royal bedchamber, counting the signatures on the latest petition received by his royal self.

"I understand that none of them are ever seen again," Queen Sandy said as the brush glided through her extremely fine blonde hair. She cocked her head to one side as she stared at herself in the mirror. "You don't suppose he kills them, do you?"

"Four thousand, two hundred and twenty-nine," King Billy said, frowning with annoyance. "That's almost a thousand more signatures than the last bloody petition! Eight hundred and seventy-three more signatures, to be exact."

"William, you're not listening to me," Queen Sandy said with an annoyed grimace.

"Eh? What's that, my dearest?"

"I *said*, you're not listening to me."

"Oh. Sorry, dearest. I was distracted by this latest petition," he replied. "They're getting worse and worse, you know. More signatures each time. 'Tis a conspiracy, if you ask me. Who *are* all these people, anyway?''

"Your subjects, my love."

"I know that," King Billy replied irritably, "but who *are* they? I mean, I have absolutely no idea, you know." He held up the petition scroll and shook it. It unrolled across the floor. "All I see here is a bloody list of names, names that mean nothing to me, absolutely nothing. I have no idea who these people are. No idea whatsoever. How do I know they even exist? How do I know someone didn't simply sit down and make all of these names up?"

"Each of the signatures is different," Queen Sandy pointed out.

"Well . . . so what?" King Billy replied petulantly. "Anyone can alter their handwriting, can't they?"

"Four thousand, two hundred and twenty-nine different ways?" Queen Sandy asked.

"Well . . . it could be the work of some gifted forger," said King Billy. "Besides, not all four thousand, two hundred and twenty-nine of these signatures are actual names. There aren't that many people in the kingdom who can read and write. A lot of these are simply *X*'s. Anyone can make a bunch of different *X*'s. How hard can it be?"

"So then you are denying the validity of the petition?" asked Queen Sandy.

"Well, how do I know that all of these signatures represent real people?" King Billy replied. "None of these names are known to me, to say nothing of all these *X*'s."

" 'Tis because none of your subjects are known to you," Queen Sandy replied, putting down her hairbrush and turning in her seat to face him. "You do not even know the names of our servants here in the palace."

"I do so," King Billy protested.

"Name three."

"There's the royal seneschal, and the royal cook, and—"

"Their *names*, not their titles."

"I always address them by their titles. 'Tis a measure of my esteem for them."

" 'Tis a measure of something," Queen Sandy replied

sarcastically, "and a rather full measure, at that. The point is, William, you are merely making excuses. You are seeking for a way to deny the validity of the petitions because you are afraid to do anything about them. And you are afraid of doing anything about them because you are afraid of Warrick."

"I am certainly not afraid of Warrick!"

"You are. 'Tis the truth and you know it. There's no use denying it."

"Well . . . perhaps I am a *little* bit afraid," admitted King Billy. "But after all, he *is* the most powerful wizard in all the twenty-seven kingdoms!"

"He is but the royal wizard," said Queen Sandy. "*You* are the king. You outrank him."

"I think he tends to forget that," King Billy replied.

"Then *remind* him," said Queen Sandy. "Be assertive!"

"Suppose he gets angry?"

"Oh, for heaven's sake, William! What if he does? Exert your authority! You are the king!"

"True, dearest, but you know how I detest emotional confrontations. They always make my stomach feel queasy."

"All these *petitions* should make your stomach feel queasy," she replied. "Each petition is more demanding than the last, and each bears more signatures, as well. If this sort of thing keeps up, soon these petitions will grow into a movement, and then the movement will grow into a revolt. I don't know about you, William, but I have no wish to see *my* head displayed upon a pike."

"You exaggerate, my dearest," King Billy said with a smile. "Such a thing could never come to pass. We are quite well protected by our palace guard, you know."

"How many men make up the palace guard?"

"One hundred and fifty of our finest soldiers," said King Billy confidently.

"And how many signatures are on that last petition?" asked Queen Sandy dryly.

"Hmmm. I fear I see your point," King Billy said. "This really is a most awkward situation. But what would you have me do?"

"Go to Warrick," said Queen Sandy. "No. On second thought, 'tis past time for you to start acting more kingly. *Send* for Warrick and *order* that he come to you with a full accounting of his actions. *Command* him to tell you what he has done with all those people. *Insist* upon a complete explanation. Each time the royal sheriff fills the dungeons, Warrick empties them again. What's become of all those prisoners? Aren't you in the least bit curious? And while you're at it, you might rescind some of these new edicts the royal sheriff keeps coming up with. It would show that you have not ignored all those petitions and that you are responsive to the wishes of your people."

"The royal sheriff wouldn't care for that," King Billy said. "He'd think that I was undermining his authority."

"He *has* no authority except that which you give him!"

"Well, I suppose that's true," King Billy admitted, "but you know how he is when he doesn't get his way. He becomes quite surly and he threatens to resign. He really can be very difficult, you know."

"Then remove him from his post and appoint another sheriff!"

"But, Sandy, dearest, he's my own brother!"

Queen Sandy rolled her eyes and sighed with exasperation. "Well, I can see that this discussion is getting us nowhere. I really don't know what to do with you, William. I've tried, by the gods, I have really tried to talk some sense into you, but despite all of my best efforts, you simply refuse to listen. You seem to care more about what Warrick might think, and what your brother might think, than you do about what your own wife thinks. Well, so be it. Since it seems you care nothing for my advice and my opinions, then there is little point in going on with this. You do what you want, William, I'm going to bed."

"Now, dearest, don't be upset," King Billy said, getting up and holding his arms out to her. Only instead of the expected hug, he wound up catching the blanket she tossed to him. "What's this?"

"What do you think? 'Tis your blanket. I wouldn't want you to catch a chill, sleeping on the sofa."

"The sofa? But, dearest—"

"Good night, William." She took him by the shoulders, turned him around, and firmly marched him out of the royal bedchamber, shutting the door behind him.

"*Sandy!*"

He heard her bolt the door behind him.

"Uneasy is the head that wears the crown," King Billy said, shaking his uneasy head with resignation. And with a long and melancholy sigh, he headed for the royal sofa.

By this point, the reader might be wondering—as was Queen Sandy—about what's been happening to all these people who have been disappearing from the royal dungeons, after being turned over to you-know-who. Never fear, your faithful narrator hasn't forgotten about them and you're about to find out exactly what *did* happen to them, but first we'll have to backtrack just a bit.

From the moment Brewster's first time machine materialized in the sky high above the Redwood Forest, deployed its automatic parachute, and floated gently to the ground, it boded ill for anyone who came in contact with it. Perhaps it was simply one of *those* machines, you know the ones I mean, those which are somehow, mysteriously, inherently *evil*. Now there are those who will insist that this sort of thinking is utter nonsense, that machines are simply devices, inanimate objects with no personality whatsoever, and in fact, your faithful narrator was once one of these sceptics. However, an unfortunate experience with a motorcycle that purely tried to kill me every time I threw a leg over it—and not just once in a while, mind you, but *every single time*—changed my thinking on that issue. Some machines are just plain nasty.

Brewster had trouble with it right from the beginning. At first, it simply wouldn't work right. Then, it worked too well, and too quickly, disappearing on its journey without Brewster. It had drifted for a considerable distance and landed in the center of a road right where Long Bill, Fifer Bob, and Silent Fred were serving their shift, lurking in the hedgerows.

"What do you think it is?" Fifer Bob said as they slowly circled the strange device.

"Some sort of magical contraption," Long Bill said knowingly.

"What makes you think so?" asked Fifer Bob.

"Well, it came down out of the sky, didn't it?" said Long Bill. "What else *could* it be?"

"I don't think we should touch it," Fifer Bob said. "It might be dangerous."

Silent Fred stood behind him, stroking his red beard thoughtfully. He did a lot of thinking, Silent Fred did. Because he hardly ever spoke, no one was ever quite certain what he was thinking about, but he sure did a lot of it.

"You think anyone's inside there?" asked Long Bill.

"*Hallo!*" shouted Fifer Bob. "*Anyone in there?*" He waited, then approached a little closer, peering through the plastic bubble. "I don't see anyone inside."

"Knock on it," said Long Bill.

"*You* knock on it," said Fifer Bob.

"Well, to knock on it, I'd have to touch it, wouldn't I?" Long Bill replied. "You said it could be dangerous."

"So you want *me* to knock on it? No, thank you. Use your staff."

" 'Tis a brand new staff," Long Bill protested.

Silent Fred neatly solved the problem by stepping up behind Fifer Bob and giving him a shove. Bob cried out as he came in contact with the machine, then pushed himself away from it as if it were burning hot. He spun around to confront Silent Fred, who merely shrugged.

"Must be okay to touch it," said Long Bill. "Now the question is, what do we do with it?"

"It must be worth some money," Fifer Bob said.

"Aye, I suppose we could sell it," said Long Bill, scratching his long jaw. "There's that wizard who lives a few days journey down the road toward Pittsburgh."

"Blackrune 4?" said Fifer Bob. "But what if he's the one who made it? We couldn't sell a wizard his own property now, could we?"

"Perhaps not," Long Bill said, "but there may be a

reward for finding it. Besides, I do not think he could have made this strange device. He's not much of a wizard, from what I hear."

"We should be taking this to Shannon," Fifer Bob said.

"Then we'd have to share the proceeds with the others," Long Bill said. "If we sold it ourselves, and kept quiet about it, we could keep it all."

"Shannon wouldn't like that," Fifer Bob said. "She'd skin us, she would."

"Not if she didn't know about it," said Long Bill.

They exchanged conspiratory glances.

"Get the cart," Long Bill said.

After a great deal of grunting and groaning and heaving and a couple of near hernias, they managed to wrestle the machine up onto a cart and take it to the wizard known as Blackrune 4, who promptly cheated them by paying them off with changeling money. (That's the kind that turns into something else after the transaction has occurred. In the case of the three brigands, they found themselves with a large bag of acorns by the time they returned home, and rather than risk humiliation by admitting they'd been cheated, to say nothing of the considerable risk of bodily harm they would incur if the other brigands found out what they'd done, they simple wrote it off as a bad business transaction and kept their mouths shut.)

The wizard known as Blackrune 4 had been the next to suffer from the jinxed machine. After trying a whole succession of divination spells in an attempt to discover the purpose of the peculiar apparatus, he managed to stumble onto a spell that tapped into its energy field, activating it by magical remote control. The result was that the machine transported him to Los Angeles without actually going anywhere itself, which meant that he was stranded. Arrested for vagrancy and suspicion of being a graffiti artist, the wizard wound up serving some time in the drunk tank, eventually becoming one of those street people who wander around talking to themselves and gesturing wildly all the time. Stubbornly, Blackrune 4 kept trying to conjure up his spells, only none of them would work. Eventually, he just went batty.

The next victim of the missing time machine was Blackrune 4's apprentice, who waited a decent length of time before deciding that his master wasn't coming back from wherever he had disappeared to, then took the time machine to the Grand Director of the Sorcerers and Adepts Guild, who questioned him at length as to exactly what Blackrune 4 had done before he disappeared. To make certain the apprentice had it right, he made him step into the machine, then spoke the spell that Blackrune 4 had used. The apprentice vanished, to reappear in New York's Greenwich Village, where after a brief period of confusion, he wound up living with a cute, nineteen-year-old performance artist and singing lead vocals in a thrash rock band. But then, he was young, and as we all know, kids are pretty resilient. So, all told, he didn't come out of it too badly. (In fact, his first album was shipped platinum.)

After the way the apprentice had vanished into thin air, the Grand Director realized that he had something fairly powerful on his hands, so he embarked upon a long series of cautious experiments. One by one, without bothering to tell King Billy about it, he had prisoners brought up from the royal dungeons and strapped into the time machine, whereupon he spoke the spell and watched to see what happened, each time hoping he could somehow discover exactly *how* it happened.

Now, the royal dungeons weren't exactly full to capacity to begin with, much to the royal sheriff's disappointment, for he dearly loved making arrests. As laid-back and mellow as King Billy was, his younger brother, Waylon, was surly and mean-tempered. Even as children, the boys were as different as two boys could possibly be. William liked to feed small animals with bread crumbs and leftovers from his meals. Waylon liked to kill and torture them in a dazzling variety of ways. In other words, he wasn't a very nice lad. And as he grew older, he didn't get any better. In fact, he got worse.

Waylon resented the fact that his brother was king due merely to the accident of having been born first. It wasn't fair, thought Waylon. And quite probably, it wasn't. Billy was born only a year earlier and he automatically got to be the king, while Waylon didn't automatically get to be anything. Billy had made him royal sheriff, but he could just as well have decided to make him nothing and there wouldn't have been anything Waylon could do about it. But then, that's the way life is. One of the most pernicious ideas ever foisted upon a gullible public is the notion that life ought somehow to be fair. It isn't, and nothing says it should be. (Trust me, I looked it up. Couldn't find it anywhere.) Unfortunately, people keep going through life thinking that it should be fair, which results in a lot of really frustrated and unhappy people. And Sheriff Waylon was certainly no exception.

The trouble was, he didn't really have a lot to do. With King Billy's *laissez faire* attitude toward government, it was actually quite difficult to get arrested in Pittsburgh. You pretty much had to do something fairly nasty. Stealing was against the law, of course, but one actually had to be *caught* stealing, and The Stealers Guild could provide a number of very helpful pamphlets to show cutpurses and alleymen how to avoid being caught. Most large cities were like that. Simply because some activity happened to be against the law, that did not mean that there couldn't be a perfectly legal guild devoted to the practitioners of that activity. The Stealers Guild was a good case in point.

The Stealers Guild met in The Stealers Tavern, on the corner of Cutthroat and Garotte, a popular watering hole for all types of questionable characters of questionable character. In fact, Sheriff Waylon hung out there quite a lot. He was on a first-name basis with the tavern keeper, all the serving wenches, and most of the regulars, as well. These regulars were all a bunch of criminals, of course, but unless Sheriff Waylon could actually catch them in the act, he couldn't touch them. (Unless, of course, he could find witnesses to testify against them, but since there was no such thing as a Witness Relocation and Protection Guild, there wasn't very much chance of that.)

"Good evening, Sheriff," the regulars would say to Waylon. "Arrest anyone today?"

Sheriff Waylon would scowl and hammer his fist upon the bar and say, "If the law had any teeth in it, by the gods, I'd arrest the whole bloody useless lot of ya!"

"Aye, 'tis a terrible thing," the regulars agreed, nodding sympathetically. "Here, have yourself a drink, Sheriff. 'Twill make you feel better."

And so the days went for Sheriff Waylon, sitting in The Stealers Tavern and suffering the humiliation of having all the criminals buy him drinks, then staggering home in a numb, drunken stupor, where he would have to listen to his wife's monotonous harangue. "If you'd only been born a lousy year earlier, *I* could have been Queen! But, *noooooo*. . . ."

However, all that changed when Waylon's big brother, the king, came to the Grand Director's alabaster tower to protest his minions snatching people off the streets for his experiments, which had brought about the first in a long stream of angry petitions. Their solution to the problem had been to use the prisoners in the royal dungeons, instead of people abducted off the streets, which had seemed reasonable to King Billy, only the royal dungeons had already been depleted. However, the Grand Director had a solution to that problem, as well. Why not introduce a few new edicts, he suggested, to tighten up on miscreants and thereby obtain a few more prisoners?

"'Twas an excellent idea, too," said Warrick. "The streets were teeming with criminals, and 'twas time something was done about it."

Don't interrupt. And wait your turn.

"You cannot avoid me by referring to me as the Grand Director or as you-know-who," said Warrick. "I know what you're up to."

Look, do you mind? I'm doing some narrative exposition here.

"Well, then, get on with it. The tale is beginning to drag."

Suddenly, an earthen vessel on a shelf where Teddy was dusting became dislodged. It fell and struck Warrick on the head, shattering and knocking him unconscious.

"Ooops," said the troll.

Now then, where were we? Ah, yes, we were discussing the introduction of new edicts to clamp down on lawlessness in Pittsburgh and keep a fresh supply of prisoners flowing into the royal dungeons. Not wanting to be troubled with thinking up new edicts by himself, the king agreed to let the royal sheriff handle that extra bit of paperwork, and that was when Sheriff Waylon truly came into his own.

With the king's naive *carte blanche*, Waylon devised a whole slew of unprecedented, new, repressive edicts, the better to ensure that there would be more laws for the populace to break. With Waylon's inherent talents for flowery legalese and obfuscation, these edicts were written in such a way that hardly anyone could understand them, which practically guaranteed numerous arrests. The effect this had on Waylon was dramatic. Almost overnight, he changed completely.

He became imbued with a new sense of purpose as his deputies started making more arrests, and he felt a great deal happier, as well. He began to comb his hair and trim his beard and, in general, pay more attention to his overall appearance. Even his wife noticed the change.

"Is that a new suit?" she asked him.

"Aye. I've bought a brand-new wardrobe, all in black velvet, trimmed with scarlet. 'Twill be my new look. Very dashing, don't you think?"

" 'Tis been a long time since you bought me a new dress."

"What's wrong with the old one?"

"What was wrong with your old suit?" she countered.

" 'Twas worn and threadbare. And not very stylish. The royal sheriff has to look the part, you know, for people to respect the office."

"What about the royal sheriff's wife?"

"Her office is to scrub the floors and do the cooking. She needs no new dress for that."

"Well, aren't we high and mighty all of a sudden? Scrub the floors and cook, is it? And I, who could have had a *score* of royal servants to do the cooking and the cleaning and new dresses by the closetful if you'd been born before your brother! But *noooo*, instead of queen, I'm Mrs. Royal Sheriff, thank you very much, and must keep inside for shame of being seen in my old rags, while my husband dresses like a bloody peacock and carouses all night in the taverns! Respect for your office, is it? I'll show you respect, you oaf!''

"Oh, by the way, my love, have you heard about the brand-new edict yet? The one concerning shrewish wives?''

"No," she ventured cautiously.

"Just signed into law this morning," Waylon said cheerfully. "Any husband complaining of a shrewish wife may have his complaint investigated and if the claim's discovered to be true, the offender is dragged off to the royal dungeons."

"And who does the investigating?" she asked uncertainly.

"Why, the royal sheriff, of course."

"I see," she replied. " 'Tis a most handsome suit, my husband. What would you like for dinner?''

Eventually, word began to spread that the prisoners in the royal dungeons were being taken to the alabaster tower of Warrick the White, from which they never again emerged. Exactly what was done with them there was something no one knew for certain, but that only whetted the public appetite for fresh rumors, which were always available from the local rumor mongers. Almost every street corner in Pittsburgh had one now, because it was a sellers market, and the Rumor Mongers Guild was handing out fresh licenses as quickly as they could have the scrollmakers make them up.

"Rumors! Get your fresh, hot rumors here!''

"I'd like a rumor, please.''

"That'll be two bits.''

"Two bits? I say, that's a bit steep.''

" 'Tis the going rate, you know.''

"Are you a *licensed* rumor monger?''

"Absolutely. Here, see? There's me scroll.''

"How do I know 'tis a genuine rumor monger's license?''

"You can read, can't you?''

"Uh . . . never mind. I suppose it looks all right. Very well, here's two bits. I want to hear a rumor.''

"Well, rumor has it Warrick's taking all the prisoners

from the royal dungeons and turning 'em into dwarves, then sending 'em to work the mines up in the mountains.''

"But I already heard that rumor last week!"

"Oh, you want the *latest* rumor then?"

"Well, that's what I said, didn't I?"

"No, you merely said you'd like to hear a rumor."

"I meant the latest rumor."

"Ah, well, you didn't specify. That'll be two bits, milord."

"I already *paid* you two bits!"

"That was for last week's rumor."

"But I already *heard* last week's rumor!"

"Well now, how was I to know that? You asked for a rumor, I sold you a rumor. You see the sign? It says, 'No refunds.' You paid for a rumor, you got a rumor."

"See here, you're trying to cheat me! I'm going to report you to the Better Business Guild!"

"Well now, milord, I'm sorry you feel that way, but you see, 'twas a perfectly legal business transaction. You requested a rumor, and you were sold a rumor. That's straight mongering, that is. If you wanted the latest rumor, you should have specified the latest rumor. I can't be held responsible."

"You're a bloody robber, is what you are! I want the latest rumor!"

"That'll be three bits, milord."

"You said two bits before!"

"We reserve the right to change the price at any time, due to prevailing market conditions. If you wish the latest rumor, I would suggest you buy now, before the price increase."

"But you've already increased the price!"

"I mean the next price increase. Which is liable to come at any minute now."

"All right, all right, here's three bits, blast you! Now I wish the absolutely *latest* rumor, you understand?"

"Right. Well, rumor has it Warrick is taking all the prisoners from the royal dungeons and stealing their life force in an attempt to come up with an immortality elixir."

"*No!*"

"Oh, aye, milord. 'Tis the very latest rumor."

"Who'd you hear it from?"

"I have it on very good authority."

"By the gods! That's terrible!"

"Aye, milord, I quite agree. Check back with me tomorrow and I'll let you know if there's been any new developments."

"Is that included in the price?"

"Well, no, milord, you paid only for the latest rumor as of today. Tomorrow it'll be a brand-new rumor. We rumor mongers have to make a living too, you know."

So with rumors flying and the demand driving the price up every day, the stories spread like wildfire through every tavern and marketplace in Pittsburgh. Amid all the conflicting rumors, one thing remained clear. Warrick's minions had stopped snatching people off the streets, but now the sheriff's deputies were doing it for him, under the justification of the new, repressive edicts. The king had not responded to the petitions after all, but had merely devised an elaborate subterfuge for Warrick's benefit. And so, poor, Bumbling King Billy got the blame and while the concept of impeachment hadn't been invented yet, regicide was a well-established practice, with a long and respectable tradition behind it. King Billy didn't know it yet, but his job—and his very life—were hanging by a thread.

In the meantime, Warrick did not concern himself with such trivial matters. (Warrick? Good, he's still unconscious. And Teddy's hiding underneath the stairs.) One after another, Warrick had the prisoners from the royal dungeons brought into his sanctorum, where he had Teddy strap them into the machine. Initially, he had simply activated the machine by magic, and watched the prisoners disappear, hoping that close observation would reveal something about what happened to them. However, that did not prove very productive, so he then attempted to reverse the spell to see if he could bring them back. However, after a number of unsuccessful efforts, he decided to abandon that approach. He tried scrying with his crystal ball, in an attempt to see if the visions in the crystal would reveal where the subjects of his experiments had gone, but no matter how hard he concentrated and focused his energies, the crystal remained cloudy and the fate of the vanished prisoners remained unknown.

Warrick then embarked upon a new course of action. He placed each of his subjects under a spell of compulsion before he had them strapped into the machine, a spell that would compel them to return to his sanctorum and reveal what happened to them. If he couldn't find a way to bring them back, he figured, he'd place a spell upon them that would irresistibly compel them to find their *own* way back. Exactly how they would manage to accomplish this was not his problem. Sooner or later, one way or another, he was certain that at least one of them would manage to return from wherever he was sending them, and then he'd know exactly what was going on.

Unfortunately, this made things rather difficult for the subjects of his experiments. As we have already established, the time machine was not designed to be operated by magical remote control, and so this method of operation had certain rather erratic results. The hapless subjects of Warrick's experiments were not all sent to the same place. When Blackrune 4 had accidentally stumbled upon the spell in the first place, he had managed to transport himself to Los Angeles. That same spell later transported his apprentice to the East Village in New York. Subsequent experiments transported Warrick's subjects to places as diverse as Tokyo, Honolulu, Paris, Reykjavik, Copenhagen, Liverpool, Tijuana, Rapid City, Albuquerque, Johannesburg, and Sydney. Once there, Warrick's hapless subjects were then faced not only with the shattering reality of a completely different universe, but seized with a powerful, irresistible compulsion to return from whence they came. Only they had no time machine to do it with.

Not to put too fine a point on it, this caused certain problems. Dropping residents of a primitive, medieval city into a modern, high-tech metropolis such as New York or Tokyo, and on top of that, imbuing them with an insane, relentless, driven urge to get back home no matter what, was akin to locking a claustrophobic gorilla inside a narrow linen closet. And considering that a large number of these people were criminally inclined to begin with, the result was a series of highly unusual incidents.

In Albuquerque, New Mexico, one of Warrick's subjects attacked a mounted policeman and knocked him off his horse, then stole the horse and led the police on a mad chase as far as Corrales, where it took six cruisers and a dozen men to cut him off and subdue him.

In New York City, a wild-eyed young man battered his way through the divider between the driver and the rear passenger section, held a dagger to the cabbie's throat, and demanded to be taken to Pittsburgh. The terrified cabbie drove him all the way to Pittsburgh, Pennsylvania, with his passenger raving all the while, and when his passenger insisted that it *wasn't* Pittsburgh, that it looked nothing at all like Pittsburgh, and if he didn't take him to Pittsburgh right away, he would fillet him, the cabbie dove out of the car and escaped with only minor injuries while the cab crashed into a bridge abutment and exploded.

In Tokyo, Japan, a strangely garbed man went berserk and ran screaming through the streets, knocking into people and picking up whatever he could find and use as weapons, causing numerous injuries until police subdued him and found someone who could speak English (for as we all know from watching *Star Trek*, everyone in the entire universe speaks English, while hardly anyone speaks Japanese), whereupon they found that the man was convinced he had been transported to the underworld, where he was surrounded by slanty-eyed demons who gibbered at him incomprehensibly and wanted to possess him. He kept babbling something about a "sanctorum" in Pittsburgh, so they gagged him and stuck him in a straitjacket and put him on a plane to the United States, where he eventually wound up in a sanitarium in Pittsburgh, Pennsylvania.

In Johannesburg, South Africa, a man appeared out of nowhere in the middle of a busy street and ran amok, dodging between vehicles and screaming until he was shot down in a hail of gunfire from passing motorists.

In London, England, a wild-eyed young woman suddenly

appeared in the House of Commons and started shouting and waving her arms about. For about ten minutes, no one could hear her over the noise made by other MP's, but eventually she got the floor and a lively debate ensued.

In Memphis, Tennessee, a pockmarked, ale-ravaged, young prostitute arrested in The Stealers Tavern for refusing to give one of the sheriff's deputies a freebie suddenly materialized onstage, behind a mike, in the middle of an Allman Brothers concert. Frightened out of her wits, she started tearing her hair and wailing about wanting to get back home. The audience gave her a standing ovation and she was hailed as a great white blues artist, given a recording contract with Atlantic Records, and about nine months later, she disappeared after giving birth to a beautiful boy with long blond hair.   ·

In Boulder, Colorado, a wiry young man mysteriously appeared out of nowhere in Scott Carpenter Park, in the middle of a Society for Creative Anachronism weapons practice session, where he grabbed a heavy wooden sword and proceeded to lay waste to the entire field. When it was all over and the grassy meadow was littered with broken, bleeding bodies, the surviving members of the medievalist group awarded him a title. The puzzled young man was then escorted off the field by several shapely young women in full armor and was not seen again for two weeks, when he was observed to be in shock, walking unsteadily, with a dazed expression on his face and three favors bound around his sword arm.

Some of these incidents passed all but unnoticed, except in the localities where they occurred, others managed to make national headlines, and it wasn't long before a certain reporter for a Florida-based tabloid of questionable journalistic integrity noticed a pattern beginning to emerge.

Now, whether this reporter was simply a throwback to another time, or had seen too many episodes of *Kolchak: The Night Stalker* was a question that was open to debate, but it should suffice to say that after twenty-five odd years in the newspaper business, he had been fired from some of the best jobs in journalism and had finally struck the bottom of the barrel, where he remained comfortably ensconced with a bottle of Jack Daniels. Outside his chosen field, he was virtually unknown, but in the journalism business, Colin Hightower was infamous.

Few people could approach the colorful uniqueness of his resume. He had once been punched in the nose by Benjamin Bradlee, and on another memorable occasion, he had been kneed in the groin by Barbara Walters. He had been shot at with a .44 Magnum by gonzo journalist Hunter S. Thompson, and Geraldo Rivera had once tried to run him over on the streets of New York City with a Kawasaki motorcycle. Anchorwoman Diane Sawyer got the hiccups every time his name was mentioned and *Rolling Stone* editor Jann Wenner was alleged to have chased him through the lobby of the Fontainbleu Hotel with a baseball bat.

The man who prompted such extreme reactions looked nothing if not placidly average and normal. Born and raised in Liverpool, Colin Hightower came to the United States to pursue a career as an investigative journalist after being fired from the London *Daily Mirror* over an incident allegedly involving Princess Margaret and a rock group called The Yardbirds. Of average height and with a stocky build, he had the rosy-cheeked, wide face of a friendly Irish bartender, with an easy smile and eyes that twinkled like those of a mischievous ten-year-old. He habitually dressed in rumpled khaki twill trousers and shapeless, nondescript sport coats, and on the rare occasions when he wore a tie, it was always at half mast, with the top two buttons of his frayed, button-down-collar shirt undone. There was never any danger of his being wooed by the television media, because he simply wasn't telegenic. Even Jimmy Breslin looked better on camera than he did. Besides, Colin's first love was always the print medium and he considered himself a purist. Damon Runyon would have loved him, but the only public figure who ever had a kind word to say about him was G. Gordon Liddy, who once described him as "a tough, old snapper who knows how to hold his liquor."

Unfortunately, Hightower's breed of newspaper reporter had died out with the birth of the Columbia School of

Journalism and Colin was as out of place in modern newspaper reporting as an Edsel at a sports-car rally. Nevertheless, he persevered, stubbornly refusing to change. For
Colin, the only thing that mattered was The Story. And
when he first noticed the strange pattern of similarities in
these apparently isolated incidents occurring at different
locales throughout the world, he began to suspect that he
had stumbled on a big one.

"Listen to this, Jack, here's another one," he said as he
barged into his editor's office without knocking. "Man
comes wandering in out of the Sonoran Desert in Tucson,
Arizona, half dead from exposure and raving like a lunatic."

"Colin. . . ."

"No, listen! Get this . . . he's dressed up in medieval
clothing, and he keeps babbling about Pittsburgh and somebody named Warwick or Warrick. He's taken to ER and
given treatment, but he breaks out and takes off again,
injuring two doctors and three nurses, and he hasn't been
seen since."

"Look, Colin. . . ."

"Don't you see, Jack? It's the same as all the others! The
weird, medieval-style clothing, the references to Warrick or
Warwick and Pittsburgh and the white tower . . . over and
over again, in all these different, seemingly isolated incidents, the same things keep coming up. Here's one in
Albuquerque, here's another one in London, and one in New
York, and another one in Tokyo—"

"All right, Colin!"

"All right, what?"

"All right, you can do the story, I give up! You're driving
me crazy. So do it, already. What's your angle?"

"I don't know yet," Hightower replied. "But I'm going
to follow up on all these common threads. Find out who this
Warrick or Warwick is, what the deal is with this tower they
keep talking about—"

"So then you're going to Pittsburgh?"

"To begin with, yeah. They've got one of these people
locked up in a sanitarium there. But I'm going to track
down each and every one of these different incidents and—"

"And it'll cost a fortune in traveling expenses," said the editor.

"So what? This is a *real* news story, Jack, not one of those World War Two planes discovered on the moon, things you've got those hacks out there dreaming up. It's off the wall, it's mysterious, and it's genuine, for God's sake!"

"Okay, okay, you've talked me into it. But I want receipts for every dime you spend, you understand?"

"You got it. You won't regret this, Jack. There's something big here, I can smell it."

"Yeah, yeah, just go. Bring me a story. What the hell, it'll be nice to do some real investigative journalism for a change. Just try not to run the bills up."

So Colin Hightower, intrepid newshawk from a bygone time, started to investigate. He had no doubt there was a story here. He had also had no doubt that this investigation would take him fairly far afield. What he did not suspect was just *how* far.

➤ CHAPTER ➤
EIGHT

"I still don't understand the part about the traveling," said Rory the dragon, sitting on the parapet of Brewster's tower, his huge, leathery wings folded back and his powerful, iridescent claws gripping the stone masonry.

It was a quiet, moonlit night, and the clearing below was peaceful, everyone having staggered home after the feast. Rory had dropped in—literally, out of the sky—to perch on Brewster's tower and chat with him about the world he came from. Rory's curiosity about Earth was due to the curious fact that dragons happen to dream about our universe, and there are many things that dragons see in their dreams about our world that they do not quite understand.

"Well," said Brewster, "you're supposed to continue dribbling as you move down the court, and if you take more than three steps without dribbling, then that's traveling, and that's a foul."

"I still don't quite understand," said Rory, in a voice that sounded like a cross between a cement mixer and a locomotive. "The point of the game is to travel down the court and stuff the little ball into the netted hoop, and yet one is penalized for traveling?"

"No, no," said Brewster, "you're penalized for traveling if you don't dribble at the same time."

"Doesn't that make the playing court rather messy?" asked the dragon.

"No, no," said Brewster, shaking his head, "you don't understand. Not drooling, *dribbling*."

"What's the difference?" asked the dragon.

"Dribbling is what it's called when you bounce the ball as you travel down the court," Brewster explained. "They simply call it dribbling. The players themselves don't actually dribble."

"Then why do they call it dribbling? Why don't they simply call it bouncing?" Rory asked.

Brewster shrugged. "I haven't the faintest idea," he replied. "I'd never really thought of it that way before."

"Oh, very well," the dragon said. "Let it pass for now. So this bouncing of the ball is known as dribbling, correct?"

"Right," said Brewster.

"And one must do this dribbling whilst one travels down the court?"

"Correct," said Brewster.

"But traveling is not permitted and is called a foul?"

"That's right," said Brewster.

"Then how in thunder does one get to the opposite end of the playing court to make a basket?" asked the dragon, frowning.

"You dribble," Brewster said.

"As you travel," said the dragon.

"Right," said Brewster.

"But traveling is a foul?"

"Correct."

"Then how do you get to the other end of the court without committing a foul?"

"You dribble. Or you could pass the ball."

"To whom?"

"To another player."

"On either team?"

"No, only on *your* team. Otherwise, the other team will get possession of the ball and they might make the basket."

"By dribbling to the other end of the court?" the dragon asked.

"Correct."

"But how do they do that without *traveling*?"

Brewster reached up under his glasses and pinched the bridge of his nose between two fingers. "I'm not explaining this very well, am I? Sports never was my strong suit."

" 'Tis a very foolish-sounding game, if you ask me," said Brian.

The dragon snorted and twin jets of sulphurous smoke streamed from his nostrils. "Nobody *asked* you, Werepot," he replied irritably.

Brian the werepot prince shifted his weight from one foot to the other as he crossed his legs and leaned back against the parapet. The moon was full and he had reverted to his human form, which was that of a handsome, well-built, young man in his twenties, with long, curly blond hair and blue eyes. He was dressed in brown and black striped breeches, high boots, a loose-fitting white blouse, and a brown velvet jacket and cape. Around his neck, he wore a necklace of sapphires and rubies.

"What's the bloody point?" asked Brian. "You're not going to be *playing* the blasted game, are you? Can you imagine how ridiculous it would look, a great, big, lumbering leviathan like you galloping down a wood-floored playing court, bouncing a rubber ball and wearing a wee, white doublet with a number on it?"

"I never said that I was interested in actually *playing* the game," the dragon replied, "I merely wish to *understand* it."

"Whatever for?" asked Brian.

"Uh . . . Rory . . ." Brewster interrupted, clearing his throat uncomfortably.

"What is it, Doc?" the dragon asked.

Brewster moistened his lips nervously and cleared his throat again. "Would you . . . uh . . . mind asking them to stop, please?" He indicated the fairies with a nod of his head, then looked away.

It had been difficult enough for him to grow accustomed

to his nightly storytelling sessions with a dragon, followed by a question and answer period, but no matter how he tried, he couldn't seem to get used to the fairies. Since meeting Rory and enlisting the dragon's aid in searching for his missing time machine, Brewster had come to look forward to the dragon's nightly visits, but fairies had a tendency to hover around dragons the way horseflies buzzed around a sweaty mare, and their behavior was something Brewster found highly disconcerting.

With the exception of their antennae and large, varicolored, gossamer wings, they looked completely human, albeit on a miniature scale, and they wore no clothing. During the day, at a distance, they could easily be mistaken for large butterflies, but at night, they glowed, which made their nudity that much more obvious at close quarters. That, in and of itself, could be a bit unsettling, as the female fairies all seemed to be uniformly sensual and beautiful and the males all handsome and rampantly endowed. What made it worse was their complete lack of inhibitions and a sex drive that any jackrabbit would have envied.

They were highly curious, but they had a very limited attention span, and a tendency to copulate at the drop of a hat. Sitting on the edge of the parapet and having apparently grown bored with the conversation, two of the fairies had started to fondle and caress each other, and as Brewster spoke, the female sat astride the male's lap, facing him, and they began to ... well, you know.

Of course, the other fairies flitting all about the dragon in a cloud began to follow suit and, in no time at all, a mass orgy was in progress. They rose up into the air, their legs entwined and their wings flapping in unison, and as they mated, the glow from them increased, so that they resembled giant fireflies with hiccups, enthusiastically bouncing up and down in midair.

"Oh, for God's sake ..." said Brewster, turning away in embarrassment. "Have they no sense of decorum whatsoever?"

"Apparently not," said Brian, "but they do seem to enjoy themselves."

"Pesky little things," said Rory wryly. He inhaled deeply,

then exhaled in the direction of the fairies, blowing them hither and yon, sending their naked, phosphorescent little bodies tumbling through the air. Brewster exhaled heavily himself, only with relief, because when he'd seen the dragon fill his lungs, he'd been afraid that Rory would breathe fire at them and the thought of all those randy, little fairies being incinerated on his behalf had alarmed him greatly.

"Well, I suppose I shouldn't impose my own standards of morality upon another race of beings," Brewster said. "I do hope they understand how grateful I am for their help in looking for my missing time machine."

"I'm not sure they've been very much help at all," the dragon replied. " 'Tis a miracle if they can hold a thought inside their empty little heads for longer than an instant. Still, I keep reminding them."

"How exactly do you communicate with them?" asked Brewster, curious.

"They read my thoughts," Rory replied.

"You mean they're actually telepathic?" Brewster asked with amazement.

"Of course," Rory replied. " 'Tis what makes them so mischievous."

"Aye, never fall asleep in the middle of a forest when fairies are around," said Brian. "They will insinuate themselves into your dreams."

"And what will happen?" Brewster asked.

"There's no way of telling," Brian replied. "With any luck, the results will merely be humiliating. But they have been known to be fatal."

"You mean they actually . . . *kill* people? Brewster said with disbelief.

"Oh, aye," said Brian. "Nasty little buggers."

"That's terrible!" said Brewster.

"They don't really mean to be evil," Rory explained. "The concepts of good and evil are utterly alien to them. 'Tis merely their way of having fun."

"The thing to do," said Brian, "is burn the garlic herb in your evening campfire, and heavily season your food with it, as well."

"So it's like the story about vampires?" Brewster said. "Garlic repels them?"

"It repels everybody," Brian replied with a shrug. "What's a vampire?"

"Dracula," said Rory. "A character from a series of motion pictures made by Hammer Film Productions, starring Christopher Lee as the undead elf."

Brewster raised his eyebrows. "The undead *elf*?"

"Aye, I saw the motion picture vision in a dream once," said the dragon. "They didn't really get the details right, but 'twas vastly entertaining, just the same."

"Wait a minute," Brewster said. "Dracula was not an *elf*. He was a fictional character created by Bram Stoker, an undead creature who survived by drinking human blood."

Brian shrugged. "Sounds like an elf to me."

"Hold it," Brewster said. "You mean to tell me that elves drink *human blood*?"

"Sure, and everybody knows that," said Brian. "They hang about at night in forest glens, sitting 'round their campfires, playing guitars, spouting poetry, arguing philosophy, and drinking coffee. The only thing they love more than drinking human blood is drinking coffee."

"*Coffee-drinking, beatnik, vampire elves?*" said Brewster.

"Aye, 'tis a foul-tasting brew," said Brian. "Unfit for human consumption, if you ask me. Keeps you from sleeping. A cup or two and you're up all night. 'Tis made from a peculiar bean grown in the kingdom of Valdez. Has a pungent sort of smell when it brews. If you're walking through the forest and you smell it, then sure and there'll be elves about."

"Methinks I smell one coming now," said Rory, sniffing the air experimentally.

No sooner had the dragon spoken than a piercing scream shattered the stillness of the night. As Brewster looked down over the parapet, he saw someone come bursting out of the trees at the edge of the clearing, running full speed, closely pursued by what at first glance appeared to be three Shetland ponies. However, a moment later, he saw the gleam of moonlight on their pearlescent horns and realized that he was getting his first glimpse of a unicorn.

The three galloping creatures looked exactly the way he'd seen them pictured in the fairy tales he'd read as a child, with gleaming, spiral horns, goatlike beards, long, flowing manes, and tufted hooves, only their white coats were matted with filth and covered with brambles and even at a distance, he could smell their rank stench on the evening breeze. It was a stink that would send a skunk running for the hills.

"I don't think she'll make it," Brian said, coming up beside Brewster and looking down over the parapet.

Brewster saw the unicorn running in the lead put its head down, lowering its horn.

"Good God! They'll kill her!" he said with alarm.

"I imagine so," said Brian.

"We've got to do something! Rory, can't you stop them?"

"Why? She's just an elf," replied the dragon with a shrug of his leathery wings.

"Rory, *please*!" said Brewster, watching as the unicorns rapidly closed in on their quarry.

"Oh, very well, if you insist," the dragon said with resignation. He sprang from the tower and spread his wings, soaring out in a swooping glide, but even as he did so, the lead unicorn caught up with the running elf. With surprising speed, the elf pivoted sharply, sidestepped the unicorn's headlong rush, and struck it on the head with something she was carrying under her arm. There was a percussive, bonking sound, and the unicorn staggered, but just then, the other two unicorns came running up and it looked bad for the elf.

With a roar, the dragon came swooping down upon them, belching fire. A blast of flame struck the ground just in front of the unicorns and almost caught the elf. The unicorns whinnied and took off in the opposite direction, galloping back toward the woods in a rapid retreat. The elf was beating at her smoking clothing, trying to put out the sparks from the wash of flame that had nearly incinerated her. Rory rose and banked sharply, then swooped down again and swept her up in one powerful claw. The elf cried out, but the dragon held on firmly, though gently, and a moment later, he set her down on the tower in front of Brewster and Brian.

"Safe and sound, if a trifle singed," said Rory.

"You nearly roasted me, you great, oafish worm!" the elf said.

"Go and expect gratitude from an elf," said Rory with disgust.

"Are you all right?" asked Brewster.

Her clothing was still smoking here and there. She was dressed all in black, with tight black breeches, short black boots, and a black leather vest held together with rawhide laces, under which she wore nothing else. Her skin was slightly blackened here and there from the dragon's smoky breath. She had a black leather choker around her neck, studded with spikes, and matching, spiked, black leather bands around her wrists. Her hair, too, was rather spikey. It was black, cut short in front and worn longer in the back, covering her neck, and large, delicately pointed elvish ears poked up from beneath it. She stood about five feet, six inches tall and she was slim, with a wiry, coltish build. Her eyes were dark and large and belligerent. In one hand, Brewster noted with surprise, she held a set of bongo drums. Her other hand rested on the slim hilt of a silver dagger in her belt.

"Who are you?" she demanded.

"He's the man who just saved your life," said Brian wryly.

"Indeed?" said Rory. "I could have sworn *I* had something to do with it."

"Oh, so now you're taking the credit, are you?" Brian said. "You were quite prepared to see her impaled until Doc asked you to intervene."

"Well then, I suppose I should thank you," said the elf sullenly. "I am Rachel Drum."

"And my name is Brewster. But my friends just call me Doc." He held out his hand.

She stared at it for a moment, hesitating, then reached out and shook it. "Well, my thanks to you, Doc. If not for your dragon, I would most surely have been spiked."

"He's not really my dragon," Brewster replied. "Rory's just a friend. And this is another friend, Prince Brian the Bold."

"Not the werepot prince?" she said.

Brian rolled his eyes. "Aye, the very same," he said wearily.

"Faith, and I thought you were just a myth," she said. "There are at least a dozen elvish songs about you."

"Ah, the burdens of fame," said Brian.

"Why were the unicorns chasing you?" asked Brewster.

"Obviously, she's a virgin," Brian said.

"I am *not* a virgin!" replied the elf.

"The unicorns knew better," Brian replied with a grin. "They would have smelled a man on you."

"I have never *had* a man on me, thank you very much," Rachel responded with distaste.

Brian frowned. "Then what did you mean when you said you weren't a. . . ." His eyebrows rose. "Oh. I see."

"Stupid beasts," said Rachel.

"You mean the unicorns?" asked Brewster.

"I think she means men," said Brian wryly.

"I *meant* the unicorns," said Rachel, "but some men might well be included in that description." She gave him a sour look, then turned to Brewster. "But not all men, perhaps. In any event, I thank you and the dragon, both. 'Tis rare for a dragon to grant assistance to an elf. Rarer still for humans."

"Perhaps that's because we humans like to keep our blood within our veins, where it belongs," said Brian.

"I've never met an elf before," said Brewster. "Do you really drink human blood?"

"Do not humans eat the flesh of other creatures?" Rachel countered.

"Well, yes, but . . ."

"Then you are predators, as well," she said. "But you need have no fear of me. I am a vegetarian."

"Better warn the bush," said Brian.

With a rustling sound, Thorny, the peregrine bush, quickly scuttled down the stairs.

"You associate with peregrine bushes, dragons, and enchanted princes," Rachel said to Brewster. "You must be the new sorcerer who has recently arrived in these parts."

"News travels fast," said Brewster.

"Elves have sharp ears," said Brian.

Rachel gave him a sour grimace.

"Sorry. No offense," said Brian, feeling his own, unpointed ear.

"I have come a long way in search of you," said Rachel Drum.

"You have?" said Brewster. "Why?"

"For the reward," said Rachel.

Brewster frowned. "I'm afraid I don't understand. What reward?"

"You have lost something of value, have you not? The fairies say so. Some sort of magic chariot? Well, I might know where it is."

As Brewster absorbed this fascinating information, Sean MacGregor and Black Shannon were absorbed in one another upstairs at One-Eyed Jack's, where they would remain throughout the night and the next day, discovering that outstanding swordsmanship was not the only thing they had in common. The three brawling, albeit somewhat dim brothers, Hugh, Dugh, and Lugh, were absorbed in a deep and dreamless sleep, more of a coma, really, which is usually what happens whenever anyone is careless enough to knock down a full mug of peregrine wine in one gulp. Harlan the Peddlar, meanwhile, had only one sip of the killer brew, so consequently he recovered fairly quickly, and as soon as the evening's entertainment—meaning the big sword fight—was concluded, he got directions from One-Eyed Jack to Mick O'Fallon's little cottage.

He drove his wagon out of town, down the winding trail leading past Mick O'Fallon's place, and he arrived at just about the same time as Mick and Robie, Pikestaff Pat and Bloody Bob were returning from the evening's feast at Brewster's keep. Unlike most nights, they had partaken of the brew only sparingly, as they had important matters to discuss late into the night, and Harlan's arrival couldn't have been timed more perfectly.

They were a bit wary when they discovered that they had a visitor, but when Harlan introduced himself and said he was a peddlar, searching for unique wares to sell, they invited him inside. Harlan wisely, though politely, refused a drink of peregrine wine and settled for a cup of Dragon's Breath tea instead, one of the non-hallucinogenic brews that Jane had concocted, and after his first taste, he allowed as to how he might be interested in carrying Jane's teas among his wares, provided an equitable, exclusive distribution agreement could be reached. He then looked over Mick O'Fallon's blades, examinining a selection of daggers, dirks, and swords, and as he was no stranger to good craftsmanship, he immediately pronounced them to be the finest that he'd ever seen.

"Understand now, under normal circumstances, I'd never be quite so enthusiastic in my praise," he said. " 'Twouldn't be good business, you see. As a vendor, one should never act too impressed with a supplier's goods, else the price is liable to go up and that would cut into your profits. However, in this case, with craftsmanship so fine, 'tis clear that you know what you're about, O'Fallon, and likewise realize the value of your work. 'Twould be insulting to a craftsman of your accomplishment to minimize the fruits of such fine labor. In truth, these are the finest blades I've ever seen, and I've traveled far and wide throughout all the twenty-seven kingdoms, and seen the works of many a fine armorer. None could compare with these. However did you manage to forge such a superior grade of steel?"

Pleased that the peddlar was well enough informed to appreciate his craft, Mick's brawny little chest swelled with pride, but he was not so proud as to reveal all his secrets.

" 'Tis a special process of me own," he replied. " 'Twas taught to me by a great wizard from the Land of Ing."

"The Land of Ing?" said Harlan. "S'trewth, and I've never even heard of it. Where is it to be found?"

" 'Tis far, far away, in another place and time," said Robie, but he fell silent when Mick nudged him.

"Ah, well, have it your way," Harlan said. "I can understand your wanting to protect trade secrets, and I wouldn't wish to pry. But I *must* have these blades to sell! You've precious little market out here in the wilds, I should imagine. With a vendor such as myself, representing your product in the cities, there would be great profits to be made. Great profits, indeed."

"Then we must discuss this matter further," Mick replied, "but first, before we do, there is another item I would like to show you, something new, and altogether different."

"Ah, yes," the peddlar said. "I have been searching for something altogether different, something no one else would have to offer. You have such an item?"

Mick smiled. "I do, indeed," he said, and he brought out the first finished example of the "many-bladed knife," complete with nickallirium grips, which he had put on and polished to a glossy luster earlier that afternoon.

Harlan's eyes grew wide when Mick put it on the table. *"S'trewth!"* he exclaimed, immediately recognizing the grips for what they were. And when Mick displayed the knife's many-bladed functions, the peddlar's eyes grew wider still.

"Never in all my days have I seen such a marvelous device!" he exclaimed. "It would seem to have more uses than the mind could conceive! You created this?"

"I crafted it," said Mick, "but to be truthful, 'twas not I who created it, but a great and wondrous armorer from a far-off land, whose name was Victorinox. The original many-bladed knife was shown to me by the sorcerer I told you of, and together we made some changes to the pattern, until we arrived at the design for this knife here."

"A most useful and marvelous design," said Harlan, turning the knife over and over in his hands. "You can make more of these?"

"Aye," said Mick. "As many as you like."

"But 'twould take a long time, surely, to forge a great number of these blades," said Harlan.

"I can craft as many as you like," said Mick, "and in less time than you might think."

"If I were to commission, say, a dozen such many-bladed knives," said Harlan speculatively, "how long would it take you to make them?"

"Oh, a day or two, at most," said Mick.

"A day or two!" The peddlar was astonished. "How is that possible?"

"Through a secret process we employ known as manufacturing," said Bloody Bob, then cried out as Mick kicked him under the table.

"A secret process, eh?" said Harlan. "Well, I must admit I'm very curious, but I shall not press you for details. 'Tis enough for me to have these blades to sell, and ensure that no one else has them to sell but me."

" 'Tis possible we might come to some sort of an arrangement," Mick said, "provided everything works out well for all concerned."

"What sort of grips would you employ for the knives that you would make for me?" asked Harlan.

"The same as you see there," said Mick. " 'Tis a rare and special knife, and as such, it deserves rare and special grips."

Harlan raised his eyebrows. "But these are nickallirium! And of an uncommon purity, to boot. Surely, the cost would be prohibitive."

"You might be surprised," said Mick. "The knives are very fine, and would undoubtedly be costly, yet not so costly that only the nobility could afford to purchase them. Nor so costly that it would preclude a good profit from the sale."

Harlan pursed his lips thoughtfully. "Indeed? One might very well infer from such a remark that you might have access to a supply of nickallirium from a source that is, shall we say, unauthorized?"

"I am not certain what you mean," said Mick evasively.

"Well, merely for the sake of argument," said the peddlar, "let us suppose that you did not come by your supply through any of the usual means. That is, you did not melt down any coins, nor did you purchase a supply from the Treasury Department of the Sorcerers and Adepts Guild, which occasionally allows the purchase of unminted nickallirium by selected craftsmen, albeit at a kingly price, for the making of such things as precious jewelry and ornamented weapons for the nobility.

"Speaking, once again, purely for the sake of argument," the peddlar continued, "one might, therefore, suppose that you came by your supply through means which would be called somewhat irregular. Such a transaction would, of course, be against the law and, as such, it could result in certain problems for a certain vendor, if you get my meaning."

"Perhaps it would," said Mick, "if such was the nature of the source."

"Aye," said Harlan cautiously. "Again, speaking purely for the sake of argument, you understand, one could not help but wonder at a source for unminted nickallirium that was not acquired through the Guild. Certain persons—not speaking for myself, you understand—might suspect that it was stolen."

"I can assure you that it was not stolen," Mick replied.

"And I, of course, would not think of questioning your word," the peddlar said. "But certain individuals might insist on proof of such assurances."

Mick and Robie exchanged glances. Pikestaff Pat cleared his throat. Bloody Bob just looked confused.

"There is another source of nickallirium that you did not take into account," said Mick after a moment's pause, with a significant look at the peddlar.

Harlan simply stared at him, then he looked around at Robie, Pikestaff Pat, and Bloody Bob, before turning back to Mick again.

"Do you seriously mean to tell me," he said slowly, "that you actually possess the secret of the Philosopher's Stone?"

"Well, let us simply say that we can supply as many knives with grips of nickallirium as the market will demand," said Mick.

"Of course, such knives could never be sold cheaply," Pikestaff Pat said.

"And they could not be sold for barter," Robie added. "The purchasers would have to pay in coin of nickallirium."

"And the profits would have to be equitably shared," said Mick. "Speaking, as you said, purely for the sake of argument, it wouldn't do to have a vendor taking more than his agreed-upon share. Such a happenstance could result in rather unpleasant repercussions."

"I think we understand one another," Harlan said, choosing his words with care, "but let us be absolutely certain of the agreement we are in the process of negotiating. For your part, you are saying that you are able to craft as many of these wondrous knives as the market will demand, exactly like the one I hold here in my hands, so that any orders I may take could easily be filled. And, not to put too fine a point on it, if I were to get greedy and be dishonest in my dealings with you, I would likely wind up lying somewhere with my throat cut, or my back broken, or some other such similar unpleasantness." He nodded. "Very well, I can accept this, as I am an honest peddlar, which is why, perhaps, I have never been a rich one.

"For my part," he continued, "I would require assurances that I would be the exclusive vendor for your products, so that my own profits would thus be safeguarded, and so that anyone wishing to purchase your goods would have to deal solely with me. I do not feel that this is an unreasonable request. Needless to say, should you find my performance wanting in any way, that is to say, should I prove unable to develop a proper market for your goods, with an acceptable profit for all concerned, you would, of course, be free at that point to negotiate some similar agreement with another vendor. But I must be given a reasonable length of time in order to develop such a market."

Mick nodded. "That is fair. I think we could live with that."

"And the same conditions would apply, of course, to any other products I might undertake to represent for you," said Harlan. "Such as this excellent tea, here. And you say you have others, as well?"

"Aye," said Mick. "There are a number of other teas we

could supply you with. We could also negotiate an agreement for your representing my Mickey Finn.''

"Ah, of course, the wine,'' said Harlan, nodding. He cleared his throat. "A unique libation, indeed. I imagine that The Stealers Tavern would pay a pretty price to offer such a potent beverage to its patrons. And you could assure me of adequate quantity in that commodity, as well?''

Mick nodded. "We could brew up as much Mickey Finn as you can sell.''

"Excellent,'' said Harlan. "Excellent, indeed.''

"What about the magic soap?'' asked Pikestaff Pat.

"The magic soap?'' asked Harlan.

"Aye, 'tis a wondrous dirt remover,'' Mick said, "that one can use for bathing and making oneself smell clean and fresh. I believe that no one else would have such a commodity to offer.''

"So? Could I see some of this rare substance, and try it out myself?'' the peddlar asked.

"Of course,'' said Mick. "We would not expect you to agree to handle our products purely on faith. You would be a better vendor for us if you believed in them yourself.''

"Aye, quite so, quite so,'' agreed the peddlar. "Well, gentlemen, I must say, this has been quite a productive evening thus far. I have been searching for unique products to offer to my customers, and you have been in need of an aggressive vendor to market your goods. I think we could help each other. Aye, I do think so, indeed.''

"Then perhaps we should proceed to the finer points of our agreement,'' Mick said.

"Aye, let's do that,'' said the peddlar with a smile. "But first, I would like another cup of this fine tea.''

The CEO of EnGulfCo International was a forceful and dynamic man, accustomed to making decisions and delegating authority. He was a powerful man, but he did not wield his power conspicuously. Heads of state frequently dropped whatever they were doing just to take his phone calls, and captains of industry looked up to him as a paragon of everything to which they aspired. Success, wealth, power, and influence. For all that, he was not a very famous man, certainly not one who would be easily recognized on the streets.

Though his name was quite well-known in business circles, and always published on those lists of the wealthiest and most successful people that the magazines come out with every year, he went to great lengths to preserve his privacy and avoided being photographed. Once, when a notorious paparazzi popped up out of the bushes and snapped his picture on the golf course, then successfully eluded his bodyguards, the CEO had managed to avoid having the photograph published by putting out some discreet feelers, finding out which magazine had bought the rights to it, and then snapping up the magazine in a masterstroke of corporate raiding. He had then fired the editor who bought the photograph, brought in a new staff, and tripled the publication's circulation. There had been several successful attempts to photograph him after that, but for some reason, the photographers could not find buyers for the prints.

Subtlety. The CEO believed in subtlety. Practiced on a big-time scale.

In this case, the CEO felt, subtlety was much more than a matter of management style. It was absolutely imperative to preserve the secret of Brewster's discovery, if indeed, what Pamela Fairburn claimed was true. And it wasn't very long before the CEO had satisfied himself that either it was absolutely true, or Marvin Brewster had somehow managed to pull off the hoax of the century. Frankly, the CEO thought, Marvin Brewster just wasn't that clever. He was smart, yes, a genius . . . but clever? No, not in that sense. As intelligent as Marvin Brewster was, the CEO thought, he was no con man. His mind simply didn't work that way. Besides, it just didn't add up.

If it was some sort of hoax or con, then what could be his motive? Money? Hardly. Marvin Brewster was an unpretentious sort of man, a man of simple tastes and with no vices that he knew of. Marvin Brewster didn't care much about money. He didn't even understand money. Besides, if money had been the issue, Brewster could have easily demanded much more than the highly substantial salary he already received, and he would have gotten it, no questions asked. He was worth that much to the company and more.

If not money, what then? Fame? Quite possibly, though Brewster didn't seem to be the type to court that fickle mistress. Recognition for his work? Ah, yes, the CEO thought, that would make sense, but for a man like Marvin Brewster, that recognition would have to be genuine, for work that was genuine. He would not measure himself against the pop icons of the time, but against men such as Galileo, da Vinci, Einstein . . . and the pride of being able to measure up to such men would preclude the possibility of attempting to fake it with a hoax.

No, thought the CEO, Brewster was too honest, sincere, and disingenuous to pull off such a stunt. And there was no way he could see how Brewster could have done it. He had simply disappeared into thin air, under the watchful eyes of guards and cameras. Houdini or David Copperfield might have found a way to do it, but not Marvin Brewster. The tapes had all been thoroughly reviewed, the laboratory had been thoroughly searched, Pamela Fairburn's phone had been thoroughly tapped . . . there was just no way that Brewster could have done it. Which meant he really did it. Disappeared, that is. Somehow, uncannily, Marvin Brewster had discovered time travel.

Of course, there was no real evidence of that, the CEO reminded himself, just to keep things in perspective. It was also entirely possible that Marvin Brewster had found a way to vaporize himself and his machine without a trace. However, in that case, the discovery could still be useful. EnGulfCo had a lot of government contracts.

Either way, the CEO was determined that no one else would have the secret. Whatever in hell the secret was. There was money to be made here. The CEO could smell it. His olfactory sense in that regard had always been unusually acute. The problem now was how to keep a lid on it.

There were only a few people in a position to blow the thing wide open. One was the head of security at EnGulfCo, however, the CEO had discovered a few things about his war record, in addition to some of his extracurricular activities in such places as Cambodia, Thailand, Rhodesia, and Belize, and there was now very little danger of the head of security stepping out of line. Another potential source of trouble was the vice-president in charge of research and development, along with his secretary. The CEO took care of that one by having the secretary transferred to a geological exploration station in Antarctica and getting his hands on certain interesting photos of the vice-president of R and D with a girl named Mavis, a black leather mask, and a bullwhip. The vice-president of R and D was married to a woman from Virginia whose father was a highly placed official in the CIA, and the CEO expected no trouble on that front.

Finally, there was the executive vice-president of EnGulfCo, a fairly powerful man in his own right, and not someone to be trifled with. Therefore, the CEO wisely chose not to trifle with him, and instead increased his stock options, sponsored him to membership in his own club, introduced him to his attractive twenty-three-year-old daughter, and promised to cut him in for a full share of the profits, which meant bringing him in on the whole deal. However, that was perfectly acceptable, for it meant he now had someone to delegate authority to. The CEO would not have liked to handle the whole thing by himself. It would have cut into his golf game.

That left only one loose end. Pamela Fairburn. And this was, as the British often said, where the wicket got a little sticky. Pamela's father was not only a wealthy and socially prominent man, he was also a close personal friend of the CEO's. This meant that any leverage exerted on Pamela had to be exerted very gently and very carefully. Unfortunately for the CEO, there just wasn't much leverage he could find to exert. Pamela was nothing if not a model of proper behavior and decorum. There was simply no dirt to be dug up on her. The CEO found that annoying. She also didn't work for him, which meant he couldn't give her orders. And she was very smart, which meant she couldn't be easily manipulated. That left him with only one string to pull. Her concern for Marvin Brewster.

He got off the elevator at the top floor and walked past the armed guards, who stiffened to attention at his approach. The special palm-scanner lock on the door to Brewster's laboratory had been changed. It now responded only to two palm patterns. His and Pamela Fairburn's. He pressed his hand flat against the scanner plate and the door slid open.

Pamela Fairburn was inside, bent over the papers spread out on Brewster's desk. She was dressed in a white lab coat over a sensible skirt and blouse and low-heeled pumps. She had pulled her hair back and fastened it with a barette, and behind her horn-rimmed glasses, her eyes were red-rimmed, with deep, dark bags beneath them. A half-empty pot of coffee stood on the warming plate of the drip percolator at the edge of the desk. The ash tray was full of cigarette butts.

"Pamela," said the CEO, coming up to the desk. She looked up at him. "You look terrible. Have you had any sleep at all?"

She shook her head and glanced toward the cot set back against the wall. "I had that cot brought in," she said. "I thought I could catch a few winks if I got tired, but I've been working straight through." She smiled wearily and shrugged. "Just became caught up, I suppose."

The CEO glanced at the overflowing ash tray and the red packages of Dunhills on the desk. "When did you start smoking?"

"Just started," she replied with a glance at the ash tray. "I'm getting rather good at it, I think."

The CEO shook his head. "There's no point in driving yourself to exhaustion, Pamela. You're doing as much as anyone could do. Perhaps I should have some help brought in. Is there anyone you'd like to work with you on this?"

She shook her head. "No, I don't think Marvin would want that. You know how secretive he is about his special projects. Besides, the more people know about this, the greater the chance of a security leak, and you wouldn't want that now, would you?"

The CEO frowned. "I'm not sure what you mean. I'm

anxious to take certain precautions about Marvin's work, of course, but—''

"You mean precautions such as having me followed and having my phone tapped?'' she interrupted him. She waved off his protest with a casual gesture. "And don't bother to deny it, I'm not a fool, you know. Those casual strollers outside my window, the van parked down by the corner, those telltale little clickings on the line . . . I do have some knowledge of electronics, you know.''

"Pamela, I—''

"Frankly, you're not really very good at this James Bond business. What did you do, hire some sort of seedy little private eye? Haven't you heard of laser scanners, dish mikes, and infinity transmitters? Honestly, if you're going to eavesdrop on somebody, the very least you could do was have the decency to be professional about it.''

The CEO rapidly realized that a Pamela Fairburn stoked on nicotine and coffee was a force to be reckoned with. Clearly, he had underestimated her. And, just as clearly, it was undoubtedly going to cost him.

"Look, Pamela,'' he began, but that was about as far as he got.

"No, *you* look,'' she replied. "I resent your attitude. I resent it very much, indeed. What did you think I was going to do, for heaven's sake, call up the *Daily Mirror* and announce that an EnGulfCo scientist had discovered time travel? Or did you think, perhaps, that I was going to get on the phone to General Electric and ask for bids on Marvin's notes? Quite aside from the fact that no one in their right mind would believe me without substantial proof of such a wild assertion, the thought I might have some sort of underlying motive of financial gain is positively insulting. I ought to box your ears for you!''

"Pamela, please, try to appreciate my position. I—''

"Appreciate *your* position?'' she said. "What about *mine*? I happen to be a responsible scientist. And quite aside from that, my first and only concern at this point is for Marvin's welfare. I've been devoting all my energies and effort to this situation ever since Marvin disappeared and this is the

thanks I get? This is the extent of your support, that you tap
my phone and have me followed?''

''Pamela, let me assure you that I—''

''The only assurances that I require from you are that you
will live up to your part of the bargain and back me up with
all the resources your company can provide,'' she snapped.
''If you want your precious little monopoly on Marvin's
discovery, that's perfectly all right with me. What *I* want is
Marvin back, safe and sound. And just in case you're
thinking of placing someone else in charge of this, you
might wish to know that I've committed certain key sections
of Marvin's papers to memory and then destroyed the
originals, so without me, you've got nothing.''

''All right, Pamela,'' the CEO said, knowing when to bite
the bullet. ''Whatever you say, we'll do it your way. I'm not
completely insensitive, you know. I'd like Marvin back safe
and sound, as well. I'm concerned about his welfare, too.
The question is, can we do anything about it?''

''We can build his time machine,'' said Pamela, ''provided
you can supply the key components.''

''Can you actually do it?'' asked the CEO.

''I'm a cybernetics engineer,'' Pamela replied. ''I can
read a bloody schematic. What's more, I can make sense of
Marvin's notes, which is probably more than anyone you've
got on your payroll can do. I understand him, I know the
way he thinks. You get me what I need and I'll build his
time machine for you, and then I'm bloody well going after
him.''

''You mean you know where he went?'' asked the CEO.

''Marvin logged everything he did,'' Pamela replied. ''I
have the precise settings he was using, right here,'' she
added, tapping her forehead. ''I've committed it to memory
and then I burned the papers, so if you want him back, and
if you want to find out how his discovery works, then *I'm*
the one you'll have to deal with. Understood?''

''Understood,'' the CEO said quietly.

''Now I've made a list of what I'm going to need,'' said
Pamela, handing him a sheet of paper. ''And number one on
that list is a fresh supply of Buckminsterfullerine. I don't

know how you're going to get it, or where you're going to get it, but I would suggest that you direct your energies chiefly toward that end, because without it, Marvin's discovery is as useless as tits on a bloody bull. You've said a great deal about EnGulfCo's vast resources and what they can accomplish. Well, go and accomplish something, and leave me to my work.''

"Right," said the CEO. He folded the paper and put it in his pocket, then turned and quickly left the lab.

➤ CHAPTER ➤
NINE

It was nearly morning by the time that Brewster and the others—

"One moment. You have been avoiding me ever since Chapter Four. Now I have been extremely patient, but my patience is beginning to wear thin. Now who is this Brewster?"

All right, now look, Warrick, this really is too much. A little interaction with the narrator from time to time during your scenes is one thing, but interrupting the narrative flow when it isn't even your turn is something else again. Admittedly, this whole business of a character interacting with the narrator is a bit irregular, but it's different and it adds a certain off-the-wall spice to the story. However, this is getting out of hand.

"You have not answered my question," Warrick said. "And don't bother with that space break, cutting to another scene trick. I have devised a counterspell and it won't work again."

Threatening the narrator is going to get you nowhere, Warrick. Trust me, it really isn't very smart. You're dealing with powers you couldn't even begin to understand.

"Is that so?" Warrick countered. "Then how do you explain my ability to break into the narrative when it's not even my scene? I have not been idle during all this time, you know. You may have less power than you think. Or I might have more than you suspect."

Don't be ridiculous. *I'm* the one who's telling this story, not you. And I'm not about to have one of my characters slipping the leash. Well-developed characters that take on a life of their own are usually an asset to a story, but now you've brought the momentum of the plot to a screeching halt. This is absolutely intolerable. I tell you, I won't have it.

" 'Twas not I who asked for this, you know," Warrick replied. "I was merely minding my own business when you began to tell this tale."

You didn't even *exist* until I began to tell this tale, for crying out loud!

"That is purely a matter of perspective," Warrick said. " 'Twould depend upon your frame of reference."

Listen, I'm not going to sit here and listen to a lecture on relativity from a fictional character! What the hell do you know about science, anyway? You're a sorcerer, for heaven's sake!

"Any branch of knowledge that is sufficiently advanced would seem like magic to one who did not completely understand it."

Damn it, don't you go paraphrasing Clarke to me! He isn't even published in your universe!

"A fact does not depend upon publication for its validity," said Warrick. "I will grant you that there is much about your reality that I do not fully comprehend, but that does not cause me undue concern. As a student of the occult, I am disposed to be flexible. Now we have some unfinished business to settle, and avoiding answering my questions is not about to make it go away. You still have not told me who this Brewster is. Is he some sort of alchemist? Does he have anything to do with this time machine apparatus? Is—"

Clang!

Warrick grunted and collapsed to the floor of his sanctorum as Teddy the troll brought the frying pan down upon his head.

"Great goblins!" Teddy exclaimed, horrified. *"What have I done?"*

He gazed at the frying pan in his hand, wondering where it had come from, and what had possessed him to strike his master with it.

"Possessed!" Teddy whispered, awestruck. His eyes darted wildly from side to side. "I've been possessed! *Demons! Voices in the ether!"*

He dropped the frying pan and ran screaming from the room.

Well, with any luck, that'll keep Warrick out of the picture for a while. In fact, Teddy hit him so hard, he'll probably have a concussion and it will take him a few days to recuperate. Poor Teddy will probably need therapy by the time this is all over, but it couldn't be helped. Besides, trolls are a little schizoid, anyway.

Now where were we? Oh, right.

It was nearly morning by the time that Brewster and the others finished listening to Rachel's tale. The first gray light of dawn was showing over the treetops and Brian reverted to being a chamberpot again. It happened right in front of Rachel's eyes and, much to his annoyance, she reacted to the transformation by clapping her hands with delight and saying, "Oh, do it again! Do it again!"

"I never did like elves," grumbled the champerpot sourly.

"Quiet, Brian," Brewster said. "I need to think." He scratched his head and frowned. "Okay, so the fairies saw three brigands loading up my missing magic chariot into a cart. From your description, it couldn't be anything else. Also, from your description, those brigands sound suspiciously like Long Bill, Fifer Bob, and Silent Fred. And then they took it to this wizard? What I don't understand is, why didn't they say anything about it?"

"Simple," the chamberpot replied. "They sold it to Blackrune 4 and they were afraid to say anything about it, for fear of what you might do to them."

"But they hadn't even met me then, and they had no way of knowing what it was," said Brewster. "Why couldn't they have simply come to me and explained what happened? I would have understood.''

"Perhaps," the chamberpot replied, "but 'tis doubtful that Black Shannon would.''

"What does she have to do with it?" asked Brewster.

"She has everything to do with it," the chamberpot replied. "Knowing how devious these brigands are, they probably cheated her out of her cut. They most likely sold your magic chariot and kept all the profits to themselves.''

"I'll have to have a word with them," said Brewster.

"Let Shannon have a word with them," the chamberpot replied. "That ought to be interesting to watch.''

"Well, the question now is where can we find this wizard . . . what was his name again?" asked Brewster.

"Blackrune 4," said Rachel. "He's not much of a wizard, really. Strictly second-rate. He lives by himself in a small cottage, with only one apprentice, about four days travel north.''

"Or at least he did," said Rory.

They glanced at him and saw several fairies buzzing around his head.

"These fairies tell me Blackrune 4 has disappeared," said Rory. "There has been no sign of him around his cottage and some time ago, his young apprentice was seen leaving in a loaded cart, heading down the road toward Pittsburgh.''

"*Pittsburgh?*" Brewster said.

"Aye," said the chamberpot. " 'Tis the capital of the Kingdom of Pitt, ruled by Bonnie King Billy. One of the largest cities in the twenty-seven kingdoms. And if Blackrune has vanished and his apprentice has departed, then it sounds as if the old wizard may have taken a journey in your magic chariot.''

Brewster sighed with resignation. "Then I guess that's it," he said in a dull voice. "It means I'm stuck here for the rest of my life.''

Shannon and MacGregor lay in bed, with their arms around each other, holding each other close. It was past noon, but they had slept late and then spent the late morning doing much the same thing that they'd done all through the night before, and now they lay basking in the afterglow of passion, simply staring into one another's eyes.

"I love you, Shannon," said MacGregor.

She smiled. "You needn't say that," she replied.

"'Tis true," he said.

"You barely even know me," she said. "All you remember is a thin ragamuffin of a street urchin that your father took in, and you see the woman I've become, but you know nothing of all the years that passed between."

"Well, that is not entirely true," replied MacGregor with a smile. "You have quite a reputation, you know."

"As do you," she said. "As for my own reputation, 'tis not one that most women would be proud of. I know what they say about me."

"Doubtless 'tis much exaggerated, as are many of the things they say of me," replied MacGregor.

"I fear not, Mac," said Shannon. "Everything they say of me is true. I am a wanton, lustful woman."

"Aye, I know," said MacGregor with a grin.

"Nor are you the first man I have been wanton and lustful with," Shannon added. "Nor the second, nor the third, nor even the one hundredth."

MacGregor raised his eyebrows. "That many?"

"Aye, and more," she said. "More than I could count, I fear. I would not wish to deceive you about my past. 'Tis quite a scarlet one."

"Well, I am no monk, myself," MacGregor said with a shrug. He chuckled. "My, aren't we a pair? An assassin and a brigand queen. 'Tis the stuff that songs are made of."

"Hardly songs that one would sing in polite company," said Shannon.

"Those are the best kind," replied Mac with a grin. "I have never met a woman like you. You handle a blade like a demon. By the gods, you would have made my father proud! And in bed, you are the very essence of a woman, a sweet and gentle lover..."

"At times not quite so sweet and gentle," she reminded him.

"Aye, 'tis true," admitted Mac. "I shall require some salve to apply upon by back." He shifted slightly and grunted with discomfort.

"Oh, forgive me!" she said. "I did not mean to hurt you."

"Ah, but it was such delicious pain!"

"I will go and fetch some salve from Mary for you," she said, and started to get out of bed, but Mac grabbed her and pulled her back.

"Oh, no, you don't! You stay right here by me. I've been hurt far worse, you know."

"I know," she said, running her fingertips across his scars. "So many times, too."

"You've never been scarred yourself, though."

She shrugged. " 'Tis merely skill," she said.

"Skill that I am lacking in, I take it?" said MacGregor.

She shrugged again. " 'Twas not I who lost the fight."

"You needn't rub it in. Aye, I lost the fight," he replied, "but then I gained a wench."

"Did you, indeed? Am I some prize to be possessed?"

"A rare and wondrous prize," he said. "But not one to be possessed by any man, no. 'Tis a prize valued all the more highly because 'twas given freely."

"Even if the prize was given out so many times before?" she asked.

MacGregor shook his head. "Nay, not like this, my love. You never gave, you took. As did I, myself. With us, 'twas different, and you know it. We each gave of each other, willingly, and joyfully, and with no reservations. We were meant for one another, you and I. We are two of a kind."

"Your speech is pretty," she said, "and it falls sweetly on my ears, yet it smacks uneasily of permanence."

"And would that be so bad a thing?"

" 'Tis not whether 'twould be bad or good," she said, "but whether 'twould be possible. I will not change, Mac. I cannot change. I am who I am and what I am. 'Tis the brigand's life for me, Mac. 'Tis the life I know and love, a life of freedom, where I can be the equal, nay, more than equal of any man. And I shall not alter it for anyone, not even for you.''

"I did not ask that you change,'' he said.

"And what of yourself?'' she asked. "You have made a life for yourself as an assassin, the most accomplished assassin of them all. Men step aside for you, and you step aside for no one. Your trade is plied in the thriving cities of the twenty-seven kingdoms, where your name is known and feared and people treat you with respect. The tavern keepers set aside their finest tables for you, and you drink their finest wine, and women vie for your attention.''

MacGregor shrugged. "It's a living,'' he said.

"Look around you, Mac,'' she said. "Look at this room. 'Tis old and dusty and the floorboards creak from looseness. Spiders build their webs in the corners at the ceiling and mice scuttle in the walls. The bedclothes are threadbare and the walls are drafty. And these are the finest accommodations this little hovel of a village has to offer. Yet this is where I live, Mac, and for all its shabbiness, I love it. This is where I belong, here with my brigand band. 'Twould be a paltry living here for the famous Mac the Knife.''

"Oh, I don't know,'' said Mac. "There is much to be said for the simple life of a small village. 'Tis true that a city offers many comforts and interesting diversions, and yet life in a large city has its drawbacks, too. There is the expense, for one thing. One has to pay for the best accommodations, and for dining in the finest taverns, and the costs of such things as weapons and supplies are greater. It does cut into one's profits.''

"True,'' said Shannon hopefully.

"And then there are all the people,'' Mac continued. "One of the disadvantages of fame is that one's face is often recognized, and far more people know you than you can know yourself. At all times, a man in my position has to watch his back. There is never any shortage of young hellions who would try to make a name for themselves by sneaking up behind me and planting a knife between my shoulder blades. In a place such as Brigand's Roost, 'twould not take very long before I knew each and every person in the village, and within a short time, I would no longer be merely a famous man among a horde of strangers, but a friend among friends. And friends watch one another's backs.''

"Aye, the people here look out for one another," Shannon said.

"If a stranger were to come to town," continued Mac, "why, I would hear of it at once, and no potential foe could enjoy the advantage of surprise. And if some wealthy client wished to employ my services, they could send some emissary to seek me out in Brigand's Roost and we could conduct negotiations in the security of a place I could feel safe in. Nor would my presence here be entirely without benefit to Brigand's Roost, I think. There are always those who like to brush up against fame, to meet someone whose life might seem more fascinating than their own, in the hope that some of that special magic might rub off on them. People would come to Brigand's Roost in the hope of meeting Mac the Knife, and perhaps buying him a drink at One-Eyed Jack's, and listening to his tales. And there are always those who seek me out in the hope that I might take them on as my apprentices and train them. I am always being sought out by young and eager aspirants to the Footpads and Assassins Guild. Some of them are fools, of course, but there are also those who have potential. I have had to turn down many of them, simply because I did not have the time. However, I am not getting any younger, and I am growing weary of stalking victims throughout the twenty-seven kingdoms. Of late, I have been thinking that it might be nice to start a school. An academy to train fighters and assassins. 'Twould be the first of its kind, you know. And there is much to be said for retiring at the peak of one's profession.''

Shannon stared at him, her eyes shining. "You would do all that for me?" she said with disbelief.

"Nay, for *us*," said Mac. "I have known many a wench, my lass. Some I have known for but one night, while others I have known for years, and yet the very moment I crossed swords with you, I knew you were the one for me. I said to myself, MacGregor, if this girl doesn't kill you, you'd damn well better marry her.''

Shannon caught her breath. ''Mac! Do you know what you're saying?''

''Aye, my love, I do. I've nary a doubt in my mind, nor in my heart. What say you? Will you join your fate to mine?''

The expression on Shannon's face was a mixture of concern and happiness. ''Think, Mac,'' she said. ''Are you quite certain 'tis not the passion of the moment speaking? I am no little wife to stay at home to sweep the floors and scrub the pots. And I have never given any thought to having children. For all I know, I may be barren. I have had many lovers, and yet I have never been with child. And my men depend upon me. 'Tis not only my own welfare I must think of, but theirs, too. I also have a price upon my head. I should think that I would be the last woman you would consider taking for a wife.''

MacGregor smiled. ''I want you for what you are, Shannon,'' he said, ''not for what I think you might become. If I need to have my doublet mended, I shall seek out a tailor or a seamstress, and if I want someone to stay at home and prepare my favorite meals, why, I shall hire a cook. 'Tis what I have always done. I need no wife for that. But a friend and lover who can not only share my bed, but watch my back and stand shoulder to shoulder with me against adversity, the skill of her blade matched with mine, now there's a wife! As for children,'' he added with a shrug, '' 'tis no great matter. If a child should come along, then think of what a bold and handsome son or daughter 'twould be. And if not, then I can lavish my fatherly affections on those three louts apprenticed to me, and on all those who will follow when I start my school. Those awful urchins running wild through the streets would make fine pupils. 'Twould give them an outlet and direction for all their youthful energies. And 'twould give me a sense of purpose to pass on what I have learned. So, once again, what say you, Shannon?''

Her eyes began to mist up. "If you truly want me, Sean MacGregor, then I am yours, body and soul."

He reached for her, but she quickly turned away.

He frowned. "Shannon, what is it?"

"Nothing," she mumbled through her tears.

He propped himself up on his elbow and looked down at her. "You're crying?" he said.

"I am *not*!" she said, the tears running freely down her cheeks. "Damn you, Sean MacGregor, if you ever tell a soul you've seen me cry, I'll cut your tongue out!"

He threw back his head and laughed. "Such sweet endearments from my wife-to-be!"

She drew back her fist to strike him, but he caught her arm and pressed her to him, kissing her. She struggled for a moment, and then her arms went around his shoulders and she kissed him back with equal fervor.

Ahem . . . now, I realize that there are some narrators out there who would, at this point, spend pages and pages of colorful, descriptive, lurid prose detailing what went on from there, but your faithful narrator believes that true romance lies not in graphic description of intimate relationships, but in gentle hints and subtle character development and the imagination of the reader. If that makes me a prude, so be it. If you want throbbing, quivering loins and heaving bosoms and heavy breathing, then go read Jackie Collins. This is not that kind of story. What we're going to do at this point is employ a narrative technique we've already encountered several times before. It's called a space break, and it's normally used for either cutting to another scene or indicating that some time has passed. After all, if you were Mac or Shannon, you wouldn't want an audience, would you? Well, all right, maybe some of you would, but I don't want to know about it. Okay, you ready? Here we go. . . .

Later that afternoon (never mind how much later), Mac and Shannon sat downstairs in the tavern, enjoying a late and hearty brunch and making plans. Shannon wanted a big wedding and a feast, with all the brigands and all the residents of Brigand's Roost and the surrounding farms in attendance, and with Dirty Mary and her fancy girls acting as bridesmaids. Mac decided that he would break with tradition and have three best men, Hugh, Dugh, and Lugh, assuming they came to in time for the ceremony. It was all happening so fast, and they were so caught up in their enthusiasm, that it was a while before Mac finally remembered that he still had a job that he had left unfinished.

"There is but one thing, my love," he said, "merely one small matter that I still have to attend to before we can proceed with our new life together. I hope that you will understand, but I do have a client for whom I have a job to do, and I have never left a task unfinished."

"I understand, of course," Shannon replied. "How long do you think this task will take?"

"Not long," said Mac. "The trail is getting very warm. I should have it all wrapped up in a matter of a few days, at the very most."

"You are stalking someone, then," she said.

"Aye, three men," he said. "Their trail has led me here, to Brigand's Roost."

"Here?" said Shannon. "Who are these three men?"

"I do not know their names," said Mac, "but I do know that one is tall, with a long face and dark hair; one is of medium height, a bit stout and balding, with a fringe of light-brown hair; and one is slim, with dark-red hair and a beard, and it seems he only rarely speaks. I also know that they play chess, for one of them has lost a game piece." He reached into his pouch. "This little wooden knight."

Shannon's eyes narrowed as she saw the chesspiece. "Why does your client want these men assassinated?"

"He doesn't," replied Mac. "He wishes them captured and brought to him, so that he might question them about some sort of mysterious, magical apparatus."

"What *kind* of apparatus?" Shannon asked.

"In truth, I do not know," said Mac. "I have never seen it. But it must be mysterious and powerful indeed if it baffles even Warrick the White."

"Warrick Morgannan is your client?"

"Aye. He keeps me on retainer, for certain special tasks.

He has been a good patron, and 'twould be wrong of me to leave this last job for him unfinished.''

"I do not quite understand," said Shannon. "If this magical apparatus is so mysterious that even Warrick cannot comprehend it, then what makes him think these three men can explain it to him?"

"Ah, well, chances are that they cannot," said Mac, "because my guess is that they stole it. They had sold it to a sorcerer named Blackrune 4, who lives not far from these parts, and who disappeared mysteriously after this apparatus came into his possession. His apprentice then brought the device to Warrick, and Warrick believes these three men who sold it to Blackrune 4 can tell him where it came from."

"They sold it, eh?" said Shannon with an edge to her voice.

"Aye," said Mac. "Ill-gotten gains, no doubt. And 'twill bring them more trouble than they bargained for."

"You can be sure of *that*," said Shannon tersely. "Come on!"

She pushed her bench back so hard that it crashed to the floor.

"Where are we going?" Mac asked.

"To have a little talk with those three men you're seeking," she replied.

"You know them?"

"Aye, I know them. They are three of my own men! And 'tis not you nor Warrick Morgannan they'll need to fear, but *me*!"

Mac hurried to catch up with her as she went outside and vaulted up into Big Nasty's hand-tooled, silver-trimmed, black leather saddle. He mounted his own horse and took off at a gallop after her as she thundered off down the road leading out of town, toward Brewster's keep.

It was all that he could do to keep her in sight as he rode, for his own steed could barely keep pace with the big black stallion, much less catch him, and Shannon rode with a determined fury, using her quirt to urge the stallion on.

They left the town behind and followed the trail as it wound through the forest, their horses' hooves digging up large divots from the ground.

"Shannon! Wait!" MacGregor called, but there was no stopping her.

Within a short while, they turned a bend in the trail and came out into a large clearing, and MacGregor saw the tower of the keep looming up ahead. He also noticed what appeared to be a busy campsite within the crumbling remnants of the outer walls. There were several fires burning, and large cauldrons boiling, and people working at a variety of tasks.

Shannon went thundering across the clearing, heedless of anyone who stood in her way. People scattered at her approach as she galloped through the camp, and Mac saw her head turning quickly from side to side, as if she were searching for someone. And then the quarry was apparently spotted, because Mac saw her yank hard on the reins and turn the stallion, and one man, of medium height, a little stout and balding, carrying a couple of buckets on a yoke, froze in his tracks as he saw her riding down upon him. Then a look of utter terror crossed his face as he dropped the yoke and took to his heels, running like a man possessed.

Fifer Bob ran panic-stricken around one of the fires, where a large spam-fat rendering cauldron was boiling, and headed for the keep. Shannon's stallion leaped right over the cauldron and the pot, scattering the brigands who were tending it, and she pursued the running brigand, apparently intent on running him down. Fifer Bob barely made it to the doors. He flung them open and plunged through, but Shannon didn't even slow down as she rode in right after him.

As Bob ran screaming through the great hall of the keep, Shannon leaned down from her saddle and snagged the back of his collar, forcing his legs to pump insanely as she ran him at an even greater speed straight toward one of the support pillars. Mac had reined in just outside and dismounted, and he came running in just in time to hear Bob's scream as Shannon ran him full tilt right into the stone pillar. The sound made as Bob connected was not unlike that of a hammer striking meat, and he collapsed senseless and bloody to the floor.

Shannon reined in and wheeled her horse around, the

stallion's hooves slipping on the stone floor, and as the crowd from outside came running in to see what was going on, she rode toward them, her eyes flashing.

"Long Bill!" she shouted. *"Silent Fred! Where the devil are you two? Step forward!"*

She spotted Silent Fred, who realized the threat too late and tried to lose himself back in the crowd.

"Oh, no, you don't!" she said, dismounting and covering the distance between them in a few quick strides. As he turned to run, she grabbed him by his hair and yanked him back. "I'll have a word or two with you, my bucko, and I'll not sit still for any of your silence! Where is Long Bill?"

There was the sound of running footsteps as Long Bill tried to make good his escape outside.

"Bill, you cur! Get back here!" Shannon shouted as the crowd parted hastily.

"Allow me, my love," said Mac, stepping up beside her, and if the brigands were surprised at the familiarity of his address, they were even more surprised when the handsome stranger reached up and drew one of his many knives from his crossed leather bandoliers, deftly flicked it around to hold it by the point, then stepped up to the doorway and threw it at the rapidly retreating back of Long Bill.

The knife spun end over end through the air on its unerring path and struck Long Bill hilt-first, squarely in the back of his head. He took two more running steps and fell to the ground, stunned.

"I assume you did not want him injured," Mac said, turning deferentially to Shannon.

"Not yet, I don't," she said through clenched teeth, still holding on to Silent Fred by a fistful of his hair. "Bloody Bob, go fetch him."

"Aye, Shannon," Bloody Bob said, and he trotted out to where Long Bill was lying, groaning, on the ground. He picked him up with one hand and slung him over his shoulder, as if he didn't weigh a thing, then carried him back inside the keep and deposited him none too gently on the floor at Shannon's feet.

"Right," said Shannon. "Help him up and bring him."

Two of the brigands supported Long Bill with his arms across their shoulders, following as Shannon dragged Silent Fred along to one of the wooden tables in the hall. She glanced down at the senseless form of Fifer Bob as she passed him and snapped, "Revive that worthless baggage!"

Red Jack and Juicy Jill went to fetch a pail of water and when they brought it back, they poured it over Fifer Bob, whose crown was not quite broken, though it was bashed up pretty badly.

"Sit them down," said Shannon, shoving Silent Fred toward one of the wooden benches. Long Bill was deposited on the bench beside him, and Fifer Bob, still stunned, was propped up against Long Bill. The other brigands gathered round.

Shannon stood back, her hands on her hips, looking down at them with a steely gaze. Mac came up to stand beside her. The other brigands still did not know who he was, and they were almost as curious about him as they were about what their three friends had done to bring down Shannon's wrath.

"Our articles state that we share all plundered booty equally," said Shannon. "We all agreed to that, did we not?"

Silence.

"Well?"

There was a hasty chorus of agreement from the others. Fifer Bob groaned and held his head. Long Bill made a quiet, moaning sound, and Silent Fred turned pale.

"Share and share alike, we said," Shannon went on. "What profits one shall profit all. A brotherhood of brigands, supporting one another, with no one holding out in greed, for 'twould be no greed among us. Was that not what was agreed?"

This time, the chorus of agreement came more quickly.

"And what punishment did we decide upon for anyone who broke with the articles we all agreed on?" she asked.

No one spoke.

"Well?" she snapped.

Lonesome John softly cleared his throat. "Uh . . . begging

your pardon, Shannon, but I do not believe that a specific penalty was ever mentioned."

"Aye," said Pikestaff Pat. " 'A punishment most vile,' was what I think you said."

"Aye, 'a punishment most vile,' " several of the others echoed, and Fifer Bob began to whimper.

"Oh," said Shannon, remembering. " 'Tis right, I meant to keep my options open. Well, we shall have to decide upon a vile punishment, for these three good comrades of ours have broken with our articles and held back profits for themselves!"

"What?"

"No!"

"They didn't!"

"Aye, they did, indeed," said Shannon. "They conspired to engage in selling stolen goods and kept the profits all to themselves, cheating the rest of us of our fair share!"

"Flog 'em!"

"String 'em up!"

"Boil 'em in oil!"

"Off with their heads!"

"Give 'em a right nasty scolding!"

Shannon turned around. "Who said that?" she demanded, but the culprit who spoke last wisely refrained from identifying himself.

" 'Twasn't what you think," said Silent Fred, moved to speech by the imminent danger of his situation. " 'Twasn't really plunder, 'twas something that we found!"

"Aye," said Long Bill. "We found it in the road, whilst we were lurking in the hedgerows. It fell out of the sky! We didn't steal it, so we thought it didn't count. We merely found it!"

"Finders keepers," mumbled Fifer Bob.

"I'll bloody well give you finders keepers!" Shannon said, drawing back her fist.

Fifer Bob hastily covered his head with his arms and whined, "Don't hit! Don't hit!"

"What's going on?" said Brewster, coming down the

stairs from his bedroom on the upper floor, where he had spent most of the day in deep depression.

"Unless I miss my guess," said Shannon, "these three curs found your missing magic chariot, then sold it, and kept quiet about it all this time."

"Oh," said Brewster. "Yes, I know. I've been meaning to talk to them about it."

Shannon's eyes widened in astonishment. "You *knew*?"

"Well, actually, I only just found out about it. Rachel told me, and then Rory's fairies filled in the rest of the details."

"Rachel?" Shannon said with a puzzled frown. "And who is Rachel?"

In answer, there came a rapid tattoo on a pair of bongo drums and everyone looked up to see Rachel Drum sitting on the railing up above them, watching the proceedings from the gallery on the second floor.

"Hey," she said, and gave them all a jaunty wave.

"An elf!" said Bloody Bob.

"Give that man a prize," said Rachel.

"What is that elf doing there?" asked Shannon.

"Sitting," Rachel said. "Do go on. Don't stop on my account. It was beginning to get interesting."

"Rachel heard that there was a reward for information about my missing magic chariot," Brewster explained, "and she came to bring me news of it. If seems some of the fairies saw Fred, Bill, and Bob loading it up into a cart and taking it to Blackrune 4. But they really shouldn't be blamed. They had no way of knowing what it was. They hadn't even met me yet, so how could they have known that it was mine?"

"Aye, we didn't know!" said Long Bill, seeing a ray of hope for a reprieve.

" 'Tis not the point," said Shannon. "Whether you found booty or you stole it makes no difference. You sold it and then you kept all the profits for yourselves, in violation of our articles!"

"But there *were* no profits!" Silent Fred said. "We were cheated!"

"Aye," said Long Bill. "The wizard was a trickster and paid us off in changeling money! We would have shared it with the rest of you, only it turned to acorns by the time that we returned, and we said nothing for fear of being mocked for being so taken in."

Shannon looked dubious. "Perhaps you may be telling the truth," she said. "Yet even so, you knew that Doc was searching for his missing magic chariot, yet you said nothing of it. Why?"

"Because we were afraid," said Long Bill. "We knew Doc was a mighty sorcerer and we feared his wrath if he discovered what we'd done, even though 'twas done in innocence. I swear it, Doc, we didn't know 'twas your magic chariot, honest!"

"Aye," said Silent Fred. "We had no idea! We took it to Blackrune 4 because we thought that *he* might know!"

"How do I know you're telling us the truth?" asked Shannon. "You'd all three lie to save your skins!"

"It really makes no difference, Shannon," Brewster said. "The fairies say that Blackrune 4 has disappeared without a trace. He must have managed to activate the machine somehow, and now both he and it are gone. I'll never find it, and now I'll never get back home."

"Perhaps not," said Mac. " 'Tis true that Blackrune 4 has disappeared without a trace, but this magic chariot of yours, whatever it may be, may not have vanished along with him. 'Tis possible that I might know where it would be."

"Who are you?" said Brewster, noticing his unfamiliar presence for the first time.

"The name is Sean MacGregor."

"Mac the Knife!" said someone, and the name was repeated in hushed tones among the crowd.

"Forgive me," said Shannon. "In my anger at these three louts, I had forgotten my manners. Mac, meet Brewster Doc, a mighty wizard from the Land of Ing. Brewster Doc, meet Sean MacGregor, the Bladesman, also known as Mac the Knife, the number-one-ranked assassin in the Footpads and Assassins Guild, and the man who is to be my husband."

In the stunned silence brought on by this announcement, Brewster stepped forward to shake Mac's hand and say, "Congratulations. I hope you'll both be very happy. But . . . excuse me, I'm not really certain if I heard correctly. Did Shannon say that you were an . . . *assassin*?"

"Aye," said Mac. "But I have decided to retire and start a school in Brigand's Roost."

"Ah," said Brewster. "I see. Well, teaching is a noble profession. But what exactly did you mean when you said that you might know where my machine . . . my, uh, magic chariot might be?"

"I was hired to find these three," said Mac, indicating Silent Fred, Long Bill, and Fifer Bob, "because they brought some sort of magical apparatus to Blackrune 4, whose apprentice then brought it to my client. My client wished to find these three, so that they might tell him where they got it, and who made it. I take it then 'twas you?"

"Yes!" said Brewster excitely. "Then it's still here? Your client has it?"

"Aye, 'twould seem so," replied MacGregor. "Tell me, this magic chariot of yours, can it make people disappear?"

"Well . . . yes, I suppose you could put it that way," Brewster said. "But if someone were to activate it, it would disappear along with them, to another place and time."

"Indeed?" MacGregor said. "And is there no way to work the spell so that 'twould make people disappear, but not disappear along with them itself?"

Brewster frowned. "I . . . I'm not really sure. I shouldn't think so. At least, not if it was operated properly. I can't really see how it would work that way."

"Supposing the means of operation employed were not the proper means," said Mac with a thoughtful expression, "but that some other spell was found to make it work, perhaps not the correct one that you intended, but one that would somehow make it function just the same. What then?"

"A spell?" said Brewster, frowning. "A spell. . . ."

"My client is a mighty sorcerer as well," said Mac. "He is Warrick the White, the Grand Director of the Sorcerers and Adepts Guild, and there have been many rumors about that he has been making people disappear without a trace, though no one knows how or why. He is the most powerful sorcerer in all the twenty-seven kingdoms, but if this magic chariot of yours is the mysterious apparatus he has in his possession, then its magic baffles even him, and 'tis you he's seeking so that he might learn its secret.''

"A spell . . ." said Brewster. "Is it possible? Using magic to . . . yes, well, in this universe, perhaps it could be . . . if the energy field could be activated by . . . I don't know. Could it? Well, if it could, then . . . there would be no way to predict how the field would. . . . Good Lord!''

"I fear I do not understand," said Mac with a puzzled frown as the others all listened, fascinated.

"This is terrible!" said Brewster. "If my machine is being used to transport people, and it somehow does so without being transported itself, then there's no way for those poor people to get back, and there's no way of telling where they've gone!''

"Then 'tis possible that it could work that way?" asked Mac.

"I don't know," said Brewster. "I suppose it could be possible, but it was never designed to be operated by . . . there's no telling what could. . . . Good God, if that's what's happening, we've got to get it back at once!''

"Hold on, now," said MacGregor. "If Warrick has your magic chariot, then rest assured that he shall not simply give it up. Nor will he sell it. This apparatus is clearly a source of some great power, and Warrick will not rest until he has deciphered the mystery behind it. He has offered a prize bounty for these three, so that he might find out where it came from, and track down its creator. He took great pains to impress me with the importance of this task.''

"I see," said Brewster. "So then you've come for me, is that it?"

" 'Twas these three brigands that I was hired to find," MacGregor said, "but undoubtedly 'tis you that Warrick seeks."

Shannon quickly stepped between them. "Stop!" she

said. "I see well where this is headed, and 'twill bode ill for everyone. Mac, none here would question your skill or reputation, but if you tried to pit your skills against a sorcerer like Doc, you would not last an instant. 'Twould be sheer folly."

"Aye," said Bloody Bob, "and Doc here is a friend of ours, as are Silent Fred, Long Bill, and Fifer Bob, for all their devious ways. We would not stand by idle if anyone made an attempt to apprehend them."

There was a strong chorus of "ayes," for which Brewster felt extremely grateful, for he'd been eyeing all of Sean MacGregor's blades uneasily and he had no illusions as to just how well his "powers" would stack up against MacGregor's. Silent Fred, Long Bill, and Fifer Bob also looked enormously relieved, for it seemed that the situation had now escalated and they were no longer the central objects of everyone's concern. It was just possible, they thought, that they might skate on this one.

"Doc," continued Shannon, "for your part, no one here doubts the extent of your abilities, but if you were to strike out against Mac, you would be striking out against the man I love, and worse still, you would incur the wrath of Warrick Morgannan, who is not only the most powerful wizard in all the twenty-seven kingdoms, but the Grand Director of his Guild, as well. All the other wizards in the Guild would doubtless stand behind him, and no matter how powerful you are, one mage against a hundred would be stiff odds for anyone to contemplate. There has to be another way to handle this dilemma, and we shall all have to put our heads together to come up with a solution to this problem."

"That sounds reasonable to me," said Brewster, thinking that going up against a hundred wizards would not only be stiff odds, it would be suicide.

"Aye," said Mac. "While a part of me would feel poorly at leaving my last contract unfulfilled, a greater part of me would have no wish to end my life in one grand and foolish gesture. Especially now that I have so much more to live for."

The look that passed between him and Shannon was not lost on any of the brigands, whose curiosity about how all this could have happened so quickly and without their knowledge was offset only by their anxiety as to how this potentially dangerous situation would be resolved.

"We shall have to hold a council," Shannon said, "and decide with care how best to proceed."

"But at least the good news is that I haven't lost my magic chariot," said Brewster. "It's still here."

"Aye, but 'tis in the hands of Warrick Morgannan," Shannon said, "and retrieving it from him will be no simple task."

"There's got to be a way," said Brewster. "Maybe we can talk to him. I'm sure he's a reasonable man."

"Warrick the White?" said Rachel, from upstairs. She gave a derisive snort. "I'd sooner reason with a rabid unicorn."

➤ CHAPTER ➤
TEN

While Brewster and the others were busy contemplating their current awkward situation, Mick O'Fallon and Robie McMurphy were busy at the cottage, finalizing their business arrangements with Harlan the Peddlar. From the blades already finished during their first production run, they had assembled a dozen more finished knives with grips of polished nickallirium, which meant that some of them would have to wait for the next production run to get their own personal knives, but business was business, after all. This was their first chance to make a profit from all the work they'd done and Harlan the Peddlar would get first crack at their inventory.

They agreed upon a selling price for the knives, which would be expensive, but still not so costly that they'd be priced out of the market. Harlan wrapped them carefully and said he'd make arrangements to get special wooden cases made up for them when he returned to Pittsburgh, so that it would make a better presentation. He also picked up a supply of magic soap, in bars, which he said he'd sell in little leather bags he'd have made up, in various colors, under the name of Doc's Magic Dirt Remover, since he felt that the name ''soap'' sounded confusing and lacked a certain flair. They all agreed upon the terms for that, as well.

Next, Harlan spent some time sampling Jane's herbal teas, all except for the hallucinogenic ones, which Mick and Robie advised him to take on consignment, but refrain from sampling until he was safely home.

"Trust me," Mick told Harlan, "you'll not want to be on the road alone when this devilish stuff kicks in. There's no telling what you're liable to be seeing."

"Will it be bad?" asked Harlan with a frown.

"Difficult to tell for certain," Mick replied. "A great deal depends upon how much you drink, and upon your state of mind. Most of us have seen pleasant and euphoric visions, but a few have seen flocks of miniature dragons with great big bloody fangs and such. Swarms of little fairies with the heads of spiders, carnivorous strawberries—"

"*Carnivorous strawberries?*" Harlan said.

"Aye, well that was Saucy Cheryl," Robie said. "She's always been a mite peculiar."

"Well, I shall take these on consignment then, and sell them as a mystical, visionary potion to be imbibed at one's own risk," said Harlan. " 'Twould be best if we could come up with a name for all these teas, though."

"But each brew has its own name," Robie said.

"Aye, but I meant for all the brews together," Harlan said. "So that the buyers will know to ask for different brews, but under the same trade name."

"How about Calamity Jane's Visionary Teas?" asked Mick.

"Nay, it lacks a certain something," replied the peddlar. He thought about it for a moment. "Ah! I have it! Celestial Steepings!"

"Celestial Steepings Visionary Teas," Robie said.

"I like it," Harlan said. "We are agreed, then. I'll take two dozen boxes of each."

"Excellent," said Mick. "Well, that gives us a good sampling of commodities to deal in, and they are all unique commodities, that no one else will have to offer, which is just what you were searching for."

"Aye," said Harlan. "My friends, I think that this could be the beginning of a beautiful relationship."

"A highly profitable one, let's hope," McMurphy said.

"I have little doubt of that," said Harlan. "In fact, I am so enthused about these products that I am anxious to load up and hit the road, so that I might start developing our market with all speed."

They helped him load up the products in his cart, and Harlan gracefully declined to have one for the road, so they toasted the success of their new venture with herbal tea, instead.

"I shall return for more as soon as I have sold this lot," said Harlan. "And I do not think 'twill take long, so best not be idle while I'm gone. I have no doubt but that I shall return with many orders."

"Good," said Mick. "Then we shall begin our production at full pace. Good luck to you, Harlan."

"To all of us," said Harlan, "though with commodities as rare as these, I do not think that we shall need it. You mark my words, my friends, for we shall all be rich before too long!"

And with that, he whipped up his horse and set off back down the road to Brigand's Roost, and from there, toward Pittsburgh. On the way, he whistled happily, and sang songs to himself, for he was certain that his fortunes were about to undergo a quite dramatic turn. Just how dramatic, he had no way of knowing, but that's getting way ahead of the story.

He passed through Brigand's Roost without bothering to stop, and in fact, he whipped up his horse and galloped through, for he was pursued all the way through town by the Awful Urchin Gang, who jeered and pelted him with dirt clods. Among them, he saw three youngsters who appeared to be quite large for their age, and whose aim with their dirt clods was uncomfortably accurate.

"Rotten little troglodytes!" he shouted. "Egg-sucking little weasels! Miserable spams!"

He managed to elude the Awful Urchin Gang and made it safely out of town, but he did not slow down until he was quite certain there was no chance of pursuit. And now all he had to worry about were highwaymen and brigands, but with Morey's Elixir of Stench at his side, he felt reasonably safe.

"If Morey could find a way to bottle up the stench of those rotten little children, then he'd really have something," Harlan mumbled to himself.

He traveled easily, not wishing to tire out his horse, and at the end of the first day, he made camp in a little clearing not far off the trail, where he built a fire and made sure to burn plenty of the garlic herb, to keep the coffee-drinking, beatnik, vampire elves at bay.

"A man can't be too careful," he mumbled to himself. "After all, I've got a lot to lose now. Can't take any risks with my new inventory."

The next day, he set off bright and early and made good time, and encountered no one on the road. But by the sixth day of his journey, he began to encounter people on the road, all traveling in the opposite direction, and all riding in carts loaded up with all of their possessions, or pulling wagons or carrying overburdened knapsacks on their backs. Their numbers kept increasing, men, women, and children, and finally his curiosity got the better of him and he stopped to ask a few of them where they were going.

"Anywhere away from Pittsburgh," one of them replied.

"And you'd be wise to turn around yourself and head the other way," another said.

"Why?" Harlan asked. "What's wrong with Pittsburgh?"

"Perhaps you haven't heard," another traveler said, "but things have changed in Pittsburgh. People have been disappearing, vanishing without a trace."

"Aye," said another, "there have been many new, repressive edicts passed by Bloody King Billy, and implemented by his brother, Sheriff Waylon. The taxes have been raised and raised again, and now a man could be arrested merely for spitting in the road, or scratching himself in public, or breaking wind, or just about any little normal thing a body wouldn't think twice about."

"Nor is that the worst of it," another traveler said.

"Once taken to the royal dungeons, one is never seen again."

"The prisoners in the royal dungeons are all brought to Warrick's tower," said another, "and rumor has it they're all turned into dwarves so they may work the mines."

"Nay, that's an old rumor," said another. "He crushes them up in a big press to make an immortality elixir."

"I heard that one last week," another traveler said. "*My* rumor monger swears he has the latest rumors, and he told me Warrick puts a spell on them and turns them into gruel to feed the soldiers of the king."

"Ahh, your rumor monger's full of it," another traveler said. "My rumor monger has it directly from the royal jailor's second cousin's nephew's friend that what Warrick really does is—"

"My friends! My friends!" said Harlan, raising his voice so that he could be heard above them. "There is no need to argue. I would be eager to hear *all* your tales. Why not take a respite from your journey so that we might break bread around a campfire and discuss these fascinating matters?"

"Aye, sounds like a good idea to me," one of the travelers said. "I've been walking for a good long while and I could use a break."

"And I see that you are all tired and dusty from your journey," Harlan said. "In fact, I might have just the thing to remedy that situation. I have recently come into possession of a most wondrous, magical new product that not only removes all dirt and filth, but leaves one feeling invigorated and refreshed, and smelling like a mountain meadow on a fresh spring day."

"Indeed?" asked one of the women in the carts. "I have never heard of such a thing. What is it?"

"'Tis called Doc's Magic Dirt Remover," Harlan said, "and I have just been taking it to market, but seeing as how you tell me things are not well in Pittsburgh, I am having second thoughts. In fact, I had planned to have this special, magical, new product taken to a leathercrafter, so that I might have special packaging made up, colorful and handy little drawstring pouches to keep the product in, yet since I have not yet had a chance to do so, 'twould be only fair if I were to reduce the price I'd planned on selling the Magic Dirt Remover for, since I do not yet have pouches for it.''

"A pouch is a pouch," the woman said, "but I have never heard of a product that magically leaves one fresh and clean. How does it work?"

"Ah, that's the magic to it!" Harlan said. " 'Tis hard for a man to describe its miraculous and wondrous properties. 'Tis something that must truly be experienced in order to appreciate its worth."

"And to experience this product's worth, one would have to buy it first, I suppose," said the woman wryly. "Nay, peddlar, I have heard this sort of pitch before."

"No pitch, my good woman, but merely the simple truth," said Harlan with an elaborate shrug. "I tell you, with a product as excellent as this one, a peddlar needs no pitch. It truly sells itself. In fact, since I am feeling well disposed today, and am enjoying the pleasure of your conversation after a long and lonely journey on the road, I will make you and you alone this one-time offer... I shall give you, my good woman, your very own *free* sample of Doc's Magic Dirt Remover, and you may be the very first among your friends to try it out with no risk to yourself. I ask you, what could be more fair than that?"

The woman's eyes narrowed suspiciously. "Free?" she said. "With no cost to me at all?"

"Nay, I shall charge you but one smile," Harlan said. "Here 'tis, my lady, your very own sample of Doc's Magic Dirt Remover, all for a pleasant look from you."

"Aye, and then I shall need to purchase the instructions for its use," the woman said warily.

"Now would I do such a thing?" asked Harlan, looking gravely wounded. "After all the trouble you have gone to, telling me about what's been happening in Pittsburgh, enlightening a poor, itinerant peddlar purely out of the goodness of your heart? Nay, I shall instruct you in its use right here and now, in front of all, so that everyone may see that Harlan the Peddlar deals honestly and fairly with his customers. You see that small creek, yonder? Well, all it takes to make Doc's Magic Dirt Remover work its spell is just a little bit of water. Merely water, which may be found in abundance everywhere, for free, and not one thing more. All you need to do is strip off your clothing in a discreet location—I am sure that several of these fine, strapping fellows here will be glad to stand guard with their backs toward you and make certain no one else approaches, as I see they are all gentlemen—then wet yourself down and rub the Magic Dirt Remover on your skin.

"As you rub, you will begin to notice how it magically turns to foamy lather, like the whitecaps on a lake during a windy day, but there's no need to be alarmed. 'Tis only the magic doing its work. As it turns to foamy lather on your body, all you need do is scrub a bit, and you will find it feels very pleasant. Then all you need to do is rinse it off with some more water and all the dirt will wash away, leaving you with a feeling of refreshment and invigoration such as you have never felt before! And 'tis all entirely safe, you have my solemn word on that."

"And you will give me this free sample to try out, with no obligation on my part?" the woman said.

"None whatsoever," Harlan said. "There you are, my lady. Your very own free bar of Doc's Magic Dirt Remover. Try it and you'll see that everything I claim for it is true."

The woman anxiously accepted the bar of soap and hastened to the stream to try it out, and while Harlan still had his captive audience, he began to tell them of the other wondrous products that he had to sell. A fire was built while they rested by the road, and some water was put on the boil, and he brewed up some of Calamity Jane's Celestial Steepings Tea, which was enthusiastically received. As they drank their tea, he listened to their tales about their journey and what was happening in Pittsburgh and how they'd all decided to move out of the city in search of a better, safer life, all the while commenting on how delightfully the brew smelled and how healthful an effect it was having on him.

The woman he'd given the free sample of soap to returned from her bath down by the creek, amazed and full of enthusiasm for the miraculous properties of the magical new product. She immediately became the center of attention as she regaled everyone with a description of how the Magic Dirt Remover had turned to foamy lather, and how wonderful it felt upon her skin, and how with a little bit of scrubbing, which felt very smooth and pleasant, all the dirt and dust had magically washed away. And, indeed, she did look very clean and had a nice, fresh smell about her. Harlan merely sat back and smiled as she sold the product for him, and by the time she finished, everyone was clamoring for some Magic Dirt Remover of their own. He sold out not only his entire supply of soap, but also his entire supply of teas, as well. And then, when he had exhausted all his other inventory, he brought out the *pièce de résistance* . . . the many-bladed knife.

When they all saw the grips of polished nickallirium, they marveled. When they saw him demonstrate some of its many uses, they were amazed. And when he allowed as to how he might be willing to let them go a bit more cheaply than he'd planned, because he'd planned to sell them along with specially made cases and it would not be fair to sell them at their original price without those cases, they all wanted to be the first to take advantage of the special discount.

He only had a dozen knives to sell, and not all the travelers were able to afford them, even with the "special discount," but as other travelers saw their camp and stopped to see what was going on, his audience increased and he managed to sell all twelve of the many-bladed knives, even getting a higher price for some of them as people began to bid against one another in an effort to get one before his supply had been exhausted. The demand was far greater than the supply, so Harlan offered to take orders.

"Understand now," he said, "that no one else will have these knives for sale but myself, so if you wish to place your order, you can do so now and pick them up in a week's time at the town of Brigand's Roost. And you need not give me a deposit now. I am an honest peddlar, and I believe that you are all honest individuals, yourselves. I will trust you and I will take your orders and you need pay only when you pick them up. And if you should change your minds, well then . . . 'twill be my loss, but then I think that I will have little difficulty selling such fine and useful items, so I do not much fear incurring any short-term losses.''

He sold out his entire inventory and took orders for more tea, more knives, and more of Doc's Magic Dirt Remover.

''Just be sure to tell everyone that you got these wondrous, useful items from Harlan the Peddlar, and that no one else has them to offer. And if you should encounter anyone who wants some of these special items for themselves, why then, I would consider giving a special discount to anyone who came to me with orders of six or more for any of these items. And for anyone who came to me with a dozen orders, why . . . for such initiative, I would be compelled to reduce the price to you still further.''

He then asked the travelers where they were going, and some replied to Franktown, while others were heading for the Kingdom of Valdez, and still others to other kingdoms, but there were more than a few who had not yet decided on their final destination.

''This town of Brigand's Roost,'' asked one of them, ''where you may be found in one week's time. Do you think there may be work there?''

''Aye, I think there may very well be work, indeed,'' said Harlan, ''for 'tis in Brigand's Roost that these very goods are made. Why, only recently, a great and powerful wizard from a far-off land took up residence nearby, and 'tis through his largesse that these products have now been made available to the general public. As of now, 'tis true, Brigand's Roost is but a small village, but as the sales of these wondrous new products will increase, the size of the village will increase, as well, and there will be new housing, and more work, and a wise man could get in on the ground floor of a good opportunity if he were to get in early, before the coming boom. As for myself, I must get back to Brigand's Roost and place some of these new orders, and replenish my own stock, so I shall leave you all to discuss these things amongst yourselves and sleep on it tonight.

And then, who knows, perhaps I will be seeing you in Brigand's Roost!''

He said goodbye to them and got up in his cart and left them, traveling all night long to get a good head start. He had to get back to Brigand's Roost and talk to Mick and Robie. He had to see about setting up a real estate office and starting a construction firm. Things were going to start happening a lot faster than he'd thought, and before anyone started getting in on the ground floor and building, Harlan was going to make sure he owned the land.

Colin Hightower stepped out of the elevator and followed the orderly down the hall. Like the orderly, he was dressed in a white hospital coat, which the orderly had supplied him with because he didn't want him to appear out of place inside the institution.

"I hope you know, I'm taking one hell of a risk, doing this," said the orderly, a trifle nervously. "The patient's not supposed to have any visitors at all, aside from staff and approved visiting physicians. Dr. Shulman would have a fit if he found out I'd brought in a reporter. I'm taking one hell of a chance here."

"All you have to do is get me in to ask her a few questions and then safely out again," said Colin, "and you'll have made a tidy profit on the deal. Easy money."

"Not so easy if we get caught," the orderly replied. "But around this time, the duty nurse usually goes back in the supply room for a little action with the security guard. We should have at least half an hour. You figure that's enough?"

"I guess it'll have to be," said Colin. "Now you're quite sure the patient isn't violent?"

"Nah, she isn't violent," the orderly replied. "She keeps trying to come on to me so I'll help her to escape, but she's never tried to hurt anybody. She's a nice girl, really. Sorta sweet. Damn shame she's so screwed up."

"You said you could get me a copy of her file," Colin said.

"Yeah, I got it right here," the orderly said, ducking into

an empty room and pulling a large manila envelope out from beneath his coat. "I took a photocopy of it, only listen, if you ever tell anybody where you got it, I'll deny it and say you tried to bribe me for a copy."

"I *did* bribe you for a copy," Colin said wryly.

"Yeah, well, just be cool with this, know what I mean? It's my ass that's on the line, not yours. I need this job. My girlfriend's driving me straight to the poorhouse."

"You have my sympathies," said Colin. "Let's hope your wife doesn't find out."

He opened up the file and scanned it quickly. It was just as he'd expected. It was the same story every time. So far, he'd followed up on half a dozen of these cases, and each time, no matter how far apart they were, the story was disturbingly, inexplicably the same.

None of the people had any idea where they really were. All of them were dressed in some bizarre, medieval fashion when they were apprehended, and all of them seemed completely baffled by modern technology. They were terrified by automobiles and traffic lights, electric signs and trains, skyscrapers and asphalt roads, and the noise and stress of modern cities. They all acted as if they had never heard a radio or used a telephone or seen a television set before. They all claimed it was some kind of sorcery. It was the strangest syndrome he had ever heard of.

Even stranger, every single one of them had exhibited an irresistible compulsion to return to Pittsburgh, though when questioned about Pittsburgh, Pennsylvania, none of them seemed to have any familiarity with the city and, in at least one case, when the individual concerned had actually reached Pittsburgh, he had claimed that it wasn't Pittsburgh at all, but some other place, and that the Pittsburgh that he came from was nothing like that whatsoever.

They all told the same, surreal story about some kind of mythical city by the name of Pittsburgh, located in the Kingdom of Pitt, which was named after somebody called Pitt the Plunderer and ruled by a monarch known as Bonnie King Billy, though other similar and less flattering versions of the monarch's name were often used. When pressed for further details, these patients all told remarkably similar stories, about some kind of fantastical, medieval city in a land of twenty-seven kingdoms, where magic abounded and mythical creatures roamed the forests. And the compulsion to return to that bizarre, medieval, fairy-tale world continued unabated in each and every one of them.

Many of the patients were quite violent and had to be either sedated or restrained, frequently both. Two of them had actually managed to escape the institutions where they were confined, but both had been recaptured. And all of them seemed to be held in thrall by some kind of being or entity named Warrick. They were terrified of him, or it, and yet they were all driven by a relentless compulsion to return to his alabaster tower.

The more Colin found out about this strange phenomenon, the more fascinated he became. What was it? Some kind of mass psychosis that struck randomly, in isolated cases, located many miles apart? What could be responsible for it? Could these people all be the victims of some kind of secret cult? It certainly seemed to have bizarre, satanic overtones, with elements of magic and the occult, and fantastic, mythical creatures. Colin had never heard of anything like it.

"Come on, we're wasting time," the orderly said. "You can look through all that later. If you want to see her, we've gotta go in now."

"Okay," Colin said, "let's go."

The orderly checked the halls, then beckoned him forward. They hurried down the corridor.

"You're absolutely sure this patient is nonviolent?" said Colin nervously.

"Hey, don't worry about it, man, she wouldn't hurt a fly. She's real simple, you know? Sweet, but not too bright. All she does all day is watch TV. The doc had a set brought in because she's safe with it and it keeps her quiet. Like I said, it's a damn shame. She's a real nice kid."

The orderly opened the door and they went inside the room. It looked like a perfectly ordinary hospital room, except for the bars over the special, shatterproof windows.

A girl was sitting cross-legged on the bed, dressed in a hospital gown and watching television with a wide-eyed expression of utter fascination. She was blonde, and fairly pretty in a pouty sort of way, with a slim, attractive figure and green eyes. She looked about seventeen or eighteen years old, but there was something very childlike about her.

"Megan, I brought you a visitor," the orderly said.

"A visitor!" the girl said, turning toward them with a beaming smile. "Oh, how nice!"

"Now remember, Megan, this has got to be our secret," said the orderly. "You know what Dr. Shulman said. No visitors. If you told anyone about this, I'd get in a lot of trouble."

"Oh, I won't tell a soul!" said Megan earnestly. " 'Twill be our secret, Andy." She gave him a conspiratorial wink.

"Be nice to the man, now," said Andy. He turned to Colin. "I'll keep watch outside. If you hear me knockin', you move your ass, you hear?"

"Gotcha," Colin said. He went over to the bed and sat down on the edge. "Hello, my name is Colin. And your name is Megan?"

"That's me," she said brightly. " 'Tis nice to be makin' your acquaintance, Colin."

"Well, it's very nice to meet you, too, Megan. I understand you come from Pittsburgh."

"Oh, yes!" she said. "You know it? No one here seems to know anything about Pittsburgh. 'Tis most peculiar. The things they keep telling me about Pittsburgh are all wrong. But I do *so* need to get back! Can you please help me, Colin?"

"Why do you need to get back there, Megan?"

"Oh, because I simply *must*, that's why! I must get back to Warrick's tower. I must tell him where I've been."

"And where have you been?" asked Colin.

"Why, here, of course! 'Tis a most peculiar place! I have never seen such magic. Like this magic box here, which unfolds the most miraculous visions! Some of them are frightening, and some are funny, and some I do not understand at all. Why do those strangely armored men fight over a small leather ball? And what is this winged creature called a Maxipad?"

"I often find those things confusing, myself," said Colin. "Tell me, Megan, do you remember how you came here?"

"Men called police brought me," she replied.

"No, I mean before that," Colin said. "How did you leave Pittsburgh?"

She frowned. "They've asked me that before," she said. "I am not really sure. I was brought into Warrick the White's sanctorum, in his tower, and there was Warrick, and his horrid little troll, and he fastened me into this strange device so that I could not move and then he spoke a spell and here I was. Oh, but I *do* need to get back! Won't you help me, Colin, please? I can be nice to you. I can be very sweet, you know. You'd like that, wouldn't you? Don't you think I'm pretty? Most men think I'm pretty. I have a pretty body, don't you think?"

She raised her hospital gown over her head and pulled it off, and Colin was suddenly confronted with a very attractive, very willing, and very naked girl.

"Yes, Megan, you are *very* pretty, indeed," he said, "but I'm old enough to be your father. I'm probably much older than your father."

"I wouldn't know," she said coquettishly. "I've never known my father. But I've had older men than you, Colin. And I think you really are quite handsome. You will help me to get away from this place, won't you?" She shifted over close to him and slid up onto his lap. "Do please help me, Colin, and I will be ever so grateful!"

She nuzzled his ear with her tongue and nipped ever so lightly at his earlobe. Gently, but firmly, Colin pushed her away.

"You're a darling girl, Megan," he said, "but it wouldn't be right, you know. I like you, and I'd like to help you, but I don't really know how to help you get back to Pittsburgh. I'm not sure I understand how you got here, or where you really came from. Is there anything else you can tell me about Warrick? Maybe that will help."

"Don't you want me, Colin?" she said petulantly. "Don't you like me?"

"I like you very much," said Colin, "but first tell me about Warrick."

"Oh, very well. He is called Warrick the White, and he is the Grand Director of the Sorcerers and Adepts Guild, and he lives in an alabaster tower not far from King Billy's royal palace in the center of Pittsburgh. He is the most powerful wizard in the twenty-seven kingdoms and I think he is a very evil man."

"Why is he evil?"

"Because he makes people disappear," she replied. "The way he made me disappear."

"But you haven't really disappeared, have you?" Colin said. "I mean, I can see you clearly. You're right there in front of me, in all your naked splendor."

She dimpled prettily. "My, how nice you talk! Why not come here and lie beside me?"

"Why don't you put your gown back on?" said Colin. "I'm afraid you might catch cold."

"Oh, I'm sure you can keep me warm," she said with a coy look.

"Let's get back to Warrick," Colin said, clearing his throat uneasily. He tried to look only into her eyes. "How did he make you disappear?"

"Why, I told you! He put me into his magical device and spoke a spell and here I am. He's done it to a lot of people, you know. Everybody says so. I never thought 'twould happen to me, for I've never done anything wrong, but then that awful deputy of Sheriff Waylon's arrested me because I wouldn't go with him because he smelled so bad, and now here I am. 'Tis not really very fair. Now I need to get back and they won't let me go. But you can help, Colin, can't you? You could take me with you? I'd be ever so sweet to you, I would."

The orderly knocked softly on the door and then opened it a crack. "Come on, man, let's go! I think I hear the duty nurse comin' down the hall!"

"Okay, one minute," Colin said. "Megan, just one more question—"

"Now, man, *now*, or we'll both get our asses busted!"

"Hell," said Colin, getting up. "I'm sorry, Megan, but I've got to go."

"You'll come back and visit me again, won't you, Colin?" she said pleadingly. "You'll come back and take me with you? We can go back to Pittsburgh and I'll take ever such good care of you and—"

The orderly pulled him out the door. "Come on, man, we gotta get out of here *now*! She stopped in the ladies' room, but she'll be out in just a minute. *Move!*"

Suddenly, a blur moved past them, knocking them both aside, and Megan took off running down the hall, stark naked.

"*Oh, shit!*" said the orderly.

They had left the elevator keyed open, to facilitate a fast exit, and Megan ran straight for it.

"God *damn* it," said the orderly as he sprinted after her, with Colin huffing and puffing to stay on his heels.

Megan must have seen the elevator in operation before, because she knew to turn the key and push the buttons. The doors slid closed just as the orderly ran up to them.

"Oh, Jesus freakin' Christ," the orderly swore. "That tears it!"

"What do we do now?" asked Colin.

"First we get *your* ass outta here," the orderly said. "Man, I never shoulda let you talk me into this! Thank God I got a second key."

He inserted his spare key into the elevator lock and hit the call button, fidgeting nervously while they waited for the elevator to come back.

"Bad enough she got away, but if the duty nurse comes out and catches *you* here, I'm really screwed," the orderly said anxiously.

"She won't be able to get out, surely," Colin said. "They'll catch her in the lobby."

"I sure as hell hope so," said the orderly. "I can probably cover myself with some kind of story, but not if you're around. Let's have the money, man, and make it quick. I gotta get you outta here."

Colin counted out the bills as they rode down to the basement, where the orderly quickly took him through the maintenance corridors and then up a short flight of stairs and outside to the parking lot.

"All right, man, you're on your own," the orderly said. "I gotta get back and make up some kinda story about how she got past me. You were never here, you got it?"

"Right," said Colin. "Thanks again."

"Just get outta here, all right?"

Colin hurried toward his car while the orderly went back into the hospital. He got into the rented car and took a deep breath to steady his nerves, then rolled down the window, lit up a cigarette, and opened up the folder that contained the pirated photocopy of Megan's file.

No last name. No known address. No known living relatives. She was a complete Jane Doe. Nothing was known about her at all, just like with all the others. And, just like with all the others, there were no surgical scars, no innoculations, and no dental work whatsoever. No ID, no records, no history at all. It was as if she'd simply dropped in from another world.

There had to be an answer, Colin thought. All these strange cases were connected somehow. The same thread ran through all of them. Sooner or later, if he kept following this up, he'd have to run into the one clue that would make everything else fall into place. It was the most baffling story of his entire career, and he was not about to let go of it. Not for anything. One way or another, he would find the answer. And then he'd bust this whole story wide open.

He started to reach for the ignition, but suddenly his lap was full of girl. A very naked girl, squirming through the window and across his lap.

"*Jesus!*"

Megan crawled across him to the passenger side of the seat and said, "Quickly, drive your magic chariot, Colin! Hurry!"

"Nothing doing, love," said Colin. "You're not going anywhere with me."

"Oh, but I am," Megan replied. "Else I'll tell everyone 'twas you who helped me to escape. And I'll scream and say you tried to have your way with me and—"

"All right, all right!" said Colin, panicking as he reached for the ignition key. "Just don't scream, all right? And for God's sake, get down so nobody can see you!"

He started the car and pulled out of the lot, his hands gripping the steering wheel tightly. Great, he thought, just bloody great. Now I've got a naked crazy woman in my car and if I'm caught, they'll lock me up and throw away the key.

He heard a throaty giggle and glanced to his right, where Megan was huddled down on the floor of the car, her legs drawn up to her chin.

"Oh, Colin, isn't this marvelous?" she said. "We're having an adventure!"

"Right," said Colin as he drove. "And I'm having a bloody nervous breakdown."

The orderly had said she was nonviolent, Colin told himself. But judging by all the other cases he'd investigated, that made her the exception to the rule. He desperately hoped she *was* the exception to the rule. What in God's name was he going to do now?

> CHAPTER >
ELEVEN

In the basement of The Stealers Tavern, among the wine and ale barrels by the flickering light of candles, a conspiracy was brewing. It was only a few hours till dawn, and the tavern had been closed for several hours. The doors upstairs were bolted and the lights were all extinguished. However, in the dank and musty basement, the senior members of The Stealers Guild were meeting in a secret convocation.

"I tell you, 'tis past time for action!" Ugly George was saying. "Our people are being clapped in prison left and right, and soon there will be no one left to pay the dues!"

"Ugly George is right," said Ferret Phil. "Not only are his alleymen all bein' imprisoned, but my footpads, too. And the members of your local are all bein' pinched as well, Fingers."

Fingers Frank agreed. "Aye, we've had ten cutpurses thrown in the slam this past fortnight alone."

"You've gotten off easy, all of you," said Lady Donna, known to one and all among The Stealers Guild simply as "La Donna," and though she was a commoner, she affected an aristocratic manner and liked being referred to as "the Lady" by the members of her local. " 'Tis my girls who've suffered worst at the hands of Waylon and his deputies. 'Tis no longer enough that they freely bestow their favors on demand. The moment any of the deputies fall below their quota, my girls are the first to be arrested, as they are the most vulnerable and the easiest to pinch.''

''Aye, I've pinched a few in my time,'' Ugly George said with a leer.

''You may jest, you lout, but 'tis no laughing matter,'' said La Donna. ''Revenues are falling off, and with the edicts driving citizens out of town in droves, business is bad for everyone, not just for us, but for all the guilds in Pittsburgh.''

'' 'Tis true,'' said Fingers Frank. ''With taxes raised and raised again, and business fallin' off, there's hardly any point to cuttin' purses, for there ain't no money in 'em!''

''What say the assassins?'' asked Dirty Dan, the tavern keeper and proprietor of The Stealers Tavern, and also secretly Director of The Stealers Guild, though it wasn't really all that much of a secret.

Mike the Mace shifted uncomfortably on his keg. He was a big man, feared and respected throughout all the twenty-seven kingdoms as the second-top-rated assassin in the Guild, but administration had never been his strong suit.

''Well, by rights, it should be MacGregor sittin' in on this here meetin' and not me, but Mac's off on a job someplace and out of reach.''

''Aye, we understand that,'' Dirty Dan replied. ''But in his absence, the leadership of the assassins in Guild matters falls to you. What is the feeling among the members of your local?''

''Well, they're none too happy with the situation,'' Mike the Mace replied. ''With Sheriff Waylon clampin' down on lawbreakers, folks are thinkin' twice before they put a contract out on anyone. Times are gettin' lean.''

''And the mood among the populace is grim,'' said Gentlemanly Johnny, the senior member of the Swindlers local. ''King Billy keeps ignoring the petitions and rarely even ventures out in public anymore. The people believe he doesn't care about them. They believe the rumors that the royal wizard is merely acting upon his instructions, conjuring some great spell at his behest. They believe the king has given his allegiance to the powers of darkness. And the sheriff, his brother, is aiding him and Warrick in these diabolical, black rites.''

"So we are all agreed, then, that something must be done," said Dirty Dan. "Yet no one here has yet dared speak the one word that is foremost in our minds.''

"Regicide," La Donna said.

"Insurrection," Fingers said.

"Revolution," said Ugly George.

"A *coup d'état*, said Gentlemanly Johnny.

"What?" the others all said together, staring at him.

"All of the above," said Gentlemanly Johnny with a shrug.

"Then we are all agreed upon a plan of action," Dirty Dan said. "The king must die. And his royal wizard with him.''

"And don't forget the royal sheriff," added Fingers.

"And the queen," said Ugly George.

"The queen?" La Donna said.

"Well . . . sure, why not? Might as well make a clean sweep.''

"Oh, well, all right, the queen, too," said Dirty Dan.

"We must foment revolution," Gentlemanly Johnny said.

"What's 'foment' mean?" asked Ferret Phil.

"Incite the people to revolt," Johnny replied.

"Oh. Right, then. What he said.''

"How are we supposed to do that?" Fingers asked.

" 'Tis very simple, my friends," said Gentlemanly Johnny. "We make the aristocracy our targets.''

"The who?" said Ugly George.

"The nobles, you great oaf," La Donna said. "Go on, Johnny. You have a plan?''

Gentlemanly Johnny got up and made a little bow. "A good swindler always has a plan, my lady. Our first step must be to prepare the good citizens of Pitt for an uprising. We shall begin here, in the capital, and once we've made a good beginning, it will spread of its own throughout the kingdom. All we need do is gently nudge our plan along. Each time the sheriff's deputies make an arrest, our people must be there, to stir up dissatisfaction after the fact. Each time a new edict is posted, our people must be there, to encourage resentment of the sheriff and the king. Each time a noblewoman purchases a brand-new dress, our women must be there, to comment on how the common folk cannot afford to clothe their children or themselves because of the new taxes. Each time a nobleman buys a horse, someone must be there to complain about their worn-out shoes. Each time an armorer receives an order for a brand-new sword or knife, someone must observe how it is meant to be plunged into the backs of the common people of the kingdom.

"In time, and not a very long time, I will wager, resentment of the king, the sheriff, and the upper classes will be at a fever pitch, and when we judge the time to be just right, we shall proceed to the next step of the plan."

"And what shall that be?" Ferret asked, his eyes aglow with eagerness.

"Only this, my friend. We shall arrange for one of our people to be arrested."

"Well, now, what's the bloody point of that?" asked Ugly George. "Our people are already bein' arrested by the score! You'd have us help the sheriff?"

"Aye, but only so that we might help ourselves," said Gentlemanly Johnny, "for this will be no ordinary arrest. It shall be planned carefully, by us, so that we control the time and place, and so it occurs in public, with many people present. We shall make certain that our people are in among the crowd, and that the sheriff's men are greatly outnumbered. When they make their move to apprehend the culprit that we shall provide for them, we make *our* move, and overwhelm them, setting free the prisoner as if it were a spontaneous action of the crowd. And mark my words, there will be those among the crowd who'll join us in the act, caught up in the fever of the moment.

"From that point on," Gentlemanly Johnny continued, "each time the sheriff and his men try to arrest someone, we shall interfere with them, and set free the prisoners, without ever identifying who we are, so that it will appear the people are rising up against the forces of the king. And once we start it, the people will continue of their own accord and follow our example. Then we proceed to the third stage of the plan."

"Go on," said Fingers eagerly. "What's the third part?"

"An organized campaign of harassment of the nobility," said Gentlemanly Johnny. "Each time a noblewoman drives by in her carriage, someone must be there to start the people jeering. Each time a nobleman sets foot out into the streets, someone must be there to start pelting him with dirt clods and pieces of manure. At every turn, their dignity must be affronted, and they must be made the scapegoats for the edicts of the king. Not only shall it arouse the people's ire, it shall arouse the anger of the nobility, as well, and they shall direct it at the king."

"Then we take over and start the revolution!" Fingers said excitedly.

"Nay, my friend, that would never do," said Gentlemanly Johnny. "We must remain behind the scenes, for in no way can this revolt be made to appear as an uprising of the criminals in Pittsburgh. It must be an uprising of the good, honest, common, working people of the kingdom."

"Then who shall lead the revolt?" asked Dirty Dan.

"Ah, that is the beauty of the plan," said Gentlemanly Johnny. "Once the flames of the revolution have been fanned, the fire shall burn freely of its own accord. The leaders will rise up among the people. Never fear, at such times, there are always men who are quick to take advantage of the situation. And if anything goes wrong and the revolt should fail, why, 'tis the leaders who'll be blamed and hauled off to the execution block, not us. All we need to do is make a small investment of our time and energies to start the venture, then sit back and profit from it." He smiled. "And business should be brisk, indeed. What say you, my friends and colleagues?"

"I move we adopt Gentlemanly Johnny's plan!" La Donna said.

"I second the motion!" cried out Ugly George.

"All in favor say 'aye,'" said Dirty Dan.

"*Aye!*" they chorused unanimously.

"Motion carried!" Dirty Dan said, slamming his truncheon down upon a keg. "I propose a toast! To the revolution! Down with Bloody King Billy!"

"*To the revolution!*" they all cried as one. "*Down with Bloody King Billy!*"

"'A punishment most vile,' she said," moaned Fifer Bob. "'A punishment most vile.' I *told* you she'd be mad, I *told* you, but did you listen? Oh, why did I let you talk me into it? It's all your fault, Bill, all your bloody fault!"

"Oh, *shut up*," Long Bill said in a disgusted tone.

Silent Fred said nothing, but then, that was not unusual. He looked utterly miserable, with his lower lip stuck out, and his face completely encrusted with filth. All their faces were covered with filth, and they looked a sorry sight, indeed, bent over and locked into the stocks in front of One-Eyed Jack's. They could move their heads a little, and they could wiggle their fingers and their toes, but otherwise they were immobilized. They were numb, and cold, and utterly degraded. All day, they'd been locked up in the stocks, tormented by the Awful Urchin Gang, who took great delight in pelting them with dirt clods, horrid muck scooped up from the hog pens, sticks and stones and anything else that came to hand (don't ask). They cut switches from the bramble bushes and whipped them on their backsides, and when they tired of that, they sat in front of them, making faces at them, spitting, and pinching their cheeks and noses painfully. Tomás de Torquemada, in his most diabolically creative moods during the Spanish Inquisition, could not have held a candle to the Awful Urchin Gang for devising painful and humiliating tortures.

"When I get out of here, I'm going to strangle each and every one of those miserable brats," Long Bill said.

"When I get out of here, I'm going to strangle *you*," said Fifer Bob.

"What if she *never* lets us out?" said Silent Fred, and the shock of hearing him speak a complete sentence was almost as great to the others as the horrifying possibility he had brought up.

" 'Twould only be a fitting reward for the likes of you three," Shannon said, and the three of them glanced up, as much as they could crane their heads back in the stocks, to see her standing in the street before them, legs spread apart and her hands on her hips. "Well?" she said. "Have you nothing to say for yourselves?"

They all looked down morosely.

"By rights, I ought to let you rot in there," she said, "remain as playthings for the urchins till they stripped the hides right off your backs. But Doc has asked me to be charitable and I must be getting soft, for I agreed to let you go."

They all looked up, unable to believe that they were getting a reprieve.

"The next time, I shall not be so merciful," she said.

"There will *never* be a next time, Shannon, we all swear it, don't we lads?" said Fifer Bob.

"Aye, Shannon, we so swear," Long Bill said contritely.

Silent Fred merely looked down at the ground and nodded.

"Well, I think perhaps you've learned your lesson," she said. "Never let it be said that Black Shannon is unjust."

She bent over to unfasten the stocks, then the three imprisoned brigands heard a soft thunk, followed by a grunt, and Shannon fell down in the dirt in front of them, unconscious.

"Shannon?" said Long Bill. And then he saw a pair of high leather boots in front of him.

"Well, well. What have we here?"

They looked up into the grinning face of Black Jack. Behind him, a group of rough and surly looking men rode up on horseback. Jack crouched down and grabbed Long Bill by the hair, jerking his face up. "This one of 'em?" he said.

"Aye," said one of the men on horseback. "I remember him stopping at the inn and arguing about a chess game with another."

"This one?" said Black Jack, jerking Silent Fred's head up by the hair.

"That's him."

Black Jack knelt in front of Fifer Bob, who looked up at him wide-eyed with fright.

"Aye, and this third one matches the description. What a pleasant surprise. All trussed up and waitin' for us, meekly as you please." He stood and turned Shannon over on her back with his foot. "So. This is the infamous Black Shannon, eh? She lays so sweetly in repose."

"She can lay sweetly with all of us tonight," said one of the ruffians behind him, and the others laughed unpleasantly.

"I won't be having none of that," Black Jack snapped.

"Why not, Jack? Where's the harm? You got what you came for. What 'bout the rest of us?"

"The rest of you signed on for a share of the bounty, and there's a right handsome bounty on this lass, as well as on the others. It won't do to bring her in as damaged goods. By all accounts, she fights like the very Devil and you'll like as not have to kill her before she'll give you what you want. Nay, lads, we'll deliver her unharmed, and the money she'll bring in will let you buy your fill of pretty wenches back in Pittsburgh. Aye, Black Shannon brought in by Black Jack. It has a proper ring to it, it does."

"Now, just a moment," said Long Bill. "Can't we talk about this?"

"Silence, dog!" Black Jack said, smashing him in the face with his gloved fist. "Release them, then bind them up together." He saw Shannon start to stir. "And tie up the lass, as well. Be quick about it. We'd best be off before we are discovered."

MacGregor crouched down as Bloody Bob held up the lantern. "Aye, there's been trouble here," he said, studying the ground. "Men with horses. At least a dozen, I'd say. They all reined in right here. Bring that lantern closer, Bob."

He moved forward, peering intently at the ground. "One man stood here. Crouched down before the stocks." He crouched down in the boot prints. "Aye, so he could see their faces." He looked around. "And here, right here someone fell. The body was moved and... Bob, come closer with that lantern!"

"What do you see, Mac?" asked the old brigand, bending down with the lantern.

"Right here," said Mac, "scratched into the dirt. The letters 'B' and 'J.'" He stretched out full length on the ground. "Aye, she scratched this into the dirt as she lay here on the ground." He got up and began to move about the site, acting out what must have happened. "She came to release them, and she stood right here, then she moved closer, came around to the side of the stocks... and was struck down from behind."

He grabbed the lantern from Bloody Bob and glanced around. "He must have waited by the corner of the building there, and come around the side. Aye, here's his track. He crept up behind her as she bent down to unfasten the stocks, struck her, and she fell here.... He must have thought that she was senseless. Perhaps she was, but she came to in time to scratch these letters in the dirt... 'BJ.'" He scowled. "'BJ.' What might... of course! *Black Jack*!"

"Who is this Black Jack?" asked Bob.

"A soldier of fortune, a bounty hunter. A killer," said MacGregor. "We've crossed swords before, but he managed to escape me. He was after your three friends, the same as I was. And now he's found them. He's brought more men with him this time. 'Twould cut into his bounty, but I think as much as he was after them, he was after me, as well."

"There's a bounty on you, too?" asked Bloody Bob.

"Nay, but there's a reputation in it for him if he kills me. But now that he's got Shannon, he's found himself a windfall. The bounty on her, together with the bounty on the others, will allow him to pay off his hired ruffians and still have plenty for himself. He'll be taking them all back to Pittsburgh."

"He won't get there alive," said Bloody Bob. "We'll fetch the others and give chase."

"They've had a good head start," said Mac, shaking his head. "'Twill be dawn before you can get back and rouse the brigands. And by the time they all get moving. . . . We may never catch them."

"They will have to camp along the road to rest," said Bob. " 'Tis a goodly journey to Pittsburgh."

"Aye," said Mac, "but they will expect pursuit. Black Jack's no fool. He will push hard, without stopping to rest, and the river's but two days journey from here. If he reaches it first, he will cross, then cut loose the ferry ropes and let the ferry drift downstream. 'Tis what I would do if I were in his place. Then there would be no catching him. You ride back hard and rouse the men, Bob, but I cannot wait for them. I must go on ahead."

"Against at least a dozen well-armed men?" asked Bloody Bob. He shook his helmeted head. "Even for you, Mac, those would be stiff odds. I'd hate to wager on your chances."

"I'll be taking my lads with me. They'll help even out the odds. At worst, maybe I can slow them down enough to allow you to catch up with the others. You'd best be off, and quickly. There's no time to lose. They must not reach the river."

"I'm on my way," said Bob, mounting his huge warhorse. "Good luck, Mac. We'll be comin' right behind you."

"Ride like the wind," said Mac.

As Bob galloped off down the road back toward the keep, MacGregor ran up the steps of One-Eyed Jack's and started banging on the door. After a few moments, Jack came to the door in his nightgown and nightcap, his empty eye socket uncovered by the customary patch and appearing very disconcerting. Mac brushed past him before Jack could say a word and bounded up the stairs to the room where the three brothers slept. He pounded on the door. No answer.

"Stop makin' such a racket!" Jack called up, from the stairs. " 'Tis the middle of the night!"

Mac ignored him and pounded on the door again. Frustrated, he rattled it and it swung open. The three brothers were all sprawled out, dead to the world. Two of them were on the bed, Hugh on his back, Dugh on his stomach, and

Lugh was sprawled out on the floor, lying on his side with his hands beneath his cheek, like a small child.

"Wake up, blast your eyes!" Mac shouted. "Wake up, I said!"

They didn't even stir.

"Hugh!" said Mac, reaching out to shake him. Nothing doing. "Lugh, damn your soul, wake up!"

He kicked the sleeping Lugh, but with no result other than a grunt from his sleeping henchman, followed by a shutter-rattling snore. Mac grabbed a washbasin from the table and emptied it upon them. Still they slept. And then he noticed the three empty jugs of Mick O'Fallon's peregrine wine lying on the floor.

"*Oh, you bloody idiots!*" swore Mac. Three whole jugs of that vile paralyzer. If it didn't kill them, they'd be in a coma for at least a week.

One-Eyed Jack stood in the doorway behind him, holding a candle. "You won't be rousing them tonight," he said. "Maybe not tomorrow, either. Never saw anybody drink like that before. Cast-iron stomachs, like my Mary, bless her heart. Drinks like a trooper, she does—"

Mac pushed past him and ran back down the stairs, cursing to himself. There was nothing else to do. He'd have to go after Black Jack and his ruffians alone.

Brewster stood up on the tower of his keep, looking down at the flickering embers of the campfires below. The grounds outside the keep were starting to resemble a shanty town. The brigands were now spending practically all their time at the keep, and instead of going back to the Roost each night, many of them had simply moved lock, stock, and barrel onto the grounds. Beyond the crumbling remnants of the outer wall, the meadow was dotted with tents and wooden shacks, and many of the brigands simply slept in the great hall of the keep below, passing out at the tables and on the floor after their nightly revels. Brewster imagined that it was rather like having a biker gang move in with you. He didn't really mind, though. He enjoyed having them around.

His whole life had been spent in fairly solitary pursuits.

As a boy, he had been obsessed with science, and while the other kids were all out playing Little League baseball or hanging out together, he stayed at home, in the basement workshop his father had helped him set up, working on experiments. When other boys were building plastic models of ships and World War II airplanes, he was building radio sets and designing circuits. And when other boys had started dating in high school, he was already in college at M.I.T., amazing his professors. All his life, he had been the classic nerd, and it wasn't until he reached his mid-twenties that other men started to regard him with serious respect and women began to find him interesting. Yet, he realized all too well that he possessed some glaring shortcomings when it came to social skills, especially where women were concerned.

Women were generally far too subtle for him and whenever they had seemed interested in him, he'd usually missed all the signals. If they became bold and came right out with it, he would become flustered. The few relationships he'd blundered into had all ended fairly quickly, due to lack of common interests or his own perpetual absent-mindedness and preoccupation with his work. Pamela was different.

Pamela was the first woman he had ever met who understood him and, more than that, was patient enough to overlook his faults. In her own way, she'd had similar problems. She was from a wealthy, socially prominent family and she was beautiful. She had attracted plenty of men, but often they were intimidated by her intelligence and self-sufficiency, and she had been unwilling to subordinate her own interests and her career to any man. In many ways, they were perfectly suited to each other.

She'd told him that she was attracted to him from the very start. He hadn't had a clue. He had, of course, noticed that she was beautiful and vivacious, and very bright, but it had simply never occurred to him that she could have any interest in him. He had remarked upon that once, soon after they started to see each other, and had been astonished to hear her say that many women found him attractive. He simply couldn't understand it.

Sometime in his mid- to late-twenties, the ugly duckling had turned into a swan, except when he looked into a mirror, he still saw an ugly duckling, awkward, shy, and introverted. When he assumed that women were merely being friendly and polite, Pamela insisted they were coming on to him. He simply never saw it.

At heart, he still felt that most people saw him as "the geek," the nickname the other children had bestowed on him in elementary school. Even after he'd become a well-respected scientist working in his own private research laboratory at one of the largest corporations in the world and making more money than he'd ever dreamed of, he still remained an outsider. Other men gave him respect and deferred to his judgement, but they never asked him to join them for a few pints at the pub, or watch a football game, or any of those other things that men do to express their camaraderie. But here, in this strange world, everything was different.

He was not only respected, but accepted. These simple, unaffected people genuinely seemed to like him. These brigands were manly men in every sense, rough and coarse and unpretentious, and even the most macho male in the modern world that Brewster came from would seem like a wimp among them, yet they all not only gave him their respect, but clapped him on the shoulder, called him Doc, and treated him with warm affection. And they were genuinely interested in everything he said and did. The women were much like the men, honest, open, and forthright, completely lacking in those devious little subtleties of modern social interaction. He had never felt so comfortable among any group of people before. It was as if he had become a part of one very large, extended family. He wished Pamela could be here, but she would feel as out of place in this world as he felt among her family and high-society friends.

"Something on your mind, Doc?"

He turned and saw Rachel sitting on the wall behind him, her ever-present bongo drums cradled in her lap. She tapped out a soft, rapid rhythm on them with her fingers.

"Oh, Rachel. I didn't hear you come up."

"Elves move quietly," she said with a grin. Since the night she'd shown up at the keep, pursued by unicorns, she had never left. No one had invited her to stay, but no one had asked her to leave, either. Brewster had no idea where she slept, but every time he turned around, there she was, watching everything with an honest, open curiosity.

At first, the brigands had been uneasy in her presence. There was a natural prejudice there. Humans and elves didn't get along. The fact that elves drank human blood probably had a great deal to do with it. However, Rachel was a vegetarian and, apparently, a bit unusual for an elf. Often, late at night, she would sit by a campfire, surrounded by curious brigands, and compose stream-of-consciousness poetry while she accompanied herself on the drums. None of the outlaws understood it, but they all seemed to find it fascinating. To Brewster, it sounded like a strange combination of Allen Ginsberg and Jim Morrison.

"I was just thinking," he said.

"About home?"

"Yes, about home, and other things."

"I've never really had a home," said Rachel, "unless you count the forest as a home, and I've always sort of wandered. Home is where my head is."

He glanced at her and smiled. "Back where I come from, they have a somewhat similar saying. 'Home is where the heart is.' But I think, for me, at any rate, your way of saying it is closer to the truth. I have never been quite so happy as when I was working. Wherever I could do my work, that was where I lived. That was really home."

"So then, in a way, this is home to you, as well," said Rachel.

Brewster shook his head. "No, not really. But in some ways, it's almost beginning to feel like it. The kind of work I usually do, I can't do here. But in another sense, the work I am doing here is equally rewarding. I admit that sometimes I feel lost here, but this is the greatest adventure of my life. In fact, it's the *only* real adventure of my life. I have always been a quiet man, a man of learning. Yet here,

I feel like a man of *action*." He looked out toward the campfires of the brigands. "I have never known people like these. They're refreshing, stimulating. They've made me realize that although I have accomplished a great deal in my life, I've never really done anything. And here, I feel that I'm *doing* something. Yes, Rachel, I miss my home, but I'm having the time of my life."

Rachel rapped out a rapid tattoo on her drums, then settled into a steady beat. *Boom-chak-chak-boom-chak-chak-boom....*

"The dreamer stood upon the tower and looked out at life,
and yearned to leave the security of dreams for what he saw.
So he came down out of the tower to walk life's broken meadows,
and found that he was living out his dreams."
Boom-chakka-boom-chakka-boom.

Brewster smiled. "I really like that. Would you write it down for me?"

Rachel shrugged. "Elves have a rich oral tradition, but we have no written language."

"Take that, Professor Tolkein," Brewster mumbled.

"What?"

"Never mind. Just mumbling to myself."

"I will remember it for you, if you like, and recite it any time you wish."

"It's a deal. Next time, I'll have to be sure and—" A shout from below distracted him and he looked down over the parapet to see a horseman come galloping at full speed into the meadow, roaring at the top of his lungs. He couldn't make out what he was yelling, but he clearly recognized the voice as Bloody Bob's. No one else could sound like that.

At once, the camp below became a flurry of activity as the brigands came running out of their tents and shacks, and out from the great hall of the keep. Torches bobbed below him in the meadow, and there was angry shouting.

"I wonder what's going on?" said Brewster, looking down.

"One way to find out," said Rachel. She hopped down from the wall and ran down the stairs. The commotion below was increasing. In the darkness, illuminated only by the moving torches and the light from the campfires, Brewster couldn't really see what was happening very clearly, but figures were rushing about down there, and there was a lot of shouting. A short while later, Rachel came running back up the stairs to the top of the tower, accompanied by Mick.

"Mick, what's going on down there?" asked Brewster.

"They've taken Shannon!" Mick said. "And Long Bill, Fifer Bob, and Silent Fred, as well!"

"Who?" said Brewster.

"Bob says 'tis some soldier of fortune named Black Jack," said Rachel. "And he had a party of men with him."

"A dozen or more," said Mick. "Bounty hunters," he spat out with angry scorn. "Bob says they'll be taking them back to Pittsburgh. Mac's gone after them alone."

"Alone?" said Brewster. "Against over a dozen men?"

" 'Twas no choice he had," said Mick. "The road to Pittsburgh is broken by the Great River two days journey from here. There's a ferry raft that takes travelers across, and if they cross the river first, they can cut the ferry loose and then there'll be no catching up with them. Mac says they've got a good head start, but if he rides hard, perhaps he can catch up with them and try to slow them down in time for the rest of us to get there."

"He'll get himself killed," said Brewster. "I don't care how good a swordsman he is, one man against a dozen or more is suicide."

"If we ride hard, we might catch them," Mick said.

Brewster frowned. "Even if he rode at a full gallop all the way, it had to take Bloody Bob almost half an hour to get here from Brigand's Roost. And it would take the rest of you at least a half an hour to reach there from here, so that's an hour lost already, not counting the time it'll take to get everyone together and mounted. Those bounty hunters already have several hours head start. They'll know the brigands will come after them, and if they know that getting to the ferry first will effectively cut off pursuit, they won't waste any time. They'll be moving fast.'' He shook his head. "I don't see how you can catch them.''

"We *must* try!'' said Mick.

"Doc's right,'' said Rachel. "'Twill be no use. The bounty hunters will be mounted on fine horses. Such men spare no expense when it comes to their arms and their steeds. Many of the brigands have no horses of their own. They'll have to double up or ride in carts. You'll never catch them.''

"Doc, there must be something you can do!'' said Mick in an agonized tone. "If they turn Shannon over to the sheriff, she'll be beheaded! And the others will be taken to the royal wizard's tower! 'Tis said no one ever escapes from there!''

Brewster compressed his lips into a tight grimace. "I don't see what I can do,'' he said.

"Will you come with us?'' Mick said.

"I have no horse, and even if I did, I'm not much of a rider, Mick. I'd only slow you down.''

With a look of exasperation, Mick turned and ran back down the stairs to join the others. Brewster could already see a number of brigands mounted down below, and the rest rushing with their weapons toward the carts.

"Damn. What we need is a helicopter. If only...'' he broke off.

"What is it, Doc?'' said Rachel.

"Yes, it might work!'' said Brewster. He glanced at his watch. "In another hour, it'll be midnight. He always comes around midnight.''

"*Rory*!'' Rachel said.

Brewster headed for the stairs.

"Where are you going?'' Rachel asked.

"To get my gun.''

➤ CHAPTER ➤ TWELVE

The brigands got themselves organized quickly and within less than twenty minutes they were riding off down the road to the Roost. The time had seemed much longer to Brewster, and now he waited atop the tower parapet, anxiously, feeling the weight of his Smith & Wesson in its holster on his belt, and he wondered what in God's name he was thinking of.

Rory would come, as the dragon came every night at around midnight. He knew that. He recalled the first time Rory came, and how frightened he had felt . . . no, *frightened* was too mild a word for it, he'd been plain scared shitless, but amazingly, his curiosity had overwhelmed his fear and he had gone up to meet the dragon. The mark of a true scientist, he thought, with a nervous, giddy sort of feeling. Let's see old Carl try that one! Wouldn't it be wonderful, indeed? He had actually made friends with the fantastic creature, and he could never quite get over the magical miraculousness of its existence. It was, in every sense, a fairy tale come to life, huge, reptilian, with iridescent scales and talons that could rip him open from head to toe as easily as he could peel a banana. And yet it possessed a droll, intellectual demeanor and an avid curiosity about his world, which it claimed all dragons saw in dreams. Meeting Rory was the most dramatic and thrilling experience of his entire life, and he never tired of the dragon's visits, and didn't care how late they stayed up talking, though usually the dragon, in a very gentlemanly manner, never stayed longer than an hour or two, at most, and always apologized for keeping him up late on the occasions it stayed longer. The brigands were frightened of the beast and always kept their distance, but Brewster had come to look upon the creature with affection, for all its fearsomeness. He had never thought that he could ever have an experience to match Rory's nightly visits. Yet now, what he was contemplating was even more fantastic.

As Rachel watched, bemused, he kept pacing back and forth across the tower parapet, talking to himself in an effort to relieve the anxiety he felt, not knowing if he was trying to talk himself into going through with his idea or out of it.

"This is crazy," he said. "I don't know what the hell I'm thinking of. I've never done anything like this in my life. I've never even *thought* of doing anything like this in life! I mean, look at me, I've got a gun strapped to my hip! A gun!"

He glanced at Rachel, who merely sat there on the wall, watching him with that mocking little look and saying nothing.

"Look who I'm talking to," he said. "I'm talking to an elf! You don't even know what a gun is. Hell, I've never even *used* a gun. I mean, I've taken a few shots at the range, but I was so nervous I couldn't even hit the goddam target and now I'm standing here with the thing strapped on my hip, like Roy Rogers, ready to ride off to the rescue when I don't even know what the hell I'm doing. Only instead of riding Trigger, I'm thinking of mounting up on a dragon! It's insane, that's what it is, positively insane. Rory might not even go for it."

"Go for what?" said a cement-mixer voice behind him, and he was so startled that he actually jumped.

He turned around and there was Rory, perched on the wall like a giant pterodactyl. It seemed impossible that anything that big could move so quietly, and yet Rory could glide in softer than the whisper of a feather.

"God, you startled me!" said Brewster.

"My apologies," the dragon said, "but you seemed quite intent upon your conversation and I didn't wish to interrupt."

"I was just talking to myself," said Brewster. "Trying to psych myself up into doing what I'm thinking of doing, which if I had any sense, I wouldn't even consider for a moment, only I just can't see any way around it. There's just no time, the brigands will never catch up to them . . ." and the whole story came pouring out of him in one mad rush.

"I understand," the dragon said when Brewster finally paused for breath. "And I am perfectly willing to help in any way I can. However, I also fully understand your reservations."

"Reservations?" Brewster said weakly. "Rory, the mere idea of it scares the daylights out of me!"

"But there is no real need for you to go," the dragon said. "I could easily catch those bounty hunters on my own and free your friends. You could wait here in perfect safety."

Brewster stared at the beast. "You'd do that?"

"Of course. What are friends for?"

Brewster licked his lips. "Wait here in perfect safety," he said. "I've lived my whole life in perfect safety. My whole damn life. The one time I ever took a real risk, I wound up here, and it's been the most wonderful adventure of my life. I'll admit I'm frightened, Rory, but I don't want to play things safe anymore. I can't just look out at life from my tower."

He looked over his shoulder at Rachel, who grinned and gave him a raised fist gesture. "That's the spirit, Doc! Seize the moment! Squeeze the day!"

"That's 'seize the day. . . .' " He stopped. "No, you know what, you're right. I like 'squeeze the day.' Wring all the life you can out of every single moment. To hell with playing it safe! For once in my life, I'm going to *do* something!"

"Climb aboard," said Rory.

"Give 'em a taste of steel, Doc!" said Rachel.

Brewster climbed up on the dragon's back. "I'll do better than that, kid. I'll give 'em a taste of lead!"

And with that, the dragon spread its huge, leathery wings and plunged off the parapet into the darkness. As Rachel ran up to the parapet to watch, she heard Doc's rapidly receding voice crying out, "*Oh, shiiiiiiit!*"

"Hmmm. Curious battle cry," she said.

Mac rode like a man possessed, not thinking of the odds he'd have to face, but worried only that his horse would give out before he could catch them. If that happened, he'd simply have to steal another one. There was an inn on the road to the Great River, and if he kept up this breakneck pace, he'd reach it shortly before dawn. He could get another horse there at their stable, assuming they had a decent one and not some broken-down old mare. What were the chances? Not many travelers on the road this time of year. He'd simply have to hope for the best. He could not afford to slacken his pace.

How much of a head start did they have? No way of knowing for sure, but the tracks back at the Roost seemed relatively fresh. He could see no tracks now, impossible in the pitch blackness of the night, but fortunately, he knew where they were going, where they had to go. They would be making for the river with all possible speed. With a sinking feeling, he realized that no matter how quickly the brigands could mount their pursuit, they would never make it in time. If it wasn't for the river, then eventually, they could hope to overtake Black Jack and his bounty hunters, but the river would defeat them if Black Jack reached it first.

The river was too deep, too wide, and too swift-flowing for horses to swim across. The only way across was by the ferry raft, and it was a mere matter of a few moments work to cut it loose. The heavy ropes that guided it across the river would be severed, and the raft would swiftly drift downstream, out of reach, and that would be the end of it. They could build another raft, and perhaps repair the ropes, or obtain new ones, and get strong swimmers to cross the river's span with them, but by the time all that was done, Black Jack would be so far ahead they'd never catch him. No, it was all up to him.

In all his life, he thought, as he galloped down the dark road through the forest, he had never met a woman even remotely like Shannon. No one had ever kindled such a fire in him. Out of all the women in the world, she was the only one for him, and now that he had found her, the thought of losing her was more than he could bear. It made no difference how many men Black Jack had brought with him. He'd kill them all, each and every cursed one of them, or die in the attempt.

There wasn't a sound in the forest as he rode, save for the steady drumming of his horse's hooves upon the hard-packed earth, *ba-da-da-dum, ba-da-da-dum, ba-da-da-dum*, like the rapid beating of his heart. He could hardly see anything in front of him. If Black Jack had thrown up any barricades in the road behind him, Mac knew that he would run right into them before he could even see them, but he was gambling that Black Jack wouldn't have wasted any time. He'd have trussed up his prisoners and thrown them over the horses, so they could move more quickly, and for Shannon and the others, it would be a jarring, brutal ride. If they had any fight at all left in them, it would be knocked out of them by the jouncing they'd receive as Black Jack and his men rode full speed for the river.

It would all be up to him. He wouldn't be able to count on Shannon, or on the three brigands, who'd be numb to begin with, from being locked up in the stocks for an entire day. And he knew he couldn't count on reinforcements reaching him in time. He had his blades, and he had his skill and years of experience behind him, but that was no guarantee of success. He decided not to think about that. All he could hope for now was that he could catch up to them in time.

He rode grimly, allowing the steady rhythm of the gallop to fill his mind. After a while, the first gray light of dawn began to show through the thick branches overhead. The inn at the crossroads was just ahead. He could change horses there. His own mount was nearly spent. The poor animal was breathing hard and gasping, and lather covered its flanks. As dawn broke, he reached the crossroads and galloped up to the inn. He reined in before it and dismounted, and no sooner had he stepped off his horse than the animal went down to its knees and fell over on its side, its flanks heaving. It would go no farther. He had run it nearly to death. He ran up to the door of the inn and pounded on it furiously.

"*Open up! Open up, damn your eyes!*"

After a moment or two, he heard someone yell that they were coming and a few seconds later, the innkeeper opened up the door, his eyes wide.

"I need a fresh horse, and quickly!" Mac said.

"Would that I could help you, good sir," the innkeeper began, "but you see—"

He suddenly found a knife blade at his throat.

"A horse, I said, or I'll slit your throat from ear to ear!"

"Pray, sir, don't kill me! If I had a horse, 'twould be yours, I swear it, but they took them all and left me none! See for yourself!"

"*Who?* Who took them?"

"A party of armed men, sir. Came by last night with four captives, they did, slung over their horses. I had but three horses in my stable and they took them all, stole them, they did, leaving me with none! Pray, sir, have pity. . . ."

Mac released the man and ran toward the stable. There was not a horse in sight. And it was impossible for him to ride his own. The animal was completely spent. It still lay on the ground, its breathing labored. Mac cursed and ran back to the innkeeper.

"Where's the nearest farm?"

"Farm, sir? Why, faith, sir, there'd be no farms here-abouts. Perhaps if you were to go down the road toward Franktown, a day's walk, perhaps. . . ."

"Blast it, where can I get a horse quickly?"

The man shook his head helplessly. "If I only knew, good sir, I would tell you in an instant, but I can think of no place nearby where you could find another mount."

Mac slumped, defeated. "That's it, then. 'Tis over. Black Jack has won. And I . . . I have lost everything that matters to me."

And then, he heard a horse's snort and the creaking, rattling sounds of a wagon approaching. He spun around and saw Harlan the Peddlar coming down the road from the Great River, whistling to himself.

Mac ran toward the wagon as it approached the inn. Harlan saw him approaching and reached for a vial of the Elixir of Stench, just to be on the safe side.

"Hallo, peddlar!" Mac cried. "Have you passed a party of armed men on the road, perhaps a dozen or more?"

"Aye, that I did, stranger," Harlan said. "Just a short while ago, I saw them heading back the way I came, toward the Great River, bearing captives slung on horseback. Say, that's a fine collection of knives you have slung across your chest there. As it happens, I represent an armorer of note—"

"Get down from your wagon!"

"What?"

Mac leaped up on the seat beside him just as Harlan drew back his hand to hurl the Elixir of Stench. Instinctively, Mac grabbed his arm. The two wrestled for a moment, then the vial dropped and shattered on the floorboards of the wagon.

"*Gahhhhh!*" cried Harlan, clapping his hands over his nose.

"*By the gods!*" cried Mac, reeling from the awful stench.

Hacking and coughing, Harlan fell back into the wagon. Mac grabbed the reins and, holding his breath, whipped up the horses and turned the wagon around. Then he cracked the whip and, holding his nose, set off in pursuit of Black Jack and his men.

The bounty hunters reined in on the rise above the banks of the Great River. "We've made it!" one of them cried, a wide grin on his face. "There's the ferry, right below!"

"Aye, once we're across and the ferry lines are cut, we can take our ease and make camp by the riverbank," Black

Jack said. He looked down at Shannon, tightly bound and slung across his saddle in front of him, on her stomach. He slapped her backside. "You're going to make me a rich man, my lass. I'll be buying a nice, new suit of clothes to attend your execution."

"My head isn't on the block, yet," Shannon said.

Black Jack caressed her buttocks. "Aye, that's the spirit, lass. Defiant to the bitter end. They'll love that in the square at Pittsburgh, when they lop your head off. Give 'em a good show. Though, truly, 'twill be a shame to despoil such a body. What a waste."

"It need not be a waste," said Shannon softly. "I am your prisoner and you can do with me what you will."

Black Jack threw back his head and laughed. "Waste not your wiles on me, my sweet. True, I find myself sorely tempted by your flesh, but the bounty on your head tempts me far more."

"I am bound both hand and foot," said Shannon. "What have you to fear from me?"

"I am not such a fool as to risk finding that out," Black Jack replied. "If I was to have my way with you, and not share you with the others, they would resent it. And if I was to let them have their turn, 'twould distract them, surely, and perhaps give you an opportunity. Nay, I shall regretfully deny myself the pleasure, and look forward instead to the greater pleasure of the reward that you shall bring me, and the fame that will go with it."

"You are a cowardly cur, Black Jack."

"Nay, merely a cautious one," he said with a grin. "Come on, men! The ferry awaits!"

He spurred his horse and galloped down the road leading to the riverbank and the ferry crossing. His men followed behind him, trailing the three horses to which Long Bill, Fifer Bob, and Silent Fred were bound.

" 'Tis all your fault, Bill!" Fifer Bob moaned as he was painfully jounced by the movement of the horse. "I don't know why I ever listened to you! See what you have brought us to!"

"Oh, *shut up!*" said Long Bill.

Silent Fred, as usual, remained morosely silent, and truly, there wasn't really much to say in such a situation. The bounty hunters rode down to the riverbank and reined in at the ferry crossing. The ferry raft was moored across from them, on the opposite bank of the river. Black Jack dismounted and cupped his hands around his mouth.

"*Halloooo!*"

From the opposite bank, the ferryman replied, and in a moment, they saw the raft move out from the other shore. Black Jack came around to the side of his horse, took a handful of Shannon's hair, and jerked her head up so he could see her face. She spat at him.

He wiped his face with the back of his hand, then hauled off and cuffed her with his fist, bloodying her mouth. "Aye, when they cut that pretty head off, I'll be in the front row to watch," he said. "My only regret is that Mac the Knife will miss the show. Pity."

"Mac the Knife?" said one of the other men. "What has he to do with this?"

Black Jack held Shannon by the hair and touched the dagger pin fastened to her breast. "He has this to do with it," he said.

"She is Sean MacGregor's woman?" one of the others said uncertainly. "You said nothing about MacGregor being part of this."

"What are you afraid of?" sneered Black Jack. "We'll cross the river and be on our way to Pittsburgh long before MacGregor even finds our trail. And even if he were to catch us, you think he could stand against all of us together?"

"Perhaps not," said one of the men, "but he may follow us to Pittsburgh and make inquiries, and find out who was in the party that brought his woman in. Then he'll be trackin' us down, one at a time."

There was uneasy mumbling among the men.

"That's right!" Shannon shouted. "Mac will never rest till he avenges me! He'll kill each and every last one of you!"

"Quiet, you!" said Black Jack, smacking her across the face, backhanded.

"She's right," one of the others said. "Mac the Knife has killed every man he's ever stalked. I didn't know he was involved when I signed on for this. I want no part of it."

"Nor I," said another.

"You are already part of it, all of you!" Black Jack said. "Ride out now, and you forfeit your share of the reward. And MacGregor may find out who you are just the same, and then he'll be on your trail and you'll have nothing to show for it! Continue on, and you'll receive your fat share of the bounty, and then together we can take care of Mac the Knife. 'Tis the only way to make sure he cannot track us down one at a time."

"You should have told us, Jack. We didn't know about MacGregor. You tricked us."

"You all willingly signed on for this!" Black Jack said angrily. "No one forced you into it. Besides, what are you afraid of? MacGregor's not so much. I myself crossed swords with him and lived to tell the tale. Had he not fled from me, the silver dagger of the top assassin would now be on my breast, as it rightfully should be!" He tore the pin off Shannon's tunic and fastened it onto his own. "There's what I think of Sean MacGregor! If he wants this back, he can damn well come and try to take it!"

The ferry was almost to the shore now.

"Any man who wishes to turn tail like a rat and run, then do it now!" Black Jack said. "And be damned for a coward. The rest of us will divvy up your share of the reward!"

There was a moment's silence, then one of them said, "I didn't come all this way for nothing."

"Nor I," said another.

"Very well, then," said Black Jack. "Half of us will go on the first crossing, the rest will follow after. When we all reach the other shore, we can cut the ferry ropes, make camp, and rest awhile. And thumb our noses at anyone who tries to follow."

As the ferry touched the shore, Black Jack led his horse down, with Shannon strapped across it, and got aboard the raft. "Bring down the other prisoners," he said.

"And have you cut the ropes once you reach the other side?" one of the others said. "No chance. Half of us will go along with you and the wench. The rest of us will remain here with the other three, as a security that you send the ferry back for us."

"A fine and trusting lot you are," Jack said with a scowl. "Very well, then. Have it your way. But be quick about it."

Six of the men dismounted and led their horses onto the raft while the others remained behind with the three brigands to wait for the next trip. The ferryman and his assistant, long accustomed to all sorts of unsavory types, kept their own counsel. Once everyone was aboard, they began to pull the ferry back across, using the lines. The other bounty hunters waited on the riverbank. The raft was about halfway across when a cloud of dust up on the rise, on the road leading to the riverbank, caught one of the men's attention.

"Look there," he said, pointing.

Black Jack looked and, a moment later, he saw a wagon come into view, make the turn, and start down the slope. " 'Tis the peddlar we passed earlier," he said, recognizing the wagon.

"Why's he coming back this way?"

"Perhaps he lost something on the road," said Jack.

"He's comin' fast."

"Aye," Jack said with a frown. "He is at that." He squinted hard, trying to make out the driver.

The wagon came straight at the other group of bounty hunters waiting on the riverbank. They had turned to watch its approach, and suddenly Jack saw one of them clutch his chest and fall. And then another. And another. The driver of the wagon had dropped the reins, and as the horses ran free, he stood in the box, throwing knives at the remaining bounty hunters, who had scattered.

"*MacGregor*!" said Black Jack.

"You said he'd never catch us!" one of the others said accusingly.

"I don't know how the devil he could have gotten here so fast," Black Jack replied.

"Now what do we do?"

Black Jack sneered. "We cut our losses and make the best of it," he said. "If some of the others manage to kill him and survive, everyone's share will be that much greater for the ones who've fallen. If not, we simply cut the ferry ropes and go on. The wench is worth ten times more than the other three combined."

He held his dagger to the ferryman's back. "*Pull*, damn you! *Pull!*"

Mac leaped down from the wagon and hurled another knife even as he landed, drawing it from his bandolier and throwing it with lightning speed, all in one motion. It buried itself to the hilt in one man's chest, and then the others were upon him. Four had fallen, but three remained, and they rushed at him together, with swords drawn. He drew his own blade and engaged them, dagger in one hand, sword in the other.

He parried one thrust and ran the man through, but at the same time caught the flash of another blade descending in a cutting stroke. He twisted to one side and felt a sharp, searing pain along his shoulder. No time to think about it, one down, two to go, and they were pressing him for all they were worth. He parried one stroke with his sword, struck the other blade down with his dagger, but the pain lanced through his arm and he could not hold onto it. His dagger fell, and he retreated, simultaneously trying to parry two blades at once. They sensed his weakness and moved in for the kill. Suddenly, a glass vial shattered at their feet and Mac's antagonists instinctively recoiled from the incredible, unholy stench. Another vial fell and shattered. Harlan was up on the box of the wagon, throwing vials of the elixir. Mac plunged his sword into a bounty hunter's stomach and the other one took off running, holding his nose and gagging. Fighting down the gorge rising in his throat, Mac drew a knife and hurled it. It struck the fleeing bounty hunter right between the shoulder blades and he fell, dead.

"I'm much obliged to you," Mac called to the peddlar. "But did you have to throw so many? *S'trewth!* The stench would fell a horse!"

The peddlar simply shrugged.

Mac turned and gazed out toward the ferry raft. It was three-quarters of the way across the river. He swore. He could swim for it, but he would never reach them before they reached the shore. And with his injured shoulder, he was not even sure he could prevail against the current. They would mount up and ride, and even if he could reach the opposite shore, he'd have no horse with which to give pursuit. He threw his sword down on the ground and cried out in exasperation. And, out of nowhere, an answering cry came, but it was a cry that issued from no human throat.

If he had known what a locomotive whistle sounded like, he might have thought it sounded just like that, but since he had never heard a locomotive whistle, he could not possibly mistake it for anything else but what it was . . . the angry roaring of a dragon.

He looked up and saw the huge beast, its giant wings fanned out full length, its tail streaming behind it, coming down out of the sun in a swooping glide, and astride its back, he could see a human figure, holding on for dear life.

"A *dragon*!" cried the peddlar. "We are done for! We'll be roasted!"

"Nay, 'tis Doc!" Mac shouted.

"The sorcerer from Brigand's Roost?"

"Aye, none other!"

Aboard the raft, they saw the dragon diving down toward them, belching fire, and the bounty hunters panicked. As a gout of flame hit the water just behind them and sent up clouds of steam, several of the men leaped, terror-stricken, into the water and started swimming for it.

"No man can fight a dragon!" one of the bounty hunters cried. "We'll have to swim for it!"

"We're almost to the shore!" said Black Jack.

"Are you mad? We'll never make it!"

The ferryman and his assistant jumped over the side.

"Grab the ropes and pull!" Black Jack commanded.

"Pull for yourself!"

The remaining men leaped into the river.

"*Blast it, I can't swim!*" cried Jack.

The dragon came swooping down over the raft and Black Jack ducked down as its talons raked the air above him. It soared up again, rising up beyond the treetops, and Jack grabbed the rope and started pulling for dear life.

"You'll never make it," Shannon said.

"If I die in flame, then you roast with me!" Black Jack cried, heaving on the rope for all that he was worth.

The dragon was coming around again, its roars filling the air. It belched smoke and fire and a jet of flame boiled the water near the raft and sent steaming clouds rising up into the sky. The dragon swooped down low, its talons reaching for Black Jack, but he ducked down beneath his horse, using it and Shannon for a shield, and the dragon soared up into the sky again.

Black Jack grabbed the rope and started pulling. The raft touched the shore and he fought to control the terrified horse as he led it onto shore. The animal shied, its eyes rolling, but Black Jack held onto the reins and swung up into the saddle.

"You'd best cut me loose and drop me, or you'll never have a chance," said Shannon.

"I'll still have a chance, with you as hostage," Jack replied, spurring his horse. The animal needed no encouragement. It took off at a dead run down the road into the woods.

"I cannot breathe fire at him in those trees," said Rory, flying high overhead. "It would set the entire forest ablaze."

"Set me down ahead of him!" cried Brewster.

"Are you certain?"

"No. But what other choice do we have?"

As Black Jack rode full speed down the forest road, he kept anxiously glancing overhead. The treetops were effectively screening him from view. So long as he kept to the trees, the dragon couldn't see him, and the forest stretched on for miles. Ahead of him, there was an open crossroads, but he could plunge off the road into the trees and work his way around it, to keep himself out of the open. He heard a great rush of wind as a huge shadow passed by overhead, and he heard the dragon's roar, but no attack came.

"Roar all you like, you great worm!" he said. " 'Twill take more than an overgrown lizard to stop Black Jack!"

The crossroads was just ahead... and standing in the middle of the road, directly in his path, was a man, dressed in a strange-looking surcoat. He seemed to be unarmed. He was holding his arms up in front of him, as if commanding him to stop. The fool, thought Jack, I'll ride right over him.

As the horseman barrelled straight on toward him, Brewster held his revolver in both hands, thinking back and trying to concentrate on the time when the EnGulfCo CEO had taken him to the firing range, after presenting him with a matched set of Smith & Wessons. The CEO was an avid target shooter, but it was the only time Brewster had ever fired a gun.

"Now, just take it nice and easy and don't get excited," the CEO had told him, after showing him the proper grip and stance. "If you've got time, and you want to make sure to place your shot as accurately as possible, fire the gun single-action, by manually cocking the hammer back with your thumb. Line up the front sight so it's squarely in the middle of the rear-sight notch, and so the top of the front sight is exactly level with the top of the rear sight. Push forward slightly with your right arm, and pull back slightly with your left, to give yourself a nice, steady shooting platform. Don't use a lot of muscular tension, though. Keep the gun steady and make sure it isn't weaving about. Once you've got the sights lined up, focus on the front sight, not the target, so that the front sight is nice and sharp and the target is just slightly blurred. Place the front sight just below the bull's-eye, take a breath, relax, exhale, and gently *squeeze*, don't jerk the trigger."

The gun fired. The .357 Magnum jacketed hollowpoint slug struck Black Jack high in the left shoulder and knocked him right off his horse, passing completely through him. The horse reared up and Brewster quickly holstered the gun and raised his arms, standing in front of the horse and hoping the animal wouldn't strike him down with its hooves.

"Easy, boy! Easy! Easy!"

He managed to catch the horse's reins and hold onto them

as the animal reared up again, and then he pulled them tight and moved in close to the horse, speaking softly, gently, trying to soothe the beast. In a few moments, the horse managed to calm down, though its eyes were still wide and frightened, and Brewster stepped close to it, gentling it, speaking softly and reassuringly.

"There, there, boy, it's all right, it's all right."

When he had the horse calmed down, he slipped his arm through the reins and came around beside it. Shannon looked up at him weakly.

"Shannon! Are you all right?"

"What kept you?" she said with a smile.

He cut her bonds and helped her down off the horse. She tried to stand, but her legs buckled beneath her.

"Don't try to stand," said Brewster. "Here, let me help you."

He took her arm and put it around his shoulders, holding onto her hand and supporting her with his other arm.

"The others?" she said.

"They're all right, I think," said Brewster. "Here, let's get off to the side of the road here so you can sit and rest."

He helped her down and she leaned back against a tree trunk wearily. She sighed and groaned. "I feel as if every bone in my body has been shaken loose." She looked up at him and smiled. "I owe you my life, Doc."

Brewster smiled sheepishly. "You'd have done the same for me."

"Perhaps," she said.

"*Perhaps*?"

She grinned. "After this, for certain. I will never forget how you stood up to Black Jack's charge and hurled your magic thunderbolts."

"My magic . . . ?" Brewster glanced down at his holstered gun. "Oh. That."

" 'Tis a truly brave and fearsome sorcerer you are, Doc. And I shall always be grateful to you." She reached up, took his face between her hands, and gently kissed him on the lips.

Suddenly, they heard a horse neigh and Brewster turned

around to see Black Jack swing up into the saddle and gallop off toward the crossroads. He jumped up and pulled his gun from its holster, ran out into the middle of the road, and drew a bead on Black Jack's rapidly retreating back. And then he lowered the gun.

"Why did you not kill him?" Shannon asked.

Brewster shook his head. "I thought I had, at first. I guess I only wounded him."

"You should have finished him," said Shannon.

"I couldn't shoot a man in the back," said Brewster. He glanced down at the gun. "I'm amazed I was able to shoot him at all."

She shook her head. " 'Tis a strange man you are, Brewster Doc. But 'tis a privilege to call you friend."

"Rory can pick us up at the crossroads and take us back across the river," Brewster said, "but I'm afraid we'll have to walk there. Think you can make it?"

"After the ride I've had, I think that I would much prefer to walk," said Shannon.

He helped her to the crossroads, where Rory picked them up and flew them back across the river, with Shannon holding onto Brewster for dear life, terrified until Rory set them down again on the opposite shore. Brewster thanked the dragon and Rory said, "Think nothing of it, old chap. It was great fun." Then he sprang up into the air and was soon no more than a faint dot receding into the distant sky.

"I knew Doc wouldn't let us down!" said Fifer Bob as he came running up with Long Bill and Silent Fred. "He and Mac have saved the day! We're back among our friends again, and free!"

"Aye, 'tis back you are," said Shannon, "but take your fill of freedom for the present, for when we get back to the Roost, I'll have the three of you in stocks until you rot!"

The three brigands looked horrified. "Oh, woe is us!" wailed Fifer Bob. "I can't take no more of those awful urchins! Oh, why, oh, *why* did I ever let you talk me into going along with your greedy, devious ways? 'Tis all your fault, Long Bill! 'Tis all your fault!"

"Oh, *shut up!*" said Long Bill.

Mac came running up to Shannon. "Shannon! By the gods, I thought I'd lost you!"

He threw his arms around her, and she recoiled in horror, pushing him away. "Blind me, what's that awful stench?" she cried, gagging.

Mac grinned weakly. " 'Tis my new fragrance. Like it?"

"Surely you jest! Doc, you wouldn't have any of your magic soap about you, would you?"

"I had a whole supply," the peddlar said, "but I fear I'm all sold out. In fact, I'm sold out of all the goods!"

"What goods?" said Shannon. And then she noticed Mac's wound. "Mac! You're hurt!"

" 'Tis but a scratch," he said. "Come, the peddlar will take us back to Brigand's Roost. We shall probably run into the others on the way."

"Aye, and it will give me an opportunity to discuss some business ventures with you," Harlan said. "I have some ideas that should prove quite profitable for all of us, I think."

"Another time, Peddlar, if 'tis all the same to you," said Shannon, getting into the back of the wagon with Brewster. "Right now, all I want to do is sleep."

Mac got in beside her.

"Mac," she said, wrinkling her nose, "would you mind very much sitting up front?"

And so, as Brewster and Shannon rest in the back of the wagon while Mac sits up front with Harlan reluctantly listening to a lecture on the money to be made in real estate, we take our leave of our intrepid characters, but only for a short while, for we'll return soon with our next bizarre installment. (After all, even narrators have to take a short break every now and then, and attend to such mundane matters as paying bills and balancing the checkbook.)

Will Colin Hightower, relentless newshawk kidnapped by the naked wench from Pittsburgh, find a way out of his embarrassing and possibly dangerous predicament and get to the bottom of the strange phenomenon he is investigating, or will he wind up with a tabloid headline all his own? Will Marvin Brewster ever find a way to get back his missing time machine from the most powerful mage in all the twenty-seven kingdoms? Will Shannon and MacGregor wed, and start a school for fighters and assassins in Brigand's Roost, so they can get the awful urchins off the streets, or will Mac's new fragrance force an indefinite postponement of the nuptials?

Will Harlan the Peddlar start a franchise operation and develop the first successful pyramid scheme in the twenty-seven kingdoms, or will the Better Business Guild cut him off at the knees? And will Brigand's Roost experience an unprecedented influx of new settlers, fleeing Pittsburgh in search of freedom from oppression, new business opportunities, and a relaxed, suburban lifestyle, or will they take one look at the grubby little village and decide to go back and take their chances with Sheriff Waylon and his deputies? And what of the plans The Stealers Guild is hatching for a revolution?

Will Warrick Morgannan discover the secret of Brewster's time machine on his own, or will he embark upon a relentless search for that machine's creator, having overheard his name by eavesdropping on the narrator again? And will he ever forgive Teddy the Troll for being the unwitting cat's-paw of your faithful narrator, or will Teddy have a nervous breakdown and start looking for an exorcist?

And what of faithful Pamela? Will she survive the devious machinations of a huge, multinational conglomerate and succeed in replicating Brewster's time machine, or will all her efforts be doomed to dismal failure? (Hint: maybe not.) For the answers to those and other irrelevant questions, be sure to join us once again for our next exasperating episode, *The Ambivalent Magician*, or Shannon and the Seven Dwarfs.